Redem

FRANCIS STUART

New Island Books / Dublin

Redemption
is published in 1994 by
New Island Books,
2, Brookside,
Dundrum Road,
Dublin 14
Ireland

Copyright © Francis Stuart, 1949, 1994
Introduction © Paul Durcan, 1994

ISBN 1 874597 08 1

New Island Books receives financial assistance from
The Arts Council (An Chomhairle Ealaíon),
Dublin, Ireland.

First published by Victor Gollancz in 1949.
Republished in 1974 by Martin Brian & O'Keeffe.

Cover design by Jon Berkeley
Printed in Ireland by Colour Books, Ltd.

CONTENTS

Chapter

The vision of Christ that thou dost see
Is my vision's greatest enemy.

WILLIAM BLAKE

To Gertrud Meissner

INTRODUCTION
Paul Durcan

"There's nothing in the world that couldn't be called a few scratches, from music to love. It's a question of making the right scratches... For me that fish was a symbol of life. Life too has that pure form. What happens has a pure form if I have the strength to regard it." (pp 23-28, *Redemption*)

There are two kinds of fiction: fiction as brilliant, mechanical, virtuoso, safe hill walking; fiction as equally brilliant but anti-mechanical, awkward, dangerous mountain climbing. *Redemption* is fiction of the second kind and its pages are ridden with risk-taking as well as with calm, measured inquiry into the fundamental question of human existence; viz. the question of Crime and Punishment. *"... the final violation is the stripping from a thing of its own air."*

In form and content *Redemption* is of the tenor and scope of Camus's *The Outsider*; Hemingway's *A Farewell To Arms;* Dostoyevski's *Crime And Punishment*. It anticipates the post-war "Beat", "Romantic", "Urban Realist" waves of fiction and poetry.

It is May 1994 as I write this Introduction and a young artist and her son along with a young priest in his prime have been murdered in counties Clare and Galway. *Redemption* tells the story of just such a murder (just such a mass of murders) and it is as much a narrative investigation of a crime as a religious meditation on it.

Reading *Redemption*, while simultaneously reading the newspaper reports of the murders in Clare and Galway, confronts the reader with a moral dilemma: we must choose – in 1994 as in 1949 – between the lies of newspapers and the truths of fiction. In *Redemption* the language of newspapers is described as "*dog rolling in dead-dog*". Crime is our entertainment because of our communal "lust for security".

In *Redemption* language is used as an exclusively utilitarian, poetic tool. What first appears as an apprentice writer's gauche

1

prose transpires to be an achieved awkwardness – linguistic re-enactments of the "right scratches". Stuart forged this technique in his novels of the 1930's until in 1948 (*The Pillar Of Cloud*) and in 1949 (*Redemption*) his technique was adequate to his meaning, and his form accommodated his content.

The enemy of fiction is rhetoric but *Redemption* is devoid of rhetoric. Stuart writes a plain prose but he goes beyond Hemingway in his capacity to infuse his storytelling with poetic magic. For example, when the murderer at the dog track attempts to glimpse the corpse of his victim through a crack in the fence he is confronted by the faces of children-at-play who innocently squeeze out a query about the names of the greyhounds as opposed to the namelessness of the hare.

Or, when the policeman looks at the faces of these same children: "*These smiles reminded him of the small clouds he had noticed earlier – smiles, which he reflected, are to be found nowhere else but on the faces of children interrupted at play.*"

Or, again, the image that could have been created by Caillebotte – the nineteenth century Precursor-Genius of twentieth century painting – of the two imprisoned lovers on their knees sorting out a sack of potatoes.

Redemption also is an open self-portrait in which the smug Arrigho is the anti-hero. The heroes and heroines of Redemption are Father Mellowes, Aunt Nuala, and Margareta.

Father Mellowes is a Van-Gogh like portrait of a Holy Fool whose greatness lies in his affinity with the women of the Gospels. "*He had a very great gentleness, and those who needed gentleness came to him.*"

Aunt Nuala is described as "*a downy, yellow wasp dying under a glass and ready to vent her venom on whatever could be stung*", while the depiction of Margareta as a "*woman with no face*" glimpsed in a foreign city during the war is a Goy etching.

Yeats, Joyce, Beckett are dead and celebrated. The author of *Redemption* lives on in "obscurity and derision" (to use the words from Derek Mahon's poem *The Forger* quoted in Stuart's later novel, *Memorial*, published in 1973); the creator of "pure form" because for ninety two years he has had "the strength to regard it".

CHAPTER I

BEASTS
OF
THE
FOREST

■ THE HOUSE where Father Mellowes had his room lay outside Altamont in an untidy garden.

"I dropped in to return your book, Father," Ezra said. Father Mellowes was seated at the big table in his room. As he took up the book and read its title, *Beasts of the Forest,* a letter slipped out of it. It was addressed to Ezra Arrigho in a foreign country. As the priest handed it to him, he said: "Isn't that a letter from your wife?"

"My wife?"

"Excuse me. You needn't tell me if you don't want to," said Father Mellowes. He went to the stairs and called Dinah, the child of his landlady, Mrs. Bamber, and sent her out for a bottle of cheap, white wine.

"I am not going back there," Ezra said when the priest returned.

"Why do you say that?" asked Father Mellowes. He spoke with gentleness. He had a very great gentleness, and those who needed gentleness came to him. Many of them did not know why they came to him, but it was in the first place because of this gentleness that was a rare thing and which they found nowhere else.

But Ezra was silent. He might have given many reasons, all with a little truth in them, but the real reason he could not find words for. As the little girl returned with the wine, she met Guard Higgins pushing his bicycle up the path to the house. The Bambers' house was a little way outside Altamont and stood in a garden where Joe Bamber grew vegetables for sale in the town. Guard Higgins had leased a plot in a corner of the garden at the back of Bamber's shed. Here he made experiments in horticulture. He was interested in the gramineal or family of grasses. He had divided his plot into small squares in each of which he grew different varieties of his fibrous-looking crop. He was experimenting on cultivating a plant, as cattle-fodder, which would thrive where nothing but the moss, heather, reeds or bracken had ever grown before.

On this summer evening he believed he was very near his goal. He had produced a seed which was sprouting under conditions which could not be worsened on the wildest or wettest bog. A few evenings before, he had first spied the tiny, bluish shoot pricking up from the almost liquid mixture in which he had a month before sown it. He had hung the pot under the tap at the back of the shed so that twenty drops a minute fell on to the soil in it. And this soil he had dug from the boggy side of a hill some miles outside the town and brought back with him in a biscuit box at the back of his bicycle.

As he was taking the clips from the ends of his blue serge trousers, Dinah told him that her mother wanted him upstairs, that he was to be sure to go to her the minute he arrived. Mrs. Bamber was in the midst of preparing a room for Father Mellowes' sister, who was arriving on a visit that evening.

"Hot is it?" Guard Higgins asked the child. He was impatient to get to his seedling. The little girl was used to the impediment in his speech, the difficulty he had in pronouncing

4

certain letters. Dinah herself was not sure of what was going on upstairs, only that it was to do with the moving of furniture.

"Bit of decorating, eh?" said the guard despondently. He could not refuse Mrs. Bamber, but he longed only to be out in his corner of the garden screened by the dark ilex trees and the potting-shed, tending his secret crop. He had visions of the mossy mountains and bogs of the country blossoming and bearing fifty- and a hundred-fold.

Directed by Mrs. Bamber, Guard Higgins moved furniture, mended the bed springs and restuck some torn paper on the bedroom wall. He did everything at a rush, dragging a wardrobe from one room to the other so that the floor shook.

"Look out, there," said Mrs. Bamber. "You needn't kill yourself!"

"Hot I says is, ma'am; put you heart into hotever your hand finds to do, until you've done it," said Guard Higgins.

Dinah listened from a corner of the room where she was out of the way. She liked these pronouncements of Guard Higgins even when she did not altogether follow them. She liked above all the stranger reiteration of the syllable "hot." This gave a sense to the words that fascinated her.

"Look out, man. Don't bring down the ceiling," Mrs. Bamber said.

"That's right, ma'am. A light touch is a magic touch," said the guard.

The moment Mrs. Bamber had returned to the kitchen to make tea for Father Mellowes and Ezra, Guard Higgins slipped out to have one look at his *Pooideal,* the name of the family of grasses to which his shoots belonged.

He stood gazing at the pot that stood on some bricks and into which a drop of water softly fell from time to time from the rusty tap. Two more shoots were pricking their blue-green points out of the slush. The guard's face, still red from his ex-

5

ertion with the furniture, reflected a kind of rapture. The child, watching him, was aware of it, of the dark leaves of the ilex, of the soft, intermittent fall of the drops of crystal on to the savage little shoots in their pot whose wet sides glowed with the same red hue as the bricks under it. She saw all as in a cavern, as though the evening was a cave and she was shut into it, shut under the glowing evening with these colours, movements and words. She heard Guard Higgins murmur, "Me beauties, me uncommon beauties," and saw him very gently begin to give the tap a fraction of a turn. The *Pooideal* had withstood the test and it now deserved a slight respite from the soaking.

Dinah lingered on in the corner of the garden after Guard Higgins had gone back to his furniture-shifting. She sat with her back to the grey wood of the shed, in the shade of the black-green ilexes with their dusty, silver glint. She listened to the soft drip of the water into the pot, she saw the patch of incandescent sky between the dark leaves, and she smelt the pungent, sad-sweet scent of the overgrown currant bushes. So much was going on, and she must have her part in it. She was irresistibly drawn to the tap. With great care and using both hands, she turned it slowly until she judged it dripped at the rate it had before Guard Higgins had come out. Let the battle between the water and the weed go on! Let it become intensified! The drip of the water she felt in her own breast; it produced an exaltation in her, like drunkenness.

Up in the room of Father Mellowes, the priest and Ezra were embarked on one of their long conversations. Ezra did most of the talking, for Father Mellowes was not much of a talker. He leant with his elbows on the table and his pale face with its thick lips was turned at a slight angle away from his guest, as though turned from the words that poured over him in a torrent. What the other said seemed a complaint or an accusation; he contested everything, even, as it seemed to the priest, the incontestable.

Long ago at home Ezra had annoyed the others by never taking anything for granted. No one knew why he argued so much. Even his mother, who was the soul of patience, had grown uneasy at his questioning of each simple statement. He had never found some one to listen to him with the patience of Father Mellowes. Of course, whether the priest really listened, he was at times not certain. At times the expression on the priest's face was absent and smiling. Ezra was off, with his passion of ridicule, passing from one thing to another, from religion to society, from society to literature.

"I am no judge of such things," Father Mellowes humbly admitted. He filled up his guest's glass with the inferior white wine. He himself only sipped from his own.

"Thanks," said Ezra. "It doesn't matter. That's not what I wanted to speak of," he went on. "All I meant to say was that life has been narrowed down and a wall built around it. But on the other side of the wall is the forest."

"The forest? How do you mean that?" asked Father Mellowes. "What sort of forest?"

"It struck me when I was reading this book. The mouse under the wings of the great horned owl whose feathers smell of death, probably because of the blood that is coated there. Biologists have noted this fact. But let us see it. The dark, noiseless swoop of death, the death smell. You don't know the death smell, Father. You only know the neatly washed and laid-out corpses. And you don't know what is going on beyond the few streets of Altamont. You don't know the deaths they've been dying and the lives they're living in other parts of the world."

Father Mellowes had a thick-featured almost negroid expression, crowned by crisp, black curly hair. Many of the poorer parishioners found comfort in his expression of gentle stupidity. When on a warm summer evening such as this they saw his big face through the grille of the confessional they were conscious that he was "a man of God." That big, pale nose turned slightly aside from the grille with the drops of sweat gleaming on it, and the full lips moving under it in the prayer of absolution—that was the sign which gave Saturday evening its peculiar solemnity for many devout people of Altamont.

Ezra was going on talking, telling the priest how he used to spend his holidays in a foreign city long ago before the war.

"I stayed in a small hotel in a back street. I got in by train at midday and went there and drank a bottle of wine with the Patron down in the dark office and then went up the narrow stairs to my room. I would be a bit tired with the journey and the wine and I would lie on the bed and hear the sounds of the city through the shutters. Then my heart would expand and expand, knowing the huge flux of life out there in the sunny city, all the men and the women, all the buying and selling, loving, loneliness, murdering, praying, lusting, drinking, hungering, all the secrets, the secrets in all the shuttered bedrooms and offices, streets and taxis, back parlours and churches, brothels, hotels, cinemas, convents and God knows where. In tired and slight drunkenness, my heart could open and receive the breath of all this, sniffing all the sweetness and the nastiness together. I would lie there and let the evening come on, waiting for the evening when it would be time to go out into the streets with the money I had in the pocket of my new jacket.

"Let the heart only open wide enough and all is given to it. There are two ways to go down a street of the big city at night. There are two ways that I know, as well as all the others that I don't know. There is the way of the shut heart, gone into a glass core reflecting everything—a little machine reflecting, registering, an exact instrument of precision like a camera, a cylinder, a vacuum-cleaner and all other small machines, carried out in highly polished glass. Then all is reflected in a blind precision, faces, stone, paper, gestures, grimaces. And there is the other way, with the heart open, dark and expanded and reflecting nothing. Being touched by what the street is and what is in it, the night in the street and the street in the night. Then there is no more sin, sin begins in the shape and form of the heart, or perhaps that is itself sin, the cylinder reflecting in a vacuum. But now there is no sin, no sin of the flesh because the flesh is no longer flesh. Girls in the street are not flesh. The girl in my room isn't flesh. Or is it flesh and something else at the same time. You should know that, Father. As is written in the song of songs: 'Thy neck is like the Tower of David builded for an armoury. . . . Thy two breasts are like two young roes that are twins, which feed among the lilies. . . .' On that evening I saw the roes and the lilies and the towers of David, there in the street, in the evening."

Father Mellowes did not know whether Ezra was mocking him.

"God does not do things by halves, as you would like to make out, Father. When he made woman he made her down to the last sensational details. It would certainly have been beyond us to have imagined such sensual depths. Or the great horned owl either, scented with death, in silent flight; that's flesh too, that's the same flesh in a different shape. Walking down the street in the strange city on a summer evening, that is what I was telling you about, wasn't it, Father? And picking up a girl and having dinner with her and bringing her back to the room in the hotel on an evening when I had the power not only to see the grubby little shape of flesh. On such an evening, I mean, when the flesh is lilies and bushels of wheat and pomegranates because the mind is expanded and dark and not the little mechanical, blind mirror, reflecting pink underclothes and under them nothing more than the reproductive machinery of the mammal. When the heart is a machine it only knows machines and reflects machines. But that night and some other nights I wasn't a reflecting machine."

"That is all about you," said Father Mellowes. "But what about the girl? Didn't you harm her?" He turned his face to Ezra's, looking at him with his grave eyes, questioningly.

"You can't harm anyone when your heart is open and dark and receptive," Ezra said. "Don't you know that? Or have you and the others finally managed to drive that rapture out of this town?"

"What did you do with her?" Father Mellowes asked gently.

"I gave her what money I had with me, that I had saved up to have a spree on, and I went home next morning."

"Did you commit a sin with her?"

"If I had passed her by in the street, looking into her face and going on and never known her or touched her or had a thought about her beyond 'That's not a bad tart, God help her,' would that have been a sin, Father?" Ezra said. "What is a sin, Father?"

Father Mellowes said nothing. Much of what Ezra said to him was never clear. But he did not think that clarity was everything. He could get, he thought, the drift of things often better without too much clarity. That did not worry him. But at the moment he did not want to give an answer to the other's question. He thought it might be a very important question and he did not want to give an answer that might be wrong. No one else poured such a dark flood of words and thoughts over him as Ezra, and he could not deal with them swiftly and easily. He had no ready-made answers as others might have. That was, indeed, why the other came to him, because ready-made answers were no answers.

"Answers must come from at least as deep down as the question," he said. "And I can't answer from there yet. I must think." He said "think," but he would not think; he would just wait. He was no great thinker. Thoughts never made anything clearer to him, but rather the reverse.

Ezra laughed. His face rippled up with amusement, as though a little gust had blown over it, darkening it. For when he laughed he seemed darker to the priest, his sallow skin deepening in tone and his grey eyes.

"Ah, leave it, Father. It doesn't signify," he said. "We're not in the confessional."

Dinah and her brother Joey had come into the room while the two men had been talking and had settled themselves at a corner of the big table with paper and crayons. They were always at home in the priest's room. They had begun to make a picture of the priest's dog, Ginger, which was sitting on the red carpet in the last patch of evening sunlight that came through the window.

Joey's picture showed a pinched and diminished form, scarcely a dog, all the lines moving together and tucked away in the corner of the white sheet of paper. The little boy regarded his work with a scowl, looking at it with one eye closed and swinging his bare feet under the table. When the two pair of feet met they grappled with each other, toe to toe, exchanging stealthy scratches, savage and tender.

Dinah's picture was quite different. In it Ginger, almost blood-red, sat at the edge of the sloe-blue pool of his own shadow. To the shadow the girl had given more care than to the dog. Something in the shape that the dark shadow had taken on the paper fascinated her. But now when she had finished she would have liked to have got rid of it. It suddenly appeared to her to spoil the picture. She tried folding it under so that it would not be seen. Ezra took the sheet and made a neat job of it for her. Father Mellowes was speaking of the picnic that he had arranged for the next day, when, after his Sunday Mass, he was taking his sister to a spot at the river to bathe. He invited Ezra.

"Mr. Kavanagh, the fishmonger from Dublin, is down here for the week-end and he will drive us in his car," the priest said.

Ezra was back at Father Mellowes' on the following morning to have a cup of tea with the priest and his sister, who had arrived by the late train on Saturday, before Mr. Kavanagh called for them with his car. The sergeant of the civic guards had also been invited.

Ezra lingered in the garden before going into the house. The sun was still low and the trees and shrubs were very still. As he paused by the shed he could see, through the loose old boards, Guard Higgins standing before his pot and carefully unwrapping something from a wet cloth. He was in uniform, being to-day on duty at the barracks. He took a slab of ice from the cloth and gently laid it on top of the semi-liquid earth in the pot so that the needle-like blue-green shoots were covered by it. Dinah was standing watching him.

"Bring down the temperature like hot bog would be like in March," he said to her. "We've got to stick to scientific methods."

He unwrapped another slab of ice, which he buried in the earth under the shade of the ilex bushes. He told the child that when the first slab melted she was to replace it by this second one.

"But supposing the other piece has melted too?" she asked.

"Don't ask questions, childeen. How the devil could it melt ad the same rade, there in the cool of the trees as the bid in the full bloody glare of the hod sun?"

Ezra stood watching the child after Guard Higgins had got on his bicycle and pedalled off into the town. Her broad, brooding face as she stood staring at the pot with the slab of ice across it attracted him. He came from behind the shed and spoke to her. He stood in the clearing between the old shed and the ilexes. It was still here as he had never felt it in many years.

Along the wall of the shed, dandelions grew and lifted their ragged golden faces into the stillness. A blackbird sang a few notes, stopped and repeated them over again.

"Listen," he said. "He is practising. What a lot of time he must have."

"He has the whole morning," said the child; "and the afternoon too."

There was time here and there was stillness. The bird-song had been the sudden, unexpected piping of peace.

"That's the first time I've heard a bird sing since before I went away," he said. To the child he could speak his thoughts.

"They sing all day," she said, looking up at him with a slight surprise.

"They make a noise," he said. "But all the time I've been back I never heard one sing till now."

"Where were you when you were away? At the war?"

"The war was there where I was," he said. "The days and the nights were full of it. The sky was black with it. It put out the sun and the moon, and it put out Margareta." He had never spoken her name to anyone, but he could speak it to this child. He could form it in his mouth and it did not choke him.

"Was she killed?" Dinah asked indifferently. He didn't want sympathy or sentiment; he could speak just because of this indifference.

"When I went to the block of flats where she lived after the raid, they had gone," he said. "There was a great pile of broken concrete and girders with a bluish, bitter steam rising up in the light of the head-lamp of a military ambulance. I waited there all night because I couldn't go away from the pile of hot rubble. On the other side of the street there were older ruins, and there I sat. In the morning I went home. I thought: 'Perhaps a message has come.' But I knew in my heart that this was the end of messages. No message can come through a thousand tons of smoking ruin. I came back and waited, gazing

13

and gazing, because the heart had to try to drink in and absorb what had happened. And yet it couldn't. The more I looked the more the heart hardened and revolted."

The little girl had stooped and picked a dandelion and put the end of the broken stalk to her tongue, tasting the bitter, milky sap that oozed from it. She made a face and said: "Our teacher, Miss Willis, says there will be another war worse than the last."

"What else does she say?"

"That the sun is a globe of gas," Dinah said, screwing up her eyes and looking up at it with the dandelion hanging from her mouth.

"But you don't believe her."

"Oh yes; she is right," said the child. Let her be right. But there were other ways of being right. Let Miss Willis have her little rightness, but she, Dinah, knew other rightnesses. Miss Willis with her globe of gas, her new war, her four times ten is forty, was right up to a point, but there was a point beyond which she wasn't right. In school Dinah was ready to pretend that that point didn't exist, to pretend complete faith in Miss Willis, but here in the garden she didn't pretend. Here she knew what the sun was.

"Shall I show you where Guard Higgins buried the other bit of ice?" she said.

"I saw him," said Ezra. But he was touched by her faith in him. She had scarcely listened to him when he had poured out his heart to her as he had done to no one before. She had hardly listened, but now she offered to reveal to him what he knew was her great secret. "I saw him," he repeated. "But he should have put the pot with the shoots there in the shade of the ilexes too. Otherwise the ice will melt in no time."

She considered for a moment and then took the pot from its brick pedestal and, carrying it tenderly between her two hands, put it down under the bushes. Then she squatted down beside it, peering at the ice that no longer sparkled, the lank thighs exposed up to the small, round buttocks.

In the house Ezra found Father Mellowes and his sister waiting for him. The priest had just got back from saying Mass in the town and they were about to begin their late breakfast. His sister was a few years younger than the priest. Her brown eyes shone out of her pale face as though they were just at an angle to catch the light. Her hair, he noticed, was done in an outmoded style, too fussily, and there was something obtrusively neat about her dress. He thought in passing: She is a virgin. There was that unripe bloom about her, the very brightness of her eyes and her skin, of something untouched.

"I told Romilly that you liked *Beasts of the Forest*. She won it as a prize for natural history at school," said Father Mellowes.

"Did you really like it?" asked Romilly eagerly.

"Oh yes. It is a relief to read about beasts. 'When the last electric sign goes out in the last city and night comes down over the earth again there will be still the forest.' Do you remember that sentence?"

Romilly nodded in her eager way that had something a little brittle in it.

They heard Kavanagh drive up in his car. Father Mellowes called over the stairs to Mrs. Bamber to show him into her sitting-room, while they quickly finished breakfast upstairs. Mrs. Bamber, who was busy in the kitchen cutting sandwiches for the picnic, left Dinah to deal with the visitor.

"Hello, hello," Kavanagh said to her at the door. "I just popped in to see if all was ready. Just popped in." He was at sea with children. It was not his nature to be silent. He believed in taking a bright tone and repeating the simplest remarks. Dinah stared at him and said nothing. He followed her into the parlour and sat down. The child stood just inside the door.

"Well, take a seat, won't you? You see I've made myself

comfortable, so why not do the same, mademoiselle? Sit you down, Miss Bamber . . ." and so on while the child perched herself uneasily on the edge of a chair.

Kavanagh was a Dublin fishmonger with two branch shops in Altamont which he visited from time to time, staying in the small flat over the shop in the main street. Father Mellowes did not keep him waiting long; he never kept anyone waiting long. He came down the stairs in his top-heavy way, the glasses on his pale face shining above his big, black-clothed body. He Brought Kavanagh back up to his room and introduced him to his sister and Ezra.

"Glad to get out of Dublin in this heat?" asked Father Mellowes, saying something, never sure what to say to this big fellow with his cuff-links and watch-chain.

"Heat? This isn't heat. Still, it's a change. Though this town's dead. Look at it. Phew! Business has gone to pot. I know this place upside down, worked here long before you ever put foot in it, Father, and I haven't seen any sign of life in it for I don't know how long," said Kavanagh.

"I think Mr. Arrigho would agree with you," said Father Mellowes with his slow smile appearing under the big, pallid nose. Kavanagh took his eyes off Romilly to regard Ezra.

"Is that so? You're a stranger here, eh? Arrigho isn't a name of these parts."

"No; I'm not from here. I'm only staying here. I've a room at Flood's hotel."

"Flood's. Shouldn't say they're any too sound, between you and me. No, Mr. Arrigho. There may be a slight after-war boom at the moment, but wait a bit—they're bound to catch it in the neck later. Whew!"

It amused Ezra to talk to Kavanagh, to feel the huge, super-ficial warmth and energy and malicious vanity of Kavanagh. He told them that he had a couple of bottles of whisky in the car to add to what he called "the hamper." It surprised Ezra to hear him say he was very keen on swimming. But he was always making too rapid and simple a picture of people, always in too much of a hurry to "grasp" them.

"In fact, I may say I used to be considered something of an aqueduct," said Kavanagh. Ezra was not sure whether to laugh. The tender, brooding smile flickered over the priest's rather heavy lips.

Kavanagh had an old car and they picked up the sergeant at the barracks. Romilly Mellowes sat beside Kavanagh in front and the sergeant got in with the priest and Ezra behind.

"Well, sergeant, how's tricks?" Said Kavanagh, leaning round and blowing his fumey breath into Romilly's face. "Excuse me, your ladyship," he added.

The sergeant answered coolly. He had accepted the invitation out of respect for Father Mellowes, who, he supposed, was getting up this outing to entertain his sister on one of her rare visits. He did not care for Kavanagh and he could ill spare the time for such parties. But he had brought with him his notebook with the calculations he was making in connection with the racing at the local greyhound track. While the others were bathing, he hoped to be able to go on with his studies of these figures.

Ezra wondered why Father Mellowes had arranged the excursion. The lake to which he had asked Kavanagh to take them was a considerable distance from Altamont and there were just as good places for bathing and picnicking in the river close at hand. He thought there was a reason for it. But in one way he knew the priest so little. From him too he was far away, even though he went there in the evenings and talked and talked about himself. But the few revealing words had never been said between them, perhaps could never be said between him and anyone again, unless a child, casual and indifferent.

CHAPTER II

THE
CAVE

■ THE LAKE lay dark at the end of a glen under hills draped with fir trees and boulders, a cool, shining shadow lying here at the foot of the great hot arch of noon. Kavanagh drove the car along the track that led on where the smooth road came to an end at the open, shallow end of the lake. They jolted on slowly with the tiny waves pouring back and forth over the pebbles and small stones below the track. Kavanagh brought the car right up to a rough stone jetty built out into the water to which there was chained a boat. They got out of the car and he helped Miss Mellowes to unpack the provisions. He unpacked a bottle of wine and read out the name on the label, "Haute Margaux," and another with a smack of the lips: "Haute Sauterne."

"By Jingo, Father, you've certainly done things stylishly; everything here is 'haute,' " he said.

After lunch they lay on the mossy ground. The sergeant settled himself with his note-book and pencil and Kavanagh began to look through some illustrated papers he had brought with him. He saw that there was not much fun to be had with Miss Mellowes. Suddenly he came on a photograph in one of them that was like a shadow filling the warm, lazy noon, falling across him, blotting out the lesser shadow of the lake. It was a photograph of the naked torso of a young, laughing negress. Her arms were held at an awkwardly graceful angle, her teeth gleamed. Her breasts were quite different to Annie's, the girl who served in his shop. Annie's breasts had the bluish-white tinge and consistency of plaice or turbot. When she stood scrubbing herself at the kitchen sink, the wet flesh of her breasts and belly had the sheen of fish. He tore the photograph out and folded it and put it in his pocket-book.

Sergeant Foley studied a column and a half of figures complete to the second decimal point. They were the times, in seconds, taken by the winners of the 525-yard races at the Altamont dog-track for the current season. The time that his own greyhound, Rainbow Cutlet, had taken in his recent trial was not written down in his note-book. This figure was noted on a separate half-sheet of paper in his pocket-book and a day scarcely passed that he did not take it out and glance at it.

"Why did your brother bring us here?" Ezra asked the girl. They were sitting on the mossy bank above the water. The dry, crumbly earth was held together by the roots of ferns and weeds with a rampart of small stones and boulders against the lapping of the water.

"Don't you like it here?" she asked.

"Oh yes. Though I'm not keen on all this 'scenery.'"

She looked at him hurt out of her dark, bright eyes. She loved an outing like this, she enjoyed the car, the picnic and she looked forward to the coming bathe.

"When I marry I shall live in such a spot as this," she said.

"Are you going to marry?"

"Yes; in the autumn." She began to talk about her fiancé, who was a widower, a Colonel Charters, much older than herself. He had a house in another glen, by another lake, with a fine library and a collection of modern pictures.

Ezra saw the big rooms, the polished floors, the rows of books and the heavy, old furniture and a view out on to a lake between the long chintz curtains. The pictures were more difficult to see; he didn't know what pictures. But in the spacious dimness of the rooms it would be really all the same what pictures hung on the walls. As long as they added to the sense of order, taste and peace on earth.

"Only you are lacking. When he has you he will have fully stocked his little earthly paradise, have completed the establishing of his heavenly Jerusalem in an Irish glen," Ezra said.

"To me it is like a dream," she said. "I was his secretary for three years in his office in Dublin. He has a business there."

She was full of enthusiasm, a pure, unclouded enthusiasm. Her cheeks were rounded, her mouth immature, unworn by pain or kisses, her dark eyes bright and expectant. Her summer dress was neat and her dark hair carefully done up in too fussy a style. He knew the moment had come either to say nothing, to say a few conventional words of good wishes or else to speak to her from the bitterness smouldering in him. He took up a pebble and threw it out into the lake. Hearing the splash, Kavanagh looked up from his illustrated papers. Father Mellowes had strolled off alone along the track towards the upper end of the lake.

"Why do you do your hair like that?" he asked.

"What is wrong with it?" She was blushing.

"I don't know." He saw her face close up and her mouth harden. She was timid, easily hurt and at the same time proud of herself. Had she not made a good match? Was she not engaged to this man of wealth and culture?

"Don't mind me, Miss Mellowes. When you prefer we can talk about the lake, only I thought that might bore you."

She was looking down at the small ripples just below them. She was still a little sulky, but she waited. She was very unsure of herself. She thought he wanted to hurt her. She was angry, defensive and, all the same, there was in her some hesitant readiness to let him hurt her that confused her.

20

"You can talk about anything you like. I am listening," she said. But she was still withdrawn into her untouched primness.

Father Mellowes came back and suggested that they take the small boat on to the lake. He had been up to the cottage and arranged it with the owner.

"There is something that I want to show you over there," he said, pointing to the cliff of the mountain that rose up from the far shore of the lake. He was standing over them, large and heavy, looking down at them with his big pale face held at its slight habitual tilt. The girl jumped up eagerly.

"What is it?" she asked.

"Wait. It's a surprise. It's something for Ezra especially."

"I know. A wild bird's nest. A hawk or an owl," she said. She was thinking of *Beasts of the Forest*.

Her brother stroked her cheek. Ezra saw that he treated her as a child. And his own derisive anger against her grew. All the way in the boat across the lake with the others he was thinking: "How does she dare to be so sure and eager and untouched?" He could not look at her. He remembered when in the sixth month of his and Margareta's incarceration in a cellar they had come to the door one morning and called him out. He had been taken with another prisoner from an adjacent cellar to move petrol cans. This was the first time he had been taken out for any other reason but to be interrogated. He had been happy moving the tins from a car into a cellar. He was allowed to carry the tins up the stairs and along the short path to the street. While he did this he was not a suspect; not to be a suspect, for a few hours, or at least not to be primarily a suspect, to be taken for work, what a sweet taste there was in that, the taste of being unharried, unhunted. When he was let back into the cellar it was like coming home. He sat down with Margareta on their bunk to their evening bowl of soup and piece of bread and they had been happy together. How many days and nights had they sat together in that cellar and in others, in air-raid cellars and in the halls and waiting-rooms of half-ruined stations. He could feel the weight of her against his shoulder as she gradually leant over against him. As he pulled the oar, sitting on the seat beside the sergeant, who was pulling the other, he could feel the weight of her tired head on his shoulder as it had been through all that waiting, sheltering, fearing and starving. The other times had been so rare. An evening of bringing home a sack of potatoes and sorting them out in their room, kneeling together on the floor close to each other, rejoicing in their great good fortune, their hands black and wet with the potatoes, the earthly smell in their noses, but with a blessed light falling around them, touching Margareta's worn young face, her old black winter coat.

This was quite a different light, the brilliant sparkle that lay over the lake. This was the Sunday light, the noon light of freedom and security and picnics and boating. There was no cellar waiting for him in this world, no one here could dream his dreams—not even Father Mellowes, for all his charity. As for his sister, no one should dare to be so untouched and innocent of all that other knowledge and experience.

She was beside Kavanagh in the stern of the small boat. Kavanagh sniffed the smell of her newly laundered dress. It was a new, clean smell. He sensed a whole new mode of life through it, different from his mode that was the smell of fish, of Annie and of petrol.

They climbed the steep bank at the farther shore. Larch trees grew on the narrow strip between the lake and the cliff, raising their thin stems out of the moss among the debris of boulders and broken granite that was piled up like ruins fallen from the rock face. Father Mellowes led them, swaying topheavily up the steep dry ground, over grey stone and grey trunks of long dead trees that had fallen from above. Ezra followed him, the others a bit behind. He liked this sunless

22

desolation. He was glad to have left the "scenery" and prettiness behind and to have lost the sense of Sunday-in-the-country that he had had during the picnic. They came under drooping larch branches to the foot of the cliff that was broken by fissures, and the narrow crevices were choked with stones and boulders that had lodged in them. Ezra saw the grey, cracked wall tower over him. The great natural chaos was beautiful to him. Father Mellowes was standing at the entrance to a fissure that was partly blocked by a rock. He felt in the pocket of his old black jacket and brought out a candle. When he lit it the small flame burnt motionless in the still air. Ezra followed him into the fissure and over some rubble of pebbles and great clods of earth, sprouting with tough, greyish grass, into the cave. He heard the others scrambling after them, the heavy breathing of Kavanagh. He felt the sudden coolness of the cave bringing back another world. He followed the small flame and stood beside the priest, who had stopped before the rock face. Father Mellowes held the candle higher and the light flickered over the black rock that gleamed as though wet. Then Ezra saw a few scratches glistening against the black, wet gleam. He saw the form of a fish against the body of darkness. And these few scratches traced the pure curve of rapture.

"Jaysus, a bloody fish," said Kavanagh, irritated and out of breath.

Father Mellowes was talking about some other signs that were in an adjoining cave, similar to those at Mellifont in County Meath.

"I'm damned if I can say I think much of it," said Kavanagh. "Just a few scratches against the rock."

"There's nothing in the world that couldn't be called a few scratches, from music to love," said Ezra. "It's a question of making the right scratches."

23

Here in his cavern the old Celt had signed the darkness with his rapture, he thought. It was his sign against the endless disaster and chaos.

"There's a lady present," said Kavanagh, laughing and nudging Ezra in the dark. In the darkness, the chill, the faint candlelight, Ezra was aware of an expectancy in him, the old listening of the blood for the terror-by-day or the terror-by-night creeping over the sky. It was as it had been when the earth had rocked and split. His hand reached out and grasped an arm in the dark, he felt the fine material of Romilly's summer dress. He gripped it when she tried to pull it away, waiting for her to cry out. He did not know why he hated her. Because she was here in this holy place, in this cellar or cavern or dungeon in her neatness and primness and did not know what it was, knew nothing, nothing, neither the terror, the weariness nor the rapture. He let her go. She had not moved or made a sound.

There was something in the form of the fish that reminded the sergeant of the tapering head of his greyhound, Rainbow Cutlet. The visit to the cave was to him little more than an interruption in the Sunday afternoon that he wanted to spend with his note-book and sporting papers.

At noon in the garden Dinah was stooping and digging up the reserve block of ice to examine it for the second or third time. In the dimness of the black ilex leaves, stuck with twigs and leaf-mould, it lay dark and damp and stinging in her hand. The piece in the pot was melting away, dwindling in the hot, dry air, burning in the needles of sunlight that, no matter where she moved it, struck into it through the foliage. Both blocks were disappearing far more rapidly than Guard Higgins had foreseen. She had known that this would be so. She had seen this catastrophe approaching even while the guard had been talking with such assurance. She took the dirty slab of ice that she had unearthed and, hiding it under her pinafore, ran with it into the house and up to the bathroom. She did not dare to leave it in the bath where her mother would find it and throw it out. She only left it in the bath while she filled her basin from her room with water and then with the ice in it hid it under her bed. There it was safer than in the warm earth.

In the kitchen she managed to grab a piece of bread and a handful of lump sugar and put them in the pocket of her wet overall. Then she set out to walk into Altamont, a journey that she had never yet made alone. When she left the familiar side of the hill where she knew all the fields and the tiny woods of young birches and the road reached the crest of the hill, then the landscape became strange and enormous. It sloped away from her into a great bright waste of unknown shapes and shadows and the summer silence said to her: "See, Dinah, what a little insect you are! Crawl on, puny midge, as fast as you can; but you'll never get anywhere."

She tried to keep her eyes on the hot, soft tarmac of the road. She trudged, suddenly weary and overwhelmed with isolation. Cars passed her, gleaming monsters of speed mocking her tiny hastening. She dare not stop to rest or shake the grit out of her shoes. If she stopped the far-awayness would close around her and break the thin thread that strung her between where she came from and whither she was going. As the road sloped down towards the town, she had the feel of the hill ever rising behind her, between her and home. The trees by the side of the road were not her trees; they were towers of a strange and bitter greenness standing up in the hot sky without sweetness to her. She was breathing through her mouth and clenching the bread in her hand with the crumbs pressed out between her fingers. When she put it into her mouth it had the taste of desolation and loneliness.

She reached the beginning of the town and trudged down the broad main street to the barracks. When she found Guard Higgins seated at a table taking notes of the loss of some geese that was being lodged by a farmer, she plucked his sleeve and whispered: "You've got to get more. It's melting away at a terrible rate."

The whispered words, the appearance of the little girl, destroyed the secret world into which Guard Higgins had been withdrawn all the morning. On his arrival at the barracks he had found a letter awaiting him with a foreign stamp. This was from a Monsieur Domais, Horticulturist at the *Jardin des Plantes* in Paris, with whom the guard had already been in correspondence and from whom he had originally obtained his seeds. He had not been able to decipher the letter. He had held it in his hands and drunk in the foreign words. They touched him in the same way as the sharp, bluish shoots of the *Pooideal*, that neither water nor ice could quen h. He had the letter folded away in the breast pocket of his uniform jacket and when he was free in the afternoon he would get Father Mellowes to translate it.

He had his Sunday lunch with Dinah in the guard-room and then, his hours of duty being over until evening, settled the little girl in an upstairs room with the sergeant's greyhound for company and hurried off to Kavanagh's fish-shop in the main street. Mr. Kavanagh, he thought, would be just finishing his dinner and would not mind coming down to open his refrigerator. He rang the bell at the door beside the shuttered shop and after a second ring it was opened by Annie Lee. Her sleepy eyes, far apart in flat cheeks that had a moist pallor, gazed at him coldly. He asked for Mr. Kavanagh.

"He has gone off for the day," she said, beginning to close the door.

"What I need is a little ice, Annie," he said, "very urgently."

"Ice?" she said, her eyes sleepily fixed on his hot face.

"That's right. If you could let me have a piece out of the shop."

"There isn't any in the shop." She spoke slowly and blankly.

"Hot does he do—hit it when he shuts up?" Guard Higgins asked.

"He locks it up with the stock in the refrigerator."

"Hot stock is that?"

"Fish," she said, standing there blank and heavy in the small, dark opening of the door.

"Haven't you the key?" he asked.

She shook her head. He began to see that she would not give it to him if she had. Words would not touch her. The only way to touch her was to come close to her, to come so close that she didn't know what to expect, a blow or a caress, and then in a kind of excited submission she would do what was wanted of her. She waited now a moment longer with an unconscious lingering hope that he would make her open the refrigerator. But he stood there stammering and stuttering.

"Where's he gone?"

"Where's who gone?" she asked, her slow, heavy fury against him gathering in her heart, pretending not to understand him.

"The boss. Didn't he say where he was?"

"He didn't have to say. I know where he is. In that joint down the street." Her fury was not only against the guard, but against Kavanagh too, who had left her alone in the dreary little flat on this bright Sunday. She banged the door and climbed slip-shod back up the stairs.

Guard Higgins got on his bicycle and went to the station hotel, where the barman said that Kavanagh had been in early in the morning and had told him of the excursion.

" 'Do you know Lough Erris?' asked our local magnate. 'As well as this bar-counter,' says I. 'Well, that's where we're off to,' says our man."

After leaving the cave and rowing back across the lake, Romilly had begun to ask Ezra about the cave drawing. She felt that no one else could explain it to her. She wanted to learn. He was conscious of this naïve desire to know things

27

in her dark, bright eyes turned to him without resentment for what had passed between them.

"For me that fish was a symbol of life," he said. "Life too has that pure form. What happens has a pure form if I have the strength to regard it. That's it. It is a desolate face, a dark, underground face like a monster's, or savage like a rock, or blank like a ruin. But regard it, have the strength to go on regarding it and it becomes not the face of chaos, but the face of God. I understood that there was an intense order in those few scratches on the wall of the cave and looking at them all else took on order for me, the rocks and the ruins."

No one had ever spoken such words to her. They did not satisfy her desire for knowledge, they did not explain anything to her. They submerged her in what was not knowledge or explanation or even conversation, but a kind of passion. She grasped that there could not be her kind of conversation between them.

"Aren't we going to bathe?" she said. She turned away and went into the wood to put on her bathing things. He did not mind her abrupt leaving of him. He knew that she was afraid of him and of him taking her where all her carefully acquired culture and her piety and book-learning would be of no avail.

Mr. Kavanagh came down from the car in a pair of blue-and-white bathing shorts whose stripes broadened where it stretched over his stomach. He walked out on to the small stone pier and stood there, short-necked and heavy. He swayed forward, gave a little push against the stone with his feet, like a bird about to fly, and entered the water with an astonishing softness. The girl appeared from the trees in a dark bathing suit. Kavanagh was swimming further out with long, easy strokes, and he called to her: "This is what I call sport. What say, miss? A good feed, a hot sun, a bit of water and to cap it all the presence of your ladyship." He stood up. The lake at this side was shallow, but on the far side it was dark and deep under the mountain. "Whew! I'm puffed," Kavanagh went on. "Out of condition, that's what."

The sergeant wondered why Father Mellowes had brought the fishmonger and allowed him to associate with his sister. Surely the priest knew of the scandal Kavanagh caused in the town by openly living with the Lee girl on his periodic visits to Altamont? Romilly stood for a moment beside Ezra on her way down to the water. Her hair was hidden in the rubber bathing cap that fitted tight, giving her face a nun-like look. She wore an old-fashioned bathing dress, but he could see the shape of her body.

"Can't you forgive me for not being your dead friend?" she asked.

He looked up at her with a shock. He knew that her brother must have mentioned Margareta to her. He had once spoken of her, very cursorily, to the priest. He didn't answer and she went on down to the water.

This was the moment at which Guard Higgins arrived, wheeling his bicycle along the track. He had not expected to find the sergeant, nor a strange young lady. The sergeant got up, thinking the guard had arrived with some urgent message from the barracks. But Guard Higgins leant his bicycle against a tree and went straight over to Kavanagh, who was standing on the stone jetty about to show them something pretty, as he thought of it.

"Well, what is it?" he asked, annoyed at the interruption.

"I don't like bothering you, Mr. Kavanagh, but—hot it is, is this: I want some ice," Guard Higgins said.

"You want what?" said Kavanagh, not relaxing his tense poise of a runner ready for the start.

"Ice," said the guard. He did not want the sergeant to overhear him.

"What the devil's got hold of you, Higgins? Have you a sup taken?"

29

"I was at the shop and the girl said the refrigerator was locked."

"I can't be bothered now. Don't you see I'm on holiday," Kavanagh said. He took a deep breath and a few quick steps and a hop which brought him to the end of the jetty. But something was wrong, the rhythm was lost, and he hesitated at the last moment and then flung himself forward in a desperate attempt to regain the lost magic of motion. He broke the water with a great splash and, rising immediately, roared at the guard: "Look here, what's your game, eh? Sneaking up with your blasted nonsense about ice. I know you and your ice!"

Guard Higgins turned away from the lake towards his dusty bicycle. But before he reached it, Father Mellowes was beside him laying a hand on his arm.

"How hot you are," he said. "You'd better have a glass of wine and a sandwich."

While he was taking the refreshment that the priest brought him from the remains of the lunch, Guard Higgins took the letter from his pocket and gave it to Father Mellowes to translate for him. It was full of technicalities and the guard listened while his hot, troubled face became placid and relaxed. Monsieur Domais ended by setting out the qualities necessary for a true horticulturist. This was a part that interested the guard especially and he asked the priest to translate it to him again.

"They must rely upon that intuitive faculty," wrote Monsieur Domais as to how the horticulturist was to distinguish between the many species of *Pooideal* "which can only be cultivated by a high degree of *la grande habitude de voir*."

Father Mellowes could not translate the last phrase, and this was the very one to which the guard attached the greatest importance. He repeated the words, trying to imitate the outlandish sound and going over them until, with the priest's help, he got it nearly right.

30

CHAPTER III

SIGNS
IN
THE
MOON

■ A COUPLE of weeks later Ezra was sitting with Kavanagh in the parlour above the fish-shop. It was Kavanagh's first visit to Altamont since the week-end of the picnic, and they were drinking Guinness while Annie prepared a fish supper in the small kitchen. She was no longer working for Kavanagh in his shop. The sergeant had spoken to her about the scandal of her relationship to her employer and had wanted to send her as maid to a family in another town. But she had run round to Father Mellowes. She had arrived one morning in her Sunday clothes and sat down heavily on the sofa.

"Don't send me out of the town," she had said. "All my friends are here."

Father Mellowes did not know what she was talking about. And when she realised that, she did not say anything about her interview with the sergeant. A look of complete innocence came into her violet eyes that had the freshness of flowers in her plump, freckled face.

"I lost my job," she said.

"I'm sorry for that. It's a pity losing a good job," said Father Mellowes. He knew nothing of the scandal. He heard very little of the town gossip.

"It's not that," she answered. She wasn't sure how much he knew about her. But when he waited she added: "I was used to him."

"You mean as an employer?" asked Father Mellowes.

"As a man, Father. That's what I mean."

"You were living together?" he asked.

"That's so," she said.

"Ah, my poor child," said the priest, his big face tilted down at her, regarding her.

"I'm in trouble," she went on.

"Ah, little one, you're going to have a child, is that it? And you've lost your job. And these two things that seem like the worst blows to you are the ways that our Lord shows His loving care for you. And was that the reason that Mr. Kavanagh gave you notice?" he added.

"No. He doesn't know about that."

"And I suppose if you told him he wouldn't marry you?"

"It isn't his," the girl said. She saw that she could confide in Father Mellowes. She had an instinct that there was depths in him in which all her worries and burdens could be swallowed up.

"There was another man, then?" he asked her.

"Yes."

"Wait a minute. We'll have a cup of tea," the priest said. He went out on to the landing and called down to Mrs. Bamber to make them a pot of tea. Annie had regarded the lithograph of St. Francis with the rays from the crucified Seraph piercing his own hands and feet. The dead white rays, the crimson wounds and the blue-black, stormy sky were beautiful to her. She had enjoyed sitting there drinking the hot, sweet tea and listening to Father Mellowes. She did not try to understand what he was saying to her. Sin and repentance were not real to her. The lithograph was real, and the large stuffed fish in a glass case in the window of Kavanagh's shop. Each meant to

32

her a certain atmosphere, a certain kind of life, the life of the flesh and the life of the spirit and she was quite ready to shift over from one to the other. The priest had asked her a question!

"Eh?" she said, starting.

"Ah, I'm sorry. You were thinking," he said.

"Oh, don't mind me, Father. I'm a terror for manners."

"If you'll excuse me now, Annie, I've got to go into the town. There are plenty of books there if you'd care to read till I come back at dinner-time."

"If you've any mending or washing, I'd rather do that, Father."

There had been a tap on the door and Sergeant Foley had come in with his greyhound, Rainbow Cutlet, covered from head to tail in a linen coat that hung down on each side to the ground. The priest's little dog hurled himself at this strange intruder. There was a mêlée of snarls and snapping and Annie burst out laughing. "The Cutlet," as he was locally called, had been out at exercise, the day of the great race was almost at hand, and the sergeant had come to ask Father Mellowes if he might use the sink in the kitchen in which to immerse his champion in a mustard bath, as the one at the barracks was too shallow.

"You'll find the very thing you want in the kitchen, sergeant. I've seen Mrs. Bamber bathing the children in it; and Miss Lee here won't mind giving you a hand, will you, Annie?" Father Mellowes said.

She did not mind. She had no resentment against the sergeant.

Kavanagh was now repeating this story to Ezra. He had heard it all from Annie when she had come secretly to the flat the night before. She was now temporarily taken on by Father Mellowes as a kind of housekeeper and had a small attic room at Mrs. Bamber's. But she had not told Kavanagh about how well she had got on with the sergeant. Of how, after they had dried the "Cutlet," she had mended the dog's coat for him that had been torn by the teeth of the priest's little mongrel, or that the sergeant had asked her to meet him on the night of the dog-races.

"That's freedom for you; that's democracy," Kavanagh was saying. "The girl can't sleep where she likes and I can't spend a week-end in my own flat with one of my own employees. But I'm not going to lie down and let them walk over me. I'll raise bloody hell in this gimcrack town before I'll let them go sneaking round taking my employees away from me."

Ezra drank the Guinness and listened. The crude, vulgar energy of Kavanagh, his anger and his lusts gave him a reality. To be in a room with most people was like being in a room with a ghost. So many people here struck Ezra as ghostly, their coming and going, their talk and expressions were ghostly and when he looked at them he saw nothing, or he saw something else. People who were not in pain, not in love, not angry, not in the grip of desire or of some secret vision; they were ghosts. He couldn't talk to them because the breath of his mouth would blow through them without touching them. But Kavanagh was ready to be touched and to be kindled, his little anger kindled by Ezra's greater anger. He seemed to sense Ezra's greater anger and to bow to it.

"I could bring business to this town. I could bring a bit of life to it," Kavanagh said. "But they'd sooner go to pot in their own petty way. They're scared of people like us, that's what. They're scared. And they'll be more scared when I'm done with them. And do you know what, if this town's finished, it's not the only one. There's many other towns all over the country that are going the same way. I've got branches in eight or ten other places and I know what's going on. I can smell it in the air. The good times are over for them, the times when you could look out of your hotel window on a fine Sunday morning and see the townspeople strolling up the main street to

34

Mass and pull down the blind again and go back to bed and have another snooze in peace and security, knowing that the day was long and there was a well-stocked larder downstairs and good company in the private bar, quiet knowledgeable fellows who could tell you the winners of the big races for the past twenty years and more. But now it's another story. No one remembers anything beyond the week before last, and if you sleep late they come rattling at the door wanting to do out the room. There's no ease and quiet. Everyone's nervous, with one eye on the next day or the next meal or the next drink. It's as if they were afraid that their new gimcrack houses and cars and wireless sets were going to go phut! Perhaps it's another war they're afraid of, one that they wouldn't be able to sit out on Guinness and rashers as pretty as they did the last. What say, Arrigho, is there going to be another bust-up?"

"Well, it can't last for ever," said Ezra. "No world has ever lasted very long. They all go down one after another and there's not much left, only a fish or a deer scratched on the wall of a cave, or some marble statues without arms, or a bit of red brick wall in a jungle somewhere. Perhaps our going down has begun and perhaps nothing can stop it. Sometimes it looks like that all right; you get the smell of it, like you said, in the air."

"You're right. We're going down," Kavanagh repeated, leaning heavily over the table, looking into the black beer. "This town's going down and it's the same tale in the others. And there's no use them blaming it on people like me. 'Kavanagh's one of those fellows who make trouble in the town and bring down its morals.' That's what the sergeant said to Annie. Hey, Annie," he called. "What was it the sergeant said?"

Annie put her head in the door. She wore a dirty white apron and had rolled up her sleeves. She smiled her slight, placid smile.

"I disremember exactly, Mr. Kavanagh. It doesn't signify. I'm here, anyhow, aren't I?"

"You're here, my girl, and they couldn't stop you," repeated Kavanagh, leaning far over the table and laughing into his glass of black stout. "And I'm going to let you into a secret, Arrigho; not now, though, wait till we've had a bit of supper. I'm going to throw a stone into their duck-pond that'll make a walloping big splash, me boy."

Ezra remembered how he had written home from the foreign city, the bombed, dying city, to his wife during the war about Margareta. He had written about bringing her back with him if they were alive after this particular catastrophe passed over. He had thought in his innocence that there would be no difficulties, that she would have found shelter and refuge with his own people. His wife had understood and agreed. But later, after she had spoken to some of the officials whose permission would have had to be had, she had written that it was impossible. She had spoken to their local priest. He had discussed with Ezra's wife the implications of letting Ezra bring Margareta back into their fold. And they had confused her with their complacent, duck-pond arguments. But in the end they have overcome her and she had written to him that she could not have Margareta. But by then Margareta was lying with a huge pile of rubble on her heart. And he could not go home. He felt no bitterness against his wife. On the contrary, she had, alone and with nothing but the words of his letters to help her, stood out as long as she could. As his wife, she was powerless; the family love, the duck-pond love was too much for her. And now he could not go back. She did not even know that he was in Ireland. She was all right. She had the house and enough money, but he could not go back and live with her.

"Let's have a bite to eat. What say?" Kavanagh said.

Annie brought in a huge plate of fish and some more bottles

of Guinness. She had tidied herself up and dusted her plump, freckled face with powder.

"Have a drink with us, Annie," Kavanagh said to her.

"You know I don't take anything, Mr. Kavanagh."

"Very well. Don't call me Mr. Kavanagh, but. That's not called for among friends. Have some port. Have something."

"All right. I don't mind a glass of port."

She was glad to be back here in the cosy, familiar atmosphere. She had often felt homesick in the past week for the little flat above the shop with its smell of stale, spilt stout and fish.

The three of them were sitting at the table; Kavanagh pulled Annie's chair nearer his own so that she was within hand-reach of him. He wanted to touch her, to lay his big hand on her. Ezra felt himself floating on a sea of black Guinness, lit by the violet eyes of Annie and scented by the greasy slab of fried fish crumbling open in white flakes on his plate. Kavanagh was opposite him, a big, smouldering shadow in the dusk of the room, leaning over the white table-cloth with an old-fashioned watch-chain strung across his broad, waistcoated torso. Ezra saw the glint of the gold chain as Kavanagh leant forward, overshadowing the bottles and Annie, brooding over them with his smouldering fire engendered by the black stout, anger, lust and some confused vision of revenging himself.

He began to speak in a low voice to Annie. She listened with her blank passivity, only turning her head slightly away from his hot, beery breath.

"Ah," she said. "I could never abide the sight of blood."

"A drop of blood, that's nothing, girl." He turned to Ezra. "Did you ever remark the holy picture that Father Mellowes has in his room?"

"I dread cutting myself," said Annie.

"Tcha! What a baby! Just a pin-prick somewhere where it won't be noticed. Here I'll show you. Give us a bit of light."

She switched on the light and came back to the table. Kavanagh took a needle from inside the lapel of his coat. He pulled up her dress over her knees and jabbed in the needle. She gave a little gasp and a drop of ruby blood appeared on her bluish white thigh.

She liked things to happen, even the sting of the needle; and she liked the thought of the bleeding picture. She liked the smell of drink on the breath of men. Heavy and passive in herself, she was like a sponge that soaked up sensation, excitement. But she pretended to be afraid of him and quickly pulled down her dress with a little squeal. He began to try to mollify her with pats and caresses, calling her a baby and holding the glass of port to her lips that were greasy from the fried fish. She drank the sweet wine passively, doing nothing beyond making the lazy movement of swallowing now and then, her head bent back and resting in the big palm of Kavanagh's hand. When he had emptied the glass into her mouth, he put it down and leant over her, looking at her.

"Don't mind any of them, Annie," Kavanagh said. He turned to Ezra. "The damned busybodies came round and spoke to her. They told her that by staying here in the flat with me over the week-ends she was causing a scandal in a respectable town." He could not get over it. He went on brooding on it.

Ezra had begun by listening, amused and detached. The quarrel between the toping fishmonger and the town had no real concern for him. But gradually he began to speak too, to be caught into the controversy in spite of himself. Whether Kavanagh followed him or not, he did not care. He spoke for the first time in all these years of the shape of the cataclysm through which he had been.

"When I walk down the main street of this town," he said, "past the small busy shops and the pubs with Guard Higgins on point duty at the corner and Father Mellowes coming down the steps from the church after hearing confessions, for a moment I too breathe a breath of sweetness. I am tempted to believe that this is peace and righteousness and that they're justified in protecting it. But it's no good. Because I know where this street leads and where all streets lead. Your sergeant and the others can't see beyond the end of their street. The words that they speak in this street would be meaningless in the other street, in the street in which I was."

"What street was that?" asked Kavanagh, fondling Annie with one hand while he held his glass of Guinness in the other.

"The street of a great city. It had been a street like the others, with tailors' dummies draped in the newest fashions in the shop-windows and restaurants with table lamps on the white cloths and a big, ugly church on the square at one end and hotels where they changed the towels in your bedroom every morning, and if a child fell and cut its knee on the pavement there was a great to-do and its mummy brought out her hanky and dabbed away the blood."

"Ha!" said Kavanagh blankly. He did not know what Ezra was getting at.

"As long as there were clean handkerchiefs to dab at scratched knees and glass in the shop-windows," Ezra went on, "the same sermons were being preached in the church at the corner as Father Mellowes preaches here.

"I knew that street as I know this street. I had been into each restaurant along it at one time or other. I had sat in the summer nights on the terraces of the cafés and seen the lights shining on to the leaves of the lime trees planted along it when it was still secure and sheltered between its shops and houses, leading to all the other streets of the world. But slowly there was a change along it. Not only that I was now alone in it, or that the bombs had ground down many of the houses to piles of rubble. A street between walls of rubble is still a street and the shape of the ruins becomes as familiar and homely as the

39

shape of the houses were. But now I began to know where it led.

"The street had its own air, its own atmosphere. Even when the houses collapsed they lay in their own dust, in their own light. Everything moves or stands in its own light or shadow, I suppose, a tree, a street, a rock, and the earth itself, and the final violation is the stripping from a thing of its own air. That is what happens to you when you're arrested; the little protective sanctum around you is violated—strange hands feel in your pockets, strange voices strip away the protective layer of space around you.

"I knew this first when the shells began to fall into the street. Shells are different from bombs. Shells are the first touch of the *others,* the sign of their presence; shells begin to strip away the familiar air and bring the first breath of the unknown darkness with them.

"It was the growing strangeness of the street that is what I remember of those days. I felt it turning into something different. Along part of it a column of tanks and heavy guns had been abandoned—for want of petrol, I suppose. I came on them there one evening, grey hulks of steel, like strange monsters washed up on a shore during a night of storm. I wasn't allowed in the streets because I was a foreigner, but I came out at night to look around. I came up out of the cellar where we were waiting, and each evening there was a new darkness in the street. It wasn't the same darkness through which the lights from the shops had shone and the buses rattled or even the darkness in which the houses had burnt after the raids. The street was being stripped of its own light and its own darkness and it lay there like the dead lie, without the halo of their own beings around them any more, exposed.

"I didn't know what was coming. There were no more newspapers and no wireless. There were only rumours, words in the darkness, names. But there were no names for the unknown shape; when they had spoken the strange names of Russian generals and Russian armies, there was still something that had not been given a name, the thing that would appear in the street at a certain coming hour of the day or of the night. There was another name being spoken like an incantation against the unknown horror: the army Wenck. In the cellars under the street and along the street at night there was this name spoken, in a question, an assertion or in irony. The army Wenck. That was the name of all that was familiar, the known, the past, fighting its way back to the city and the street. The army Wenck was the name of all that was known and familiar, the familiar pain, the familiar ruins and the familiar hunger and the small familiar joys and securities still left amid the ruins and the hunger. And the other names were the names of death, of the angel of death, of Astoreth, and they had the sound of the last trumpet. The horribly strange sound of something announcing the unknown doom.

"And in the street at night there were always new signs and new portents. No one knew what they meant, except that they meant the end coming nearer. There were the German lieutenant and sergeant hanging under the bridge of the elevated railway with a placard with words on it that confirmed the hopelessness of those who read it furtively as they passed. 'Found without arms in face of the enemy.'

"In face of the enemy. Those too were words that were mysterious and horrible. The street was now in face of the enemy! The street that had led to a bridge across the railway and beyond that to a leafy avenue that in its turn went out to a suburb now led only into the jaws of the enemy.

"I as a neutral might not have any enemy, but I had lived for five years in the street; through the war I had lived there and its smells and its ruins were familiar to me and I too was touched by the passing of that world. For a street is a world, with its air and its shape and its order. And it is a great shock, no matter how detached one may be, to see the actual hour in which order passes away and chaos appears. It is a shock in the depth of the heart. The heart cannot absorb the shapelessness of chaos, it is shocked, it is like a great scandal to it."

"That was what he said to Annie," Kavanagh interrupted. "That we were causing a scandal in this town."

"There were a couple of days and nights when I didn't leave the cellar," Ezra went on, "because we heard that foreign workers had been shot for being out in the street. All the people of the house were living in the cellars, Germans and foreigners together. The cellar had become a thoroughfare; holes had been broken through into the cellars of the next-door houses and it was possible to go from street to street through the cellars. I stayed two or three days in the cellar with the others from the house, sometimes in the dark and sometimes with a bit of candle burning. There in the cellar there were no more pretences; I had a glimpse of how a tribe must live in their huts in the depth of an African forest. All the escapes, the cinemas and radios and books, were gone and privacy was gone; no one lived any more in the little civilised isolation of his own room and his own possessions. There was no more dressing up or washing. If we stank, we stank. At least it was the stench of life and not the other stench that was beginning to drift through the streets.

"We were a little tribe in the midst of the forest on the edge of death. There were no more differences between us except what could be seen or felt. We were not Germans or Poles or Irish or railway officials or dressmakers or schoolteachers, but we were still men and women because the man and woman difference is a thing of shape and sensation and shape and sensation were left. Indeed, there was only shape and sensation. The shape of the shadows in the dark cellar, the new shape of time, flowing slower and slower, like a river at its mouth beginning to meet the pressure of the sea, and the shape of our own cramped bodies. The underground darkness was full of sensation as the day or the night up above in the world seldom is. The two dry slices of black bread which we could eat once every twelve hours were a sensation, they were sweeter than manna, and the quivering of the darkness from the bombs and the shower of shells that they called Stalin organs was a sensation in the spine and in the guts, like a tree whose roots are shaken by a storm. And when we prayed it was a different praying to most of the church praying; it was a turning of our dirty, pale faces to the face of darkness beyond the cellar-darkness; it was the feeling in the trembling of the cellar and the falling of the plaster, the passing of the angel of death and the angel of the end. And if a man took the hand of the girl huddled next to him it was another touch from the old touching, the old mechanical caressing.

"But even down there we could sense the progress of the battle.

"Soldiers came through, passing down the street through the cellars, their dull-painted, steel helmets like dark hoods over their faces in the shine of their electric torches. And they were questioned, questioned. And the same blank look in reply, tinged with impatience, and then the long, empty, noisy hours again with no one coming through, with whispers and only the minute break of going out into the passage to make water.

"It was about the third night that I went up and out into the street again. Now it had changed again. In two days there was a change that normally would have taken centuries. There were corpses lying in the street and no one paying any attention to them. Even two days before, when someone was killed they were picked up and carried away. Death had still been an accident, a part of disorder to be quickly tidied up. Now there was only disorder; chaos and death were beginning to be in the street, not as something accidental, but as part of the street.

43

There were women with basins and buckets and a few men with knives cutting up a dead horse in the middle of the street. I went back to the cellar and got a basin and a knife and hacked away between the white bones, filling the basin with slabs of dark flesh. That was the treasure of those nights, the dark slabs of flesh, and it was lusted after more than the flesh of women. There were many living women and girls in the streets and only a few horses. There was a crowd round the horses with buckets and basins, and those who had not basins took the wet chunks of meat in their arms, hugging them to their breasts. In the morning the dead were still lying in the street in the full light of day and I stood and looked at a group of four or five bodies in their dusty sleep, a child and young woman and an old woman, drinking in this new shape, the shape of death that was strange and shocking and fascinating at first, as the shape of a woman's naked body at a window had been to me long ago as a boy. But as I walked down the street I had learnt this new shape, death-in-the-street, the dead sharing the street with the living and making again something different out of the street, signing it with their dusty, still and huddled sign.

"We feasted on the meat in the candle-lit cellar and the girl next me kissed my hands and pressed them to her breast in rapture at satiating her hunger.

"That night I was out in the street again. There were a lot of shells falling, and while I was sheltering under the remains of the bridge of the elevated railway I got a piece of shrapnel through my shoulder. There was a dressing-station further up the street and although it was a military station I went there with a sergeant who had been wounded in the leg and, as I was helping him, they let us both in. They couldn't do much for us; there were no bandages, no antiseptics, only the candle-lit rooms with the shadowy, blanket-covered forms. There was only one sister, and as she was washing the sergeant's leg wound he talked to her. He was a small, thick-set little fellow of forty-five and he had a way with him, an air of knowing a great deal of what was going on.

" 'What are they holding out for? Do you really expect the army Wenck to break through from the West?' the sister asked. She could hardly hold the basin of water for tiredness.

"The sergeant shrugged his shoulders and smiled his weary, knowing smile.

" 'We heard the capitulation would come to-night,' said the nurse. 'They are said to be discussing terms.'

" 'Terms!' said the little sergeant with his thin smile. 'All I know is they have thrown in the Norwegian S.S. Division, all big, young fellows of twenty or so. I saw some of them in the Friedrichstrasse area.'

" 'There's no sense in it; no sense,' said the girl, slopping water from the basin to the floor in her weariness.

"Afterwards the sergeant and I sat in the hall. The outer door was ajar and the street was just beyond, and we were both drawn towards it, not wanting to be far from it. We sat in the hall and through the door came the night air from the street with the smoky tang that had been in it for weeks. And there was a faint smell of excrement; it had been there, too, for days, like the scent of savoury, slightly rotten cooking, and I did not know whether it was only a memory in my nose lingering from the cellar or whether here, too, there was no sanitation. Now and then the sergeant asked me to go to the door and have a look out; he couldn't move so easily because of his leg wound.

"It was a clear night with a waning moon and I could see along the street. The smooth black surface of the wide street gleamed and it seemed very quiet. There was always the background of noise, but that we were used to and there were no new noises and no shells. Only the street lying empty with its dark, traffic-polished surface leading away into the night. Such a moment of quiet there had not been in these weeks, and I stood there alone and came to myself as I had not in all that time. In the long hours in the cellar I had only been capable of waiting with the others, dreaming of food, of a bed, waiting for the hour of eating the two slices of bread or the two cold potatoes, drinking in every scrap of rumour. But now in the street outside the dressing-station I felt a change in myself. I had strength again, and not drifting here and there with each pang of hunger, each wave of sleeplessness, each new whispered announcement. It was as if I had got strength at the last minute. But so it is with me; all happens to me at the last minute.

"When I came back the sergeant had got hold of an old civilian suit and was putting it on, slowly drawing the trousers on over his stiff leg.

" 'How's it look?' he asked.

" 'Worn. But that doesn't matter if it fits.'

" 'Not the suit, man, the street.'

" 'It's quiet,' I said. 'It's quieter than it's been for a long time.'

"He was taking papers and things out of the pocket of his uniform, tearing them up, tearing up his soldier's *soldbuch,* and laying a few things aside, a comb and some money and a small tattered New Testament. There was an envelope stuck in it as a marker and he opened it and said to me: 'Do you know that all this was prophesied in the Bible. Listen.' He held the small book close to the hurricane lamp on the table and began to read: 'Then he said unto them: Nation shall rise against nation and kingdom against kingdom and great earthquakes shall be in divers places, and famines and pestilences; and fearful sights and great signs shall there be from heaven. . . . For these be the days of vengeance, that all things which are written may be fulfilled. . . .'

"And these words were themselves a sign to me," Ezra went

46

on, "coming in and hearing these words I knew what it was that I had seen in the street."

"What was it?" Kavanagh asked. Annie, too, was listening with her big, freckled face against Kavanagh's shoulder.

"I had seen how these things must be if we were not to go on swimming round our duck-pond. We dare not be given too much security. As soon as we have a little security, we settle down by our duck-ponds, and it doesn't matter whether it's a religious duck-pond, a cultural duck-pond or an economic duck-pond. It's all the same old mud. The little duck-pond writers, the duck-pond reformers, and the little white duck-pond God with its neat crown of thorns. That's our great genius: to tame! We have our tame God and our tame art, and it is only when the days of vengeance come that there's a flutter around the pond."

"A flutter around the pond!" repeated Kavanagh with a cackle. Ezra looked at the big, slightly bemused face with a momentary dislike. He knowing nothing of the price paid in horror, in starving and sweating and bleeding, had no call to use the words that Ezra might use without offence.

"After the days of vengeance there comes a new breath. Here and there, among those who have survived, comes a new vision, further than the duck-pond vision. That's the only hope for us now: a new vision and a new god. That's what I saw that last hour before the end, with the wide, empty street waiting under the moon. It was a strange moon, the colour of flesh bled bluish-white. And then I went back to the dressing-station and the little sergeant was reading those words out of the book he had come across emptying out his uniform pockets: 'And there shall be signs in the sun and in the moon . . . and upon the earth distress of nations, with perplexity, the sea and waves roaring.' "

CHAPTER IV

THE
VARIED
SHAPES
OF
VIOLENCE

■ EZRA STOPPED speaking to take a swill of the black stout. By now Kavanagh was slightly drunk. Not really drunk, though, because what Ezra was saying kept him from drifting down on the dark tide of Guinness in his blood.

"At midnight the sergeant and I were still sitting in the hall of the flat that had been turned into a hospital," Ezra was saying. "I was thinking of going back to the cellar. 'Hold on a bit,' the sergeant would say. 'You've got all night, haven't you?' But I had seen the sign in the moon and I wanted to be back in my own corner——"

"What sign was that?" asked Kavanagh.

"That's only a way of speaking. It was a sign in myself," Ezra said; "the sign that I was ripe for what was coming. And the moment you are ripe for what is coming, it comes. Death, pain, love, whatever it may be."

"That's a queer word," said Kavanagh. "What about all the others who weren't ripe, as you call it?"

"I don't know. There are two faces to reality, and I have seen them both. There was the bloody face of the sister as I saw her a little later, one of all the faces of the raped, the dying, the

48

horror-stricken and the other face, the face of 'Not a sparrow falls without the Father——' and whoever has seen these two faces as one is finally delivered and at peace. But I haven't. And now I never shall.

"I wanted to go but I kept staying on to keep the sergeant company. We had been talking and we stopped talking. There was a new sound from the street, a soft, even sound after all the loud and intermittent sounds of the time before. I peered out from behind the door. I saw dimly a column of men pass down the other side of the street.

" 'What is it?' asked the sergeant. I didn't know, and yet I knew. I did not want to give it a name. To name the hour for which all had been waiting in fear and trembling.

" 'Well, what is it, man?'

" 'The Russians,' I said.

"We were speaking lower. 'Did you see them?' he asked. I thought that in spite of all his air of knowingness even he had still a hope about the army Wenck. We heard more of them passing and then the door was pushed open and some of them came in, in their baggy, belted uniforms. They had come. The Apocalyptic rider on the pale horse had dismounted and come through the door into the hall and gone on into the wards. There was a sentry at the door, and the sergeant and I went back into the ward, where a Russian colonel was standing talking in German to the chief orderly and a soldier with a tommy-gun stood just behind him. Then the officer went into the small room where we had had our wounds dressed by the sister, and the soldier stood outside the closed door. In a few minutes they came out again and the colonel went upstairs with his body-guard and the sister went about her duties, silent. I was spoken to by a big, slouching fellow in German and I showed my pass-port which, being printed in English, French and Gaelic, he could not read. But he did not want to read it. That was the first thing I learnt about these Apocalyptic hordes. They had

49

not yet come to the complete faith in documents and documentation that the Germans and Americans and English have. He looked at me out of his small, peasant eyes and repeated after me, 'Irländer,' and seemed to think it over and think me over. He handed me back my papers and slouched off down the room, the gun dangling from his big hand, stooping over a mattress now and then as the fancy took him and demanding the papers of the man lying on it, but then hardly looking at them, dangling the gun and kicking the straw of the mattress with his big boot.

"The colonel's orderly came down and went back upstairs with the sister. All the time I wanted to get back to the cellar. My few belongings were there. I felt that the end had come and caught me far from home.

"'Wait a bit,' the sergeant told me. 'Wait an hour or two and let things settle down.' I would have been still waiting if I'd waited for that," Ezra went on.

"An hour or two," repeated Kavanagh in his own slow way, wiping his mouth. "An hour or two, ha!"

"The little sergeant and I went back and sat in the hall. 'This is the best place to be, in a hospital,' he said.

"The long, long waiting was over; the end had come. The sergeant had heard that the city had capitulated. No more bombs would fall, no more shells; the rocking of the earth that loosened the roots of the heart in your breast was over; the earth was still. I could see out into the street past the sentry lounging at the half-open door and it was still. But it was not the beginning of peace. 'There was silence in heaven and on earth for the space of half an hour.'

"The sister came downstairs. Her face was scratched and bitten and bloody. I went to the door and stood outside it, looking up and down the street. I did not want to seem to be in a hurry. I must move like these men moved, easily, slouching without haste. There were two of them outside the door talking and I stood beside them. I felt the breath of violence in which we stood and moved and had our being. The former, explosive violence had passed away and there was this new, quieter, more intimate violence in the air of the street. All these years we had moved in and breathed the air of hatred, of violence and the threat of violence. Not only the explosive violence, the violence that came down out of heaven, but the other soft-footed, official violence. I knew much about the shape of violence and I could sniff it around me, in all its different shapes and forms. If you have a kind of quietness and suppleness in you you can often slip through under the very jaws of violence, but if you haven't, if you're nervous and excitable and if your movements of body and of soul are too quick or too set in one direction, then you're lost from the start. I had lived with it, in a city where all the offices in all the official buildings were ante-rooms of violence, and, waiting outside them, waiting for one's turn, however quiet you tried to be, your armpits got damp. That was the mechanical, statistical violence, and you couldn't escape it if, because of your papers, you came into one of the doomed categories. That was the violence of order, the terrible statistical violence of the great machine of order and it had its lair in every street, in dusty corridors and offices and its threat was in every ring of the bell, in every strange voice.

"In the street as long as I had lived there had always been the unseen presence and pressure of violence like an invisible hand laid on the heart. Even in my room it was there, the slight pressure always there, subtly altering the shape of everything, squeezing everything a little bit smaller. Just as long before I had sometimes been in another great city and I had lived in the pressure of another hand laid on me, the hand of sex. Sex was then the great mystery for me; it was in the belly, in the house and in the streets. And later in this other city and in this other street it was violence.

"I thought about this as I stood at the door of the dressing-station and tried to sense the new violence that had come to replace the old. And I felt that this new violence was not so statistical, and you might escape it not so much by having the right papers, the right signatures, but by the way you moved and looked, by keeping a small centre of quiet in you.

"As I say, I know all about violence and its different shapes. I have sat waiting in corridors with violence hidden on the other side of a door and known it there, known in my stomach that it was there, unseen, and waited, gone dead and numb between chest and belly with the touch of its invisible hand in my guts. You get so that you can sniff it from far away, when it's hidden away behind doors and walls. You can walk down a street full of shops and traffic and the sun shining and the old women calling the lastest editions of the papers, and you can know in a slight sensation below the ribs that behind all this, like a boy who has wound up his train and sits back watching it go, there is violence. I got so that I could sense it in the very stone of the houses, in the reflection of the windows. And I hadn't completely escaped it, either. For some months I had been locked away with the others, though later I had been let out again to walk in the street or sit in the cafés and restaurants, moving in the pseudo-freedom of a world in which everyone is numbered and registered and summoned from time to time into one of the ante-rooms of the great machine. I had lived all this time in this order of brooding, hidden violence that was broken through from time to time by the other violence, the open violence of destruction. It had a different face, but from its mouth came the same breath of the pit, and when the cellar rocked you knew it was the same hand that rocked it as the cold hand that grabbed you in the guts as you waited for your turn outside one of the closed doors in the big building down the street.

"And to-night the hand of violence had another grip. So far

I had only caught a glimpse of it in the night air and in the marks of its claws on the face of the nurse, which was no more than a touch in passing. I leant up against the door lintel and smoked my cigarette to the end, and as I threw the butt down I moved off into the street, trying to make my movements quiet and familiar as I think I would try to move in a lion's cage. The two soldiers stopped talking together. I did not look back, but strolled on very slowly, and I heard them talking again and at that moment I had a kind of love for them, because they had left me alone.

"I walked down the street. It had changed since I had walked up it with the little sergeant limping on my arm some hours before. There had been that silence, as for the space of half an hour, and in that space the last wall had fallen that had surrounded it, that had made it, in spite of all, still a street in a city with still some faint air of being sheltered, as towns and cities were once shelters. But now it was a space open to all the winds that blew.

"I knew this even more certainly when I reached the cellar. It was no more a shelter. It was a ravaged pit. But how easily and subtly the body accepts all so long as it can still breathe and stretch itself and talk. Some get over it in talking and some in silence; the ones who talk, quicker. The girl who had shared my corner for the last weeks showed me the scratches on her arm and began to talk to me. She huddled up close to me and I put my arm around her and listened to the quick, warm words against my cheek. They had taken her and raped her in the flat above. But already rape, that a few hours ago had the shape of the unknown horror, similar to the shape of death, was something familiar, a thing like the corpses lying in the street, that after all could be in some way come to terms with, and turned out not to be the final horror. You adapt yourself to it, you become a girl-who-has-been-raped. You pass in a short time, in that 'space of half an hour,' from being one thing to being the other. As the street did. It is the moment of passing over, of giving up what you were, and knew and which was the form and sign under which you had lived, almost the *you*. But not quite the *you*. Even under the other form, the new raped form there was still the *you*, and quite quickly it conformed itself and was chattering, making the same gestures, pouring out tea made from the packet the soldier had given. But the hand trembled. She spilled some tea on the blanket that she had pulled over us, and she showed me her bare wrist. 'They are taking all the wrist watches and jewellery,' she said. 'Their arms are covered with watches to the elbow. As long as I don't get a dose,' she went on, 'I don't mind getting pregnant. I can cure that, but I'm afraid of getting a dose. You're lucky your girl is lying under the ruins,' she said. 'She's better off.'

"She was being a little false, a little sentimental. I knew I was not lucky and that I would never be lucky again. If I had had Margareta with me there in the cellar, then I would have been lucky, let her have been twenty times raped, let her be scratched and bitten and raped, but there under the same blanket, pouring the tea, or with no tea, with nothing, then I would have known the unfathomable gift of luck. But I let the girl go on, chattering in her quick whisper with my arm around her, her breath on my cheek: 'I know of a place in the ruins,' she said, 'and I'm going out there to hide as soon as it begins to get light. I'm too sore to stay here and have that done to me again.'

"In the next days I got to know what rape looks like as you can't know it from hearsay, as you can't know what raids are and death-from-explosion is from hearsay. Violence never takes the shape that you imagine it will. The first rape I saw was the body of a young girl on the floor of the cellar, spread-eagled, not like a girl any more, like something nailed to a wall, a skin or a rug or some rags with the bare legs sticking out of them.

54

But not a girl's body; and what they were doing to her wasn't like what you had thought it would be like. It was like some mechanical operation, pumping up a tyre or like the drilling that goes on in the street, with a little group of workmen standing round; only all went silently, quite silent and against flesh instead of concrete."

Kavanagh was listening, rapt in the dark miasma produced by the Guinness against which appeared the varying face of violence that Ezra had conjured up for him into the quiet parlour. One heavy arm lay across the table-cloth, which was already stained with stout and grease, and the other arm encircled Annie. When Ezra paused to drink from his glass or light a cigarette or go to the lavatory, Kavanagh leant over the girl, whispering. He was stirred by this tale of Nineveh. Why had his path not led down that street? Why was he condemned to walk down these mean streets of Altamont and the other towns where he was frustrated and diminished? He should have been there, where Ezra had been, there at the beginning of the end. He saw himself there in the foreign darkness, among ruins. He did not know what ruins were, what a razed street looked like. He knew he had only his small vision of darkness; the constricted night in which he sometimes moved through the back streets of Dublin, visiting mean houses in the rain, leaving again later in the deserted night, limping home past the rows of shuttered shops with the thirst in his bowels damped but unslaked. He turned savagely to Annie: "You know what you have to do, eh? Take a needle and prick yourself like I showed you—or if you can't manage to draw enough blood like that, take a safety-razor blade. And then with a match or a pencil dab a drop or two of the blood on the holy picture, see? On the hands and the feet of St. Francis, that's the ticket. That's all. Then wait, lie low. I'll do the rest. All you've got to think of is to keep the blood on the holy picture. There'll be a to-do, there'll be a holy, bloody fiesta when the word gets round, as it will, first through the urchins who are always in and out of the Reverend Father's room. As soon as he washes off the blood, you wait till the stage is clear and on you dab it again."

He got up and limped into the bathroom to fetch a blade.

"Ah, me bould Moss Kavanagh," said the voice within him, mocking, "what a bloody, great fellow you are with your needles and matches. Matches! Jaysus! Matches!"

He fetched the blade all the same. He laid it on the table. He wanted to go on listening to the words of Ezra. But Ezra had not much more to say. One picture remained, for some reason, still at the surface of his consciousness, ready to be told among all the others that had sunk into him and were too absorbed into him to be told.

On the last evening that he had been in the cellar before he had moved back up to his room in the flat above, the second evening after the end of the war, a figure had appeared in the doorway. It had stood there in a long, well-fitting coat, with pale leather gloves and a cane in one hand, exuding a faint fragrance of eau-de-Cologne in the evil-smelling cellar. It had stood looking at them and had nodded to them and then turned and gone, followed by the little group of soldiers who accompanied it. Not one of them huddled in the cellar had known what to make of it. There was a hum of talk around it. Did it herald the end of the war? For at that time they had not known that the war was over. Or the end of the sack of the city? And then there was the question whether it had really nodded at all.

Kavanagh was standing at the window. The house was at a corner and the window at which he stood looked out on a side street and over the roofs of Altamont towards the hills. The other window faced on to the main street. From where he was, Kavanagh saw the cold, grey flush of dawn. The blackness of night had turned to ash piled on the hills and dully reflecting the still far-away flame of day. He limped to the other window. When he had drunken a few pints of stout, his limp always became more noticeable. From this window there was nothing to be seen but the oceanic darkness. That was better. Kavanagh did not yet want the dawn. He did not yet want the day that would bring him back to the shop, to the mean street of the provincial town from the other street down which he had followed Ezra in the Doomsday darkness. His heart had expanded as Ezra's words had touched it. He felt it would burst if it could not be stilled. It needed darkness; he had been brought by Ezra to a place on the edge of depths that seemed half-familiar to him. Had he seen them in dreams? There was still the night left. From this window the night was still long —long enough for him to go down into it with Annie and be stilled. Be stilled? That was a queer word, too. He stood staring out at the darkness that already seemed a shade less profound. He could see the low roofs of the shops in Main Street. Was there still enough of the night left in which to do that that would save him from the drabness of the coming day?

Yet when Ezra rose to go, Kavanagh tried to keep him. He knew that when he went he would take with him some of the breath of darkness, of the *Dies Irae* darkness, and that what was left of the night would be lessened and diminished. They split one more bottle of stout together, and then Ezra crossed the street to Flood's hotel.

Kavanagh sat on at the table. He heard Annie washing at the sink. He would show them! He would desecrate their little pieties with her body and blood. He would slake his lust by befouling their miserable altars!

When she had finished washing, she walked naked through the parlour to the bedroom. "Going to bed," she murmured.

"You might remember that this is the parlour, girl, and put something on when you're going through it," he said. He

57

hated her for taking him so much for granted, for taking this night for granted, for not being affected by Ezra's words, for not being afraid of him.

"What for? Aren't you used to the sight of me?" she said.

"More than used. I'm sick of it and that's a fact." But it was not true. He was seeing her for the first time.

In this smouldering, mouldering way, the quarrel which on his part was only a polite pretence had dragged on as he undressed and got into bed with her. He smelt the kitchen soap that she had used. She lay quite still and breathed through her mouth. Kavanagh had turned to her savagely in the dark. To-morrow he must return to Dublin, and there was so little darkness left between him and the long, drab day that would dawn. He had other nights, of course, but each night it would be more difficult to wrest from her what he wanted. He thought of the soldiers sacking the city, their arms covered in watches. What was there left for him to do, to get? He could not sack a city. But he could at least raise quite a little bit of trouble in this town.

He would smear their holy pictures for them with the blood from her big, bluish-white thigh! He was a little drunk; not with the stout, though. That was a surface drunkenness. Dawn was at the window; but now he had no more fear of the sober, pious light of the small-town day. Let the light fall on the street, on the black clothes of Father Mellowes clip-clopping down the steps of the church from saying Mass, *dominus vobiscum, ite Missa est,* on the women doing their shopping, the bacon machine slicing the rashers while they waited, thin, thick or medium, fat, streaky or lean, the jingle of the till, of the bicycle bells in the street, of the bell rung by the servers at Mass. All the tinkling, clinking, chattering day that was ebbing back into the street, but before which there was still these hours of silence. In the grey silence he had yet time to burrow into the secret flower of chaos whose pollen was blood.

CHAPTER V

THE
BLEEDING
PICTURE

■   Ezra lay in bed in his room,
number eighteen, in Flood's hotel. His breakfast had been
brought by the dark little chambermaid called Eileen who was
very pious. She moved, he thought, with a small, pious step
and put down the tray with a small, pious clatter, neither slap-
dash nor lingering.

Now he had a room with a bed on which he could lie, and
what he wanted would be brought to him, coffee, marmalade,
the *Irish Times,* a poached egg, a bottle of stout, his letters, his
laundry. In the big imitation marble basin, the heavy furniture,
the long narrow windows there was the shape of security. He
did not believe in it. He did not believe in the rock on which
Flood's hotel had been built, the rock of nineteen-hundred or
thereabouts, but while it lasted he was ready to enjoy it.

A few mornings after the night he had spent at Kavanagh's,
Romilly Mellowes asked for him at the desk downstairs. He
came down and brought her into a small reception-room at the
back of the hotel that was always empty and had a smell that
reminded him of the smell inside the brougham of his great-
aunt when he used to drive with her as a child. Romilly had
come to ask him if he would give her German lessons while
she was at Altamont. The Colonel whom she was to marry

had many German books and she wanted to be able to understand at least a little about them when she began to make a catalogue of his library.

"But perhaps you have no time," she said. He had never before had so many hours day after day to a measured rhythm that was the very rhythm of this false security. "Breakfast from seven till half-past nine," it said on the menu. "A shilling extra charged for meals served in the bedrooms." It amused him, this great pretence of security, this being able to say that wet or fine, winter or summer, from such an hour to such an hour, the tables would be laid, the kettles boiling, the rashers frying. He did his writing in the mornings and he had the whole, long afternoons free. In the rainy weather—it rained a great deal in Altamont—he sat reading in his room until it was half-past six by the station clock, when he went out and bought the evening paper that came on the train from Dublin and had a drink in a pub before dinner. He had time to give her lessons. He picked up a dirty menu card that was lying at the table and gave it to her to translate. When she said: *"Von sieben bis halb zehn,"* the words had an other meaning. That language belonged for him to another time, the words had something mixed in with them, a fear. Even the simplest German words, hearing them in the security of Flood's hotel, had still about them the sound and taste of those days. *"Bis acht Uhr,"* Margareta had said, leaving him at the corner of the wintry street, smiling from the turned-up collar of her coat. All the words were coming back, but they were no longer quite the same words; they had another meaning as well, as though somewhere in the middle or at the end of each something was added, like a faint bell-stroke, tolling.

He had filled his room with books; there were books on the old-fashioned mantelpiece, on the chest-of-drawers and on the floor. With his books and his typewriter, a fire in the grate in cold or wet weather, and his meals served on a table beside it

60

when he wanted, he spent whole days in the room, not even going across the street to the pub opposite and not even bothering to send down for the evening paper. Sometimes he spent a whole day without going downstairs, without going beyond the bathroom and lavatory that were a few steps down the passage from his room, building an invisible wall between himself and the world. Perhaps because he had seen so many walls fall or be blown down and had lived in a place of broken walls or no walls—except prison walls, for there were always enough walls left to make prisons—he was a little obsessed by the problem of walls in general. Time and walls and violence —these were things which he had a great feeling about, whose shape and ways and disguises he had studied, not with thoughts, but with sweat and blood.

The afternoon that Romilly came for her first lesson was one of those wet days that he had spent entirely in his room. He hung her wet mackintosh in the bathroom and pulled up a chair for her beside his own at the fire. She began to tell him something in halting German, helping herself out with English.

"There's a very queer thing that I'll try and tell you," she said. Before she began he knew what it was.

"It's the picture of St. Francis that hangs in my brother's room—*in dem Zimmer meines Bruders. Blutstropfen sind darauf erschienen.*" The heavy German words, as though themselves coming from a wound or causing one, dropped into the rather stuffy quite of his room.

All the words were coming back again. He had only to stay in his room and all would come to him in it. There was no hope of being left alone.

She began to tell him that for the past few days Father Mellowes had noticed a secret excitement in the children, in Dinah and Joey and the others that were always about the house and garden and in and out of his room. He had not had time to take any great notice of them, but yesterday when he came back from the town for lunch there was a little crowd of people gathered in the garden outside the house. In his room he found the children, standing round as though awaiting him or someone else.

"Hello. Whatever's up?" he had asked.

"It's the holy picture, Father," Dinah had said.

"I seen it too," said another child. All had begun to talk. He had turned them all out except Dinah, and he had called Romilly from her room.

She was sitting there in her neat clothes in the big fusty armchair by the fire, and she was Margareta as she had been on her first visit to him at his pension, as women were on their first visits, sheathed in their own air, in their clothes, in their words, like a gift brought in and left wrapped-up, not opened. They came and sat in his chair, leaning back in it, at ease, but all the same never seeming to weigh it down, hardly touching it, their limbs light like flame.

She went on telling him about the holy picture, seeking for the German words, sometimes dropping back into their own language, her eyes bright. She enjoyed the excitement. Her dark eyes were lit by the thought of the commotion.

Dinah had told them that the wounds on the hands and feet of St. Francis had dripped with blood. Father Mellowes had gone over and examined it. There had been no blood on it, but around the garishly painted stigmata there had been marks made by dirty little hands.

Ezra saw that, in spite of the scepticism of her brother, she half believed in the miracle. She spoke of *der heilige Franziskus,* sitting there in her untouched bloom, bud-like in the neat leaves of her clothes, her rounded cheeks pink in the warmth of the fire.

The German words were turning syrupy with echoes of prayers learnt during her year in the convent. There was the convent behind her and marriage with the cultured Colonel in front of her, and she could speak German prettily, expressing her half-belief in miracles in it very nicely. There had been the Lithuanian girl in the cellar saying in her German that was not so pretty as Romilly's: "I'm too sore to have that done to me again. I'm going out to hide in the ruins." He spoke those sentences to Romilly and told her to repeat them. It amused him to hear her say them so prettily. She did so and asked: "Why? What does it mean?"

"I just happened to remember them. They mean that bleeding pictures are an anticlimax."

Father Mellowes had gone to the bathroom and, bringing a sponge, had wiped the marks from the shiny surface of the lithograph.

"There. That's all right again now," he had said to the little girl. Then he had gone out on to the landing, where a host of small, eager faces were raised to his. The children had hoped that he might be about to announce something hitherto unheard of and extraordinary.

"Now, you ruffians, you're going to get a drop," he had told them, but gently, with gentleness shining on his glasses. "It isn't the end of the world this time, not even the return to earth of *der heilige Franziskus*. Run off! Shoo! You'll have to make do with the same old games a bit longer. Everything's not going to be turned inside out after all."

"I saw it," one of the smallest boys had repeated obstinately. The children had felt that they were being excluded from something momentous and exciting. They had not taken seriously a word that the priest had said to them.

On their return to the garden, they had been set on by the adults with a flow of questions. The children had given different versions of what had happened in the few minutes since Father Mellowes' return. Some had said he had rushed for a sponge and a basin of water; that afterwards they had seen the water in the basin a deep red. One had averred boldly that

63

the priest had told them that, St. Francis was about to return to earth again and another that he had forbidden them playing any noisy games, because, this little informant had added, "holy miracles were happening."

Eileen came in with the tea things on a tray, putting it down on the table beside Romilly. The deft, pious movements of the girl, the faint scent of the buttered toast and the muted ringing of bicycle bells in the gathering dusk filled the room. As Romilly lifted the cosy from the tea-pot, Ezra said: "I still can't get used to this sort of time—your time, tea-time and fire-light time. But I suppose we may as well enjoy it while we can."

"What other time is there?"

"*Acht Uhr,* alert; *neun Uhr,* alarm; *zehn Uhr,* starvation; *elf Uhr,* arrest on suspicion; *zwölf Uhr,* provisionary liquidation."

As they had tea, Romilly told how she and her brother had sat down to lunch and the priest had spoken about other things. But when Annie had come in to clear away the dishes he had asked her when anything strange about the picture had first been noticed.

"The day before yesterday. It was one of the kids that saw it."

"And was the cause of it too, I wouldn't wonder, with jammy fingers."

"It wasn't jam, Father."

After lunch he had had to go into the town. The crowd hanging around the house had grown.

"What do you want?" he had asked gently of those nearest him. No one answered; there was a shuffling and a doffing of caps.

"What they wanted," Ezra said, "was a miracle, excitement and sensation."

When Father Mellowes had come back towards evening, he

found his landlady, Mrs. Bamber, sitting in his parlour. She had lit a small red lamp and placed it on the mantelpiece under the picture. She had a newspaper folded on her knee, the *Altamont Advertiser*, but she had apparently felt there would have been something disrespectful in opening and reading it.

"What's wrong now?" Father Mellowes had asked.

Without a word, Mrs. Bamber had pointed to the picture. Father Mellowes had gone up to the lithograph and examined it. He had seen what looked like a drop of blood clinging to each of the saint's outstretched hands.

Ezra was aware as she talked that she too half believed in and hoped for the miracle. He saw it in her dark eyes, bright with a child-like, naïve shine.

"Better believe in bleeding pictures than in Altamont with its holy pictures that neither bleed nor sing nor dance," he said. "There's nothing bleeding or singing or dancing in anyone here except in some of the children and in Kavanagh, the fishmonger."

"Oh, that horrible man."

"Horrible? I like him."

"But you, Mr. Arrigho," she said. "What do you want here? Why do you stay here at all?"

"Because it's not worth the trouble of going anywhere else. Besides, it amuses me here, just to stay here and look at things, to sit back and see what's going on. In myself and in the world, in books and in other people."

"And what do you see?"

"Contradictions mostly, and confusions. In the world darkness and violence in wait, violence driven out by violence, but never overcome, simply lurking round the corner. And in myself a particle of the great violence, too, and also a particle of anti-violence, of a hatred of violence that is still not quietude or patience. And in other people more confusion and the apathy that is the counterpart of violence, and here and there a little singing and dancing and a lot of bleeding."

"And in me?" she asked.

"In you, Miss Mellowes, there is a great deal of virginity that neither sings nor dances, and no bleeding and nothing that has yet touched or been touched by God or man."

"Your Margareta, did she sing and dance?"

"A few thousand tons of rubble on your back stops all singing and dancing."

He had thought that she would not come again. Yet she had come. She had come back at the appointed time of her next lesson, taking off her mackintosh, sitting down and drying her wet ankles at the fire. She had gone on with her report, partly in her slow, soft German and partly in her own tongue, of the events at Mrs. Bamber's, which were by now the talk of the town.

Quite a little crowd were constantly outside the house, in the garden under the priest's window. Women came and said the Rosary, talked together and stared up at the window, waiting for Father Mellowes to come down, and after an hour or so they drifted off again and others came. Mrs. Bamber herself had removed her votive lamp at the request of the priest, but she was in and out of the room bringing Father Mellowes cups of tea at all hours or performing other little attentions that he did not want and that, in any case, Annie was there for.

Father Mellowes wiped the picture every morning, and sometimes in the day too there were the blood-drops clinging to it, like red pearls, "*rote Perlen*," Romilly said.

When her brother came and went he was always stopped by someone in the little throng. They did not ask him any direct questions; they never even referred to the picture at all. In true Irish fashion, they spoke of other things but with a certain intonation, a mixture of wheedling and awe. Then a girl with a bandaged hand had asked him for his blessing and an old fellow bent over a stick had said: "For the love of Christ, Father, lay your hand on me back."

The dog, Ginger, did not like the crowd, the coming and going. He followed the priest everywhere with his red tail between his legs and snapped at the children.

Kavanagh, on his next week-end in Altamont, discovered the success of his plan. But it gave him little relish. On the Saturday evening he met Annie outside the town because he judged it better at this point not to risk her being seen coming to the flat over his shop. They walked along a path across a waste lot on the outskirts of the town near the greyhound race-track. The sky was cloudy and dark over the few scattered, ill-kept allotments and labourers' cottages. There was not a tree or bush or the shelter of a wall. They stopped on the open track and turned to each other and Kavanagh put his arms around the girl.

"Look out, Moss. We might be seen," she said.

"There's not a soul about. Anyhow, we could be admiring the sunset, couldn't we, eh?"

His hands were on her back and buttocks beneath her coat, and he was wearing a raincoat that half enveloped them both.

"There's no sunset," she said. There was a yellowish light behind the clouds low down over the wooden fence of the greyhound track. He stood there, his heavy head and shoulders turned away form her as though regarding the sky, and his lower body pressed to hers in a passion intensified by the exposure of the place, the flat, littered piece of land. Annie pulled herself free and they went on, walking fast. They went towards a hollow along which a railway siding ran. There was a line of railway wagons standing on the siding and between these and the shallow embankment there was just room to walk.

Kavanagh limped down, pulling Annie after him. The place had been used as a latrine, and excrement lay in the coarse tufts of grass and between the ends of the railway sleepers.

Kavanagh turned again to the girl desperately and clumsily, both of them slipping on the muddy slope. They were struggling together to commit their act of fury. The heavy, dark trucks loomed over them on their iron wheels, in a kind of motionless brutality of couplings and axles.

CHAPTER VI

FLOOD'S
HOTEL

■ EZRA WAS LYING in bed in room number eighteen with a singing in his ears, a boiling in his nose and his tongue tasting bitter. He was quite glad to be ill here where it was easy to lie and let the bones ache and flesh burn. It was a relief to be able to be ill after all the times that he remembered when he dared not be ill, when there had been no shelter or space of time in which to lie and let the illness go through him. Only thus being ill, but not too ill, could he taste and touch the security of this life. He let himself sink sensuously into the security of being ill in his room in a small hotel where he had money to pay for all he needed and where he was served gladly enough by Eileen and no one waited impatiently for him to be up again. Because in his heart of hearts he did not believe in the endurance of security, or at least not in this old-fashioned, blind, provincial security, he was all the more ready to indulge in it while it was still there.

Father Mellowes came to visit him, sitting on a chair beside the big hotel bed, with the pale face held at its peculiar, grave tilt.

Ezra asked him about the picture. "Why is it that you are so convinced that it is not a miracle?" he said.

"God is not a conjuror, Ezra," the priest said, "and doesn't deal in tricks. Tricks are not miracles. Miracles cast their shadows before and after them, they grow and blossom like a tree in spring, but they don't happen with the jerky, sleight-of-hand suddenness of a rabbit coming out of a hat."

Ezra laughed in spite of the pain in his head as Father Mellowes went on: "If blood comes out of a picture as a rabbit comes out of a hat, it isn't a miracle; it's a trick." He was worried over the "trick." The last thing he wanted were such "tricks."

"Your sister half believes in it," Ezra said. Father Mellowes did not answer, and Ezra went on: "You should not let her come here to me any more. I tell you that now which I mightn't tell you if I were well."

"She is not a child and you are not a man of violent passions," said the priest.

"Not of sudden passions," Ezra corrected him. "I am a married man," he added with that warm smile that was at the same time always slightly mocking, "and I don't believe in marriage."

"Is it not that you don't understand it?" the priest said. "Christian or Catholic marriage is a great mystery, being the meeting-place of the two great streams of life. Now that you are ill and the day is long perhaps you will not take it as officious if I tell you about marriage.

"You have read many books, Ezra—more books than I have," Father Mellowes went on, glancing at the piles about the room; "and haven't you found in all the books—that is, of course, in all the books worth reading, and I dare say they are few enough in the end—that there have only been two heroes?"

"I've never thought about books in terms of heroes," Ezra said.

"Heroes is perhaps not the best word. I am never sure with words. Words are a great stumbling-block," went on the priest. "As soon as it becomes a question of words, as in the pulpit, I am seeking and searching and not knowing where to turn for the next one. Therefore I say 'heroes,' but perhaps I mean something else. Have patience with me, and leave me my heroes, and I'll try to make you recognise them.

"There is the book of man and the book of God, the earthly books from the Greeks, through Shakespeare up to now; let us say, to our own James Joyce. I am not presuming to give any literary opinions, mind you. And there are the other books, the heavenly books, from the Gospels to Eckhardt and on to the autobiography of St. Thérèse of Lisieux. In all the earthly books the old white Worm is curled at the centre. Be the story as it may, there is the Worm lying at the centre, the ravening Worm that eats down kingdoms and spins out history. You follow me, Ezra? You see whither I'm stumbling? The Worm I mean is the ravening Worm out of the pale cocoon, the old Worm that spins out and spews out the web of life."

"More or less."

"The snaily crawl and puny thrust of the white Worm is the power that moves the world," said Father Mellowes. "When all the syllables whispered through the grill of the confessional are put together, what is the shape that emerges? Isn't it the Worm, Ezra? Open the history books and the poetry books and whose is the face that shines out from them? Clytemnestra's and Cassandra's, Lucrezia's and Electra's, Peggy O'Reilly's and Helen's or, if you like, Mrs. Leopold Bloom's; and all these faces, beautiful or ugly, are in a trance at the white Worm. The trail of the worm is a silver slug-track across the centuries and the civilisations," said the priest, "and civilisation has been the sacrificial service of it. We sacrifice to

71

it and worship it under all its disguises. It is our invisible king and the hero of all the books, the small, pre-historic monster roosting in the fork of the tree of flesh.

"Such is the power of the Worm, Ezra, and the other power is the power and the blood of our Lord. And in the end there are these two powers and no others, these two over against each other and only once and and in one way are they brought together. One way is given us, Ezra, wherewith to submit the white Worm to the blood of Christ so that its power is sweetened and its blindness given light, the one way and sacrament of marriage and the nuptial Mass."

"You have a strange way of speaking sometimes, Father," said Ezra. "Is that how you speak from the pulpit? I will come one day to hear you in the pulpit. But as to what you say, it is a very fine fable, Father. If you had lived like me in hotel rooms, in pensions and lodging houses, as sub-tenant in rooms of somebody else's flat and overheard and overseen what goes on, instead of being told about it all through the grille, as you say, then you'd sing a different song, Father.

"I've seen marriage at close quarters and at the other four quarters," said Ezra, "and I've met it in the passage and lived next door to it, with a thin screen of paper between, hearing its every cough and kiss, so to put it, and I've had it around me in the night at its nakedest and seen it dress up on Sundays and set off to its church. I've breathed it in and sweated it up and smelt it and tasted it, Father, your holy marriage, in many, many holes and corners, furnished flats and detached villas. I've had plenty of opportunity to follow the slug-track of your white Worm, Father, after it's had the holy ceremony performed over it, and I can only tell you that there has been some miscalculation in ·your ancient receipt, Father. I have been married in the church and I have been married outside the church, and I tell you, Father, if a man and a woman can manage to be together and become a new flesh and a new

72

spirit, stronger and more peaceful and more patient than they were apart, that is the one true marriage, the true marriage rhythm, the singing and the dancing and the bleeding all in one, and it can neither be started nor stopped by any priest before any altar."

But these words were less near to him than the heat of his body between the sheets, the burning in the soles of his feet and the aches crawling along the bones under the flesh. He was glad when Father Mellowes came, but he was glad when he was gone again. Then it was twilight in his room and the web of quiet was woven thicker, the priest's visit had added to it. Ezra lay flat and the web of quietness in the room, with its threads of firelight, of bicycle bells, of far-away voices through the solid walls, was drawn around him. The stress of time was relaxed. The afternoon faded into evening with the gentle movement of the time of convalescent rooms or of children's playrooms or of gardens. He had many memories of gardens. He traced again the minute paths of a garden that he had had in the mountains. It had been a small, level piece of ground enclosed by a low wall of loose stones. Outside was the slope of the high hills, boulders, bracken and a mountain stream. Out of the wilderness he stepped down the three big stone slabs of steps into a little space of orderly luxuriance. The narrow path was white with the gravel from the river at the bottom of the valley, and he could pace this path round the garden sheltered from the wind, wired against the rabbits, and his steps were light with the white gravel under them and the delphiniums sang together in the hush of evening behind the loose stone walls like nuns chanting their office behind their grille. In the hush half outside of time, the hush that has begun to be mixed with timelessness.

In this stillness Ezra roamed from one garden to another, and each had its own secret. The crab-apple tree of his aunt's garden standing outside the window of her small sitting-room on an autumn afternoon with the tiny apples glowing red, had its own meaning, to grasp which he had had to go far and through much and then come back again in memory, as he was doing.

On the following afternoon, Kavanagh came to see him. He brought some newspapers and what looked like a bottle of rum.

"I heard from Annie you were sick," he said. "A touch of influenza, eh? I know how you feel: cooked, boiled. Like a boiled onion. I'm getting them to make you a glass of hot toddy. What do you say to that? And if there's anything else you fancy, say the word. I was going to bring you something from the shop, but I thought I'd pop over and ask you first— when you're sick it's not everything that you fancy."

The whole day, on and off, Ezra, beginning to be hungry again, had been thinking of stuffed crabs. He had been asleep and had been woken by Kavanagh's knock, and was now in a warm, heavy doze in which he seemed to see a menu-card on which was written: Boiled onions, stuffed crab, hot toddy.

"Stuffed crab? I tell you what," said Kavanagh. "I haven't any in the shop; there's no call for them here in Altamont; but I'll pop down to the bar and ring up my Dublin manager and get him to send down half a dozen on the evening train. There'll be just time, and you'll have them with your dinner. What say?"

Did he stay away so long? Did the call take so long to put through or did he stay drinking downstairs in the bar? Or was it in reality, by his time, by the bar time and the street time, only a few minutes before he was back again? Ezra did not know. By the time of gardens and of unsailed oceans and of the oceans of sleep and the inland seas between sleep and waking in which he lay it was very long. Long enough for him to walk through several other gardens, over lawns, over one lawn that he had long ago tried to make into a croquet lawn;

were the rusting hoops still in the corner of that outhouse at home? And what was home? Was "home" what the crab-apple tree meant? But that had grown in another garden, in another And what was home? Was "home" what the crab-apple tree meant? But that had grown in another garden, in another country, or was it in another part of the same country? All the letters of his mother, the punctual monthly, weekly letters coming to him in far, foreign mornings, saying nothing and saying all, were they "home"? And where were they? They were there bound by a piece of too-loose elastic in a cardboard box, where? There where the croquet hoops were, or the apple-tree that was probably now cut down, or the young bay tree that he had planted in a tiny round bed in the centre of the garden in the mountains; they were there in the luminous darkness at the shore of the ocean of sleep.

Kavanagh came back. The stuffed crabs, packed in ice, would be on the six-thirty. He settled himself in a chair and looked round the room: "A gimcrack place, Flood's. Too much wicker-work," he said. "Gimcrack" seemed to Ezra an inappropriate word. It was, on the contrary, solid and rock-like, and the only piece of wicker-work was the basket chair in which Kavanagh was sitting. Eileen tapped at the door with the hot drink for Ezra.

"Eh? What's that?" said Kavanagh, looking up, as though he had forgotten all about it. He had been remembering his walk the other afternoon with Annie. His small eyes had had such a light in them as he looked at her that Eileen said to her colleague downstairs: "You'd have thought I was on fire."

"I'll tell you what," Kavanagh said. "You might bring me up a few sandwiches. And put a bottle of wine on the tray, will you, girl? Any wine." But after she was already closing the door after her with her precise movement, he shouted in his loud yet muffled voice: "Red!"

When she brought the wine and sandwiches, he reached out

his arm and encircled her in it, but she slipped tranquilly out of his grasp. She had no fear of him. Kavanagh was known at Flood's and "well liked." She did not dream of taking his ways amiss. After she was gone, he got up and poured the burgundy into a tumbler which he found on the basin, ignoring the wine glass with which the tray was laid.

He began to speak of Annie: "Do you know, Arrigho, there's a devil in that girl that stirs the blood up in me, boiling and burning and howling for her till there are times when I wish her dead and every limb of her rotten, and a reign of peace and decency left in this town again."

"I thought it was the decency and respectability of Altamont that you couldn't stand," Ezra said.

"You're right, of course. You're right there." Kavanagh was not clear what he really wanted. He had begun to look up to Ezra and to want to emulate him. He found in Ezra a quality that he could not define, but that he sensed was a resentment greater and less blind than his own. In his leisurely way, which Kavanagh secretly admired, he had managed to be in the midst of great events. He was glad to be near him, to do something for him. He opened the papers that he had brought and sought in them for items of interest to read to the patient. But there was little there of what, to his mind, might have sped the hour or two till dinner. No large-scale brigandage, crimes of passion or reports of heavyweight fights.

"Dull. Tcha! Nothing at all—the situation in central Europe, the situation in Asia." He suddenly thought he would take a room here at Flood's too. There was very little point in him staying at the flat over the shop now that Annie could not come to him there. He would take a room here over the weekend and be near Ezra. He could keep an eye on him until he was on his feet again. He rang the bell and when the girl came asked her if there was a room that he could have on the same floor.

"There's number twenty, Mr. Kavanagh," she told him.

He engaged the room. He would bring what he needed over later. He settled the pillows behind Ezra. Ezra saw the fleshy face with its thin, mobile lips and the small eyes that had a reddish glitter bent over him as Kavanagh straightened the bed-clothes. And Kavanagh did not impinge on him. His presence in the room was not burdensome and it did not break the web of quiet.

"Number twenty's a nice room," he said. "I had it when I was first here, and later I moved into this one because it gets more sun."

"I don't set great store by rooms," said Kavanagh, "as long as they've got a bed and a table and a pot under the bed."

"That's according to one's nature. For me rooms are everything, rooms and gardens, all places that are enclosed. Walls, those have a fascination for me," Ezra said. "Think of all the worlds enclosed by walls, all the various worlds that walls can make."

"You've had your share of various worlds."

"Rooms and gardens and then, again, cells," Ezra went on. "Were you ever locked up in a cell, Kavanagh?"

"I was not, then," said Kavanagh. "Were you?"

"I have been in cells, and that's the nearest you come to the grave before you die. That is the most complete cutting off of your life, and violation. To be a suspect is to have the delicate membrane of your spirit torn away from you. We repose in the web of our own spirits; as a tree reposes in its leaves and a bird in its feathers.

"To be arrested, to stand in an office while they go through your pockets and examine the papers they have taken from your room, that is the horror of violation, of becoming a suspect.

"To stand in an office, in one of those large, bare rooms, arrested, searched, questioned and suspected, where every

77

piece of furniture, every chair and inkpot and electric bulb is a thorn piercing into your quick, because the secret web in which you repose and are yourself has been torn away, that is the first horror. You stand there, plucked, stripped, violated between the walls of that room and each movement, each word of the officials is your deflowering. We were there, Margareta and I, and we were taken and shut away in cells, and the time of prisoners closed over us. We were there in our narrow cells, in that place where space is shrunken to a few steps and time is a great grey swamp. To lie there in the blankets with the dirty white wall just in front of your face and the grey stagnation of time soaking through the walls and through your bones, that is the second horror."

"And the third horror, what is that?" asked Kavanagh after a moment's pause.

"The third and final horror is the hour of execution. But of that no one can tell. And that takes place in a yard, also between walls, or against a wall.

"Oh, there are walls and walls," Ezra went on. "Walls within walls; and then again there are wall-less ruins. That's what I do here at times; I lie and think of all the walls, the scribbled over, white-washed walls of cells, the walls of the rooms taken over by the security police with the former pictures still hanging on them, outside walls and inside walls, red-brick walls seen across the street through a thin rain (those are the Irish walls as I used to think of them), and walls papered with flower patterns and lit by firelight, old, dark fire-lit walls like this wall; and then garden walls. That was what I longed for, to be again between garden walls, to walk slowly in a garden while out of the still air I spun my web around me again."

Kavanagh got up and put some more coal on the fire. He poured some more of the drink from the hot-water jug into Ezra's glass and gave it to him in the bed.

78

"All that's over and done with. You're among friends now, eh, Ezra, me boy?" he said. He took his gold watch out of his waistcoat pocket. "I'll slip across to the station now and get the crabs off the train. Is there anything else you want before the shops shut?"

"The evening paper."

"The paper. Right you are."

Kavanagh finished the wine in his glass, wiped his mouth, put on his grey hat, which was turned down in front over his eyes, took up his stick and limped out of the room.

Ezra lay listening to the faint, evening noises from the street and the muffled sounds that came from the hotel. He was feeling all right again. He could quite well get up, but there was such repose in staying in bed, in this world within a world, that he decided he would remain in it another day.

He got up and went along the pasage to the bathroom. The hotel bathroom was part of this world of incredible repose and security. He lay in the hot water and thought of his wife. He had been back in Ireland a year now and had not let her know. But sooner or later he must go and see her and come to some sort of "understanding" with her.

It was hard to come back from the places where he had been and to come to an understanding with someone who had remained in the world of the living and of the judging. If she had not been his wife, then she might have been able to have opened her heart to him at the time of his need, when he had written to her. But as his wife she could not accept Margareta. To be a wife is to be incapable of the final, unjudging friendship.

He had wanted one letter from her. When he had been a suspect, when he had felt himself branded with suspicion of he did not know what, he had wanted one word to set against all the other words that he imagined were somewhere written against him in the secret files of some office: sabotage, espionage, treason, subversion, revolution, conspiracy, plot-hatching, and God knew what. But because of Margareta his wife had not been able to write the words of comfort. For himself alone she had written, but that had not served him. For her there had always been marriage and giving in marriage, because she had never been brought down to the place where man stands exposed and mocked, a suspect, and there is only hatred and the stagnation of time and the face of death.

He came back to his room. Eileen had re-made his bed in his absence and he sat by the fire in his dressing-gown. He did not believe in a relationship in which the woman was neither a real lover nor a real and final friend, but a third thing, a wife, something between the two. Let Father Mellowes speak about the two great life-streams coming together in marriage; that might be theology or it might be poetry, but it did not satisfy him. A woman must meet him in the extreme depths of union one way or the other. Let her go with him into the sensual violence and darkness and with him rejoice in it; let her be with him there, and from there let them turn back together to the light and the day and live in the day together, in the day and in the night, and then he would ask of her no more. Or let her be incapable of that, let her then be his friend, but then to the final extreme of friendship.

Kavanagh returned with the crabs and a couple of dozen oysters that he had also had sent from Dublin. He went over to the basin and, taking off his jacket, began to open them with a special knife that he had fetched from his shop.

"It's a grand night," he said, "with a big moon sitting right up bang over the station. When I was a boy I'd be out on an evening like this with a gun. It's a queer thing the fascination a hare or a partridge can have for a man; the way a woman can, too. When a man gets out in the fields of an evening with a gun or a girl he's a different creature to what he is sitting up on his backside in a room. It's like what you were saying about gardens, Arrigho. It's the power of Nature, I dare say. Now, me boy, I think we've got a dinner for you that you'll fancy."

CHAPTER VII

EVENING
SHADOWS

■ ON THE following Friday,
the eve of the Altamont dog-races, Ezra went with Father
Mellowes and his sister in a hired car to visit the colonel whom
Romilly was going to marry. Father Mellowes had asked
Ezra to accompany them and so had Romilly, and Ezra, not
really wanting to go, had nevertheless given a passive agreement. So he came to be sitting between the priest and the girl
in the big old-fashioned car driven wildly over the mountain
road. The Colonel's house lay on the slope of a hill above a
lake and a wide glen. It was an old house raising its wet
granite walls in the dim seclusion of the valley and of the long
years, and the Colonel had taken it and remade it and had
gathered around him all the machines of ease and taste and
beauty.

He brought them into a large room overlooking the garden
and, in the distance, the lake. The room was spacious, with
pale walls and softly gleaming furniture. All was shining
softly with the gleam of peace and plenty, the hang of the
brocade curtains at the long windows, the lie of the rugs upon
the polished floor had taken on the shape and lineaments of
spacious ease. There were no dark corners, nothing unthought-
out. The Colonel himself was small and spruce and pleased.

He was pleased with the smooth running of all this, and he stood beside Romilly at the window with his strong white hand on her shoulder, showing them the view of the distant lake that was part of the design, of the smooth-running beauty, as his engagement to her was also part of it. He showed them the other rooms, the library with its rows of books that were part of the whole design too. The books and the shaded silver candlesticks on the dark dining-table, the gleam of porcelain and polished taps in the bathroom and the beds with the snow-white pillows and silky green bedspreads, all radiated the glow of peace and prosperity, of taste and assurance.

For lunch there was clear soup and lamb, greenish-white wine in tall glasses and an expanse of dark polished table and ease and assurance and a little more wine, but not much, and crême caramel, and the lake shining through the windows.

The Colonel was talking of politics, saying what was reasonable and sound, saying all the things that Ezra could never have thought of to say. He spoke of charity, goodwill and tolerance, and it was all very good and it was all no good. But he never spoke of anything too long; he passed from one topic to another with a kind of spacious ease.

He began to speak of his housekeeper. "A very capable woman, but a pilferer," he said. "She takes things home with her. Caught her clearing off the other evening with the best part of a cold chicken. You'll have to take the matter into your hands, Romilly, when you come here," he added.

Romilly nodded. She was silent, a little uncertain and awed as she always was at these visits, but to-day with an added uneasiness because of Ezra. On her previous visits with her brother there had been nothing but approval and admiration in her. She would come here to the Colonel and hers would be the head on the white lace pillows, hers the face in the light of the shaded candles at dinner-time. That would be marriage: the affluent, shaded, dimly-glowing table, the softly shining pillow, the breeze from the lake, the Colonel's hand laid with such easy assurance on her shoulder.

"Lamb and marriage for lunch," thought Ezra; "candle-light and marriage for dinner. All runs beautifully smooth; there isn't a hitch or a hint of doom." Unless somewhere in some book, but that was bound away between covers. He had caught sight of a Baudelaire, of *Les Fleurs du Mal*, and there was an ivory-and-oak crucifix in the library. But the cross had long since ceased to be a living symbol of the lurking violence. And there had been the tip of the cold wing of a chicken peeping out of the housekeeper's basket.

As for the white Worm of Father Mellowes, there was not a dark corner in which it would dare show its ugly snout; it would crawl elegantly under the silken bedspread and white sheets like a pig in a silver sty.

"What humanity wants," said the Colonel, "is not conferences and pacts, but someone showing a little goodwill and faith. Don't you agree with me, Arrigho?"

"Certainly, Colonel. And as for humanity, you can divide it into three categories: the inhuman, the injudicious and the boozers. The inhuman, now they would require a discourse to themselves; then the injudicious, that is my own branch; and of course the boozers, the Moss Kavanaghs," he added to Father Mellowes.

Romilly gave him a quick, troubled glance.

"That's a peculiar division that you make," began the priest with his patient gentleness.

"Isn't it as good as any of the others, Father? Take the case of the better-known ones: black, white, yellow, or: men, women, children. Or again: capitalists and workers, or Christians, agnostics, atheists and Copts."

Strangely, he felt drunk. Perhaps he really had been ill and not just lying in his bed out of a sense of repose, and perhaps there had been more wine than there had seemed to be.

"Yes; there are too many divisions," said Romilly quickly and earnestly. She began to talk very seriously to the Colonel, her dark, bright eyes turning from time to time with a quick, uncertain glance to Ezra.

They moved into the sitting-room and there was coffee in small cups and the Colonel talking a little, not too much, sound and clear, taking everything into consideration except one thing, except the one nameless thing that could not be taken into consideration, Ezra thought, and so upset all consideration.

"I want peace and quiet," the Colonel was saying; "a few books and some gramophone records. I'm not saying I'm entitled to it, mark you. But if I can have it shouldn't I jolly well take it?"

"That's right," said Ezra.

All was right and all was wrong, but he had better lie low.

"I've never had time to read all the books I wanted to," the Colonel was saying. "I want to brush up my French and German and dip into the great classics in those languages again. I can tell you I look forward to our reading such writers as Racine and Corneille, Goethe and Schiller together, Romilly, my dear. I hope she's showing herself a diligent pupil, Arrigho, so that she'll be able to help me along over the gaps in my own knowledge of these languages."

"Ich bin zu wund, das wieder zu ertragen. 'Wund'—that is a better word than just 'sore,'" Ezra thought. I am so damn sore. . . . I am so wounded, but wounded was not the same thing. The names that the Colonel mentioned gave him a sense of weariness.

"I'd like you to come and have a look at the spare bedrooms, Romilly," the Colonel was saying, "and see what you think about the colour schemes I had in mind."

A silence fell on Father Mellowes and Ezra when they were

left alone. After a bit the priest said: "You don't like it here, Ezra?"

"I don't have to like it. I'm not marrying the Colonel."

Father Mellowes smiled his gentle smile. "He will make Romilly a good husband. And he is not a worldly man, for all his wealth. He is a good Catholic. She can live here a life of quiet goodness, bearing children and bringing them up and at the same time cultivating her own mind and spirit."

"You may be right, Father. All the same, I cannot quite believe in this 'quiet goodness' of yours. But let it be. Let her bear the Colonel's children and keep an eye on his house-keeper —she'll take some watching, that woman—and read Racine and Schiller with him. Look at the mountains there, Father, beyond the lake," he said suddenly. "Look at the line they make against the sky. Isn't it a chaotic, unorderly shape? But it's beautiful, it's something that if you lived here you'd never get tired of. When you were weary of all the rest, you could still look at that line and rest your heart."

" 'I lift up my eyes to the hills whence cometh my strength,' " quoted Father Mellowes. "And we need strength, Ezra; I need it. I need strength for my little flock. If I had more strength, they wouldn't be left often hungry so that they roam around after all sorts of weeds and poisonous plants."

"Is the picture still bleeding?" Ezra asked curiously. The priest nodded.

"And what do you suppose will be the end of it?"

"The end? There will be no end. The commotion will just die down and it will be forgotten," said Father Mellowes. "I came across another case, many years ago when I was a curate in another part of the country, of a bleeding picture—or, rather, a statue—in the next parish. There was a great to do about it and now I completely disremember what was the outcome. I can see the little statue very clearly and the damp, dark stain on the white plaster folds of the mantle just where

86

the heart might be said to beat. But if you ask me what was the outcome of the whole business I couldn't tell you."

Romilly and the Colonel came back talking of wallpapers and curtains and chintzes. She was so neat and clean and untouched in her summer dress, and the Colonel was so spruce and clean in his tweed jacket and flannels that Ezra couldn't help admiring them both, though with amusement.

"We're going to have a balcony from one of the bedrooms out over the garden," Romilly told her brother. "That'll be your room when you come and stay with us."

"Ah, a balcony. I wouldn't know what to do with a balcony, Romilly," said Father Mellowes. "I've no call for such things."

"You could read your Office on it."

But he liked his shabby little room at Mrs. Bamber's with Annie and the children running in and out. He liked the big, dingy church in the main street and the musty smell of the confessional.

They drove back to Altamont in the afternoon. The priest had some sick calls to make that evening. Romilly suggested starting her German lessons again and Ezra told her she could come at six.

Out on the waste land between the allotments and the siding were Kavanagh and Annie. They had been walking in the autumn dusk, caught together in a dark stream of words, of pictures, boasts and taunts which they exchanged in this strange and desperate game. It had begun as usual with hints and jokes and implications. Annie had made play with veiled allusions to other lovers and Kavanagh had begun to boast of the houses in Dublin along the river, of the whisky flowing and of the upstairs rooms into which he had been locked and shut up with city girls, powdered and drunk and sweet-smelling, with the gulls crying outside the window in the grey city-dawn and the Guinness barges going down the Liffey. But his words never seemed to be winged and barbed as were Annie's. He recounted his tales in his muffled voice, but as he told them they seemed to him dreary and without savour, without power to wound and rouse her. Her words were going into him, were like hot irons in his veins and guts, burning. She told of this man and the other, at first vaguely but later, herself excited by her own memories, more explicitly. But she spoke always in her slow, heavy way, smiling her sly, innocent smile now and then, speaking as though she was telling of baking a cake or selling fish across the counter. They wandered along the desolate path, absorbed in this game that for Kavanagh was half an agony, being drawn ever deeper into it with their nerves and senses, prolonging it, drawing it out towards its inevitable end.

Annie was speaking of a man called Laughlin, a cattle-drover. "A great, coarse brute of a fellow," she said, strolling along beside him, her hands in the pockets of her old raincoat.

"Did you go with him?" asked Kavanagh, trying to make his voice sound casual, fearing that if she heard the tension in it she would stop speaking.

"Go with him, is it? It all depends what you mean by going with him. With him it was as if I was a heifer that he was driving up a lane. But there was a grand, big meadow at the end of it," she added with her small, violet child's eyes smiling at him.

All the others had had her and had known her, had known the secret of her that was still a mystery to him. She was telling him casually of the repeated robbery of his one great treasure; he was listening to one long, agonising account of other men who, in passing as it were, had turned aside and taken what was his, knowing what he had never really known, and perhaps now could never know and have and make his own. He wanted to bring her down into the cutting, but first he wanted to draw out the terrible game a little longer. He wanted to rouse and touch her with his city debauches, but his tales were over before they had rightly got going, they were over and he was listening to her again, limping along, trembling, his voice hoarse and muffled, asking her this detail and that, not knowing what to ask, asking everything as though by knowing more and more he could at the last, at the last, retrieve all.

The arc lamps were lit beyond the fence of the greyhound racing-track. It crossed his mind that to-morrow night the dog-races were taking place and that the long-awaited Altamont Dog Derby would be decided. But all that was as nothing now, because there was something else to be decided first on which all that and all beyond it hung.

He drew her down with him to their old spot between the railway wagons and the slope. There came a sound of hammering from the track and the light fell in pale narrow strips between the wagons on to the embankment. One of the shafts of light caught Annie's upturned face as she lay with her head bent back into one of the coarse tufts of grass. She was staring up with her placid indifference into the dusky evening sky.

"Are you never afraid, Annie?" Kavanagh asked.

"Afraid? Afraid of what?" she asked vaguely, innocently.

"Afraid of me. Or of other things. Of getting into trouble, for instance, my girl."

"I'm in trouble now," she said. "That lad of yours in the shop got me into trouble. But I'll get out of it again."

"In the shop? That bastard?" cried Kavanagh, poised above her, like a clumsy bird of prey about to settle on her. Her blouse was unbuttoned and the thin shaft of light caught her breast. It shone just below him, a fragile bunch of whiteness that it might be still not too late for him to gather.

As he took off his jacket his hand touched the knife that he had put in his pocket the evening before after opening the oysters in Ezra's room. His fingers closed over it and, as he embraced the girl, crushing her, he kept it in his hand. It gave him the power over her that his flesh alone did not have. What power? He felt the power, but did not know its shape, its face. There was only the white, indifferent upturned face of Annie that he loved, loving it with an agonising hatred.

Ezra was stretched on his bed and thinking about going across the street to have a drink at the Corner House when Kavanagh entered the room. He sat down on the bed.

"Good evening, Arrigho," he said, leaning forward towards Ezra as though about to confide in him some secret. But then he straightened himself again and took from an inside pocket what Ezra, at first glance, thought was a red ball grasped in his hand. It was a handkerchief completely saturated in blood. Kavanagh held it in the palm of his hand under the lamp.

"Know what that is?" he said. "That's Annie's heart's blood. I killed her." He had put the handkerchief back in his pocket. Ezra slid his feet from the bed and into his down-at-heel slippers.

"What time is it?" Ezra asked after a moment. What had the time to do with it, though? Was it a futile attempt at measuring the unmeasurable? The time of arrest, the moment of death, the hour that the murder was committed. Kavanagh took out his gold watch. He was sitting on the bed beside Ezra, his game leg stuck out in front of him.

"Five. No; it's stopped. It must be later."

He began to tell Ezra all that had happened, precisely and exactly going into everything relevant. Ezra listened with a strange feeling of having heard the story before. But that may have come from knowing the end before the story began and having seen the bloody handkerchief. Or had he always had a premonition of hearing a story like this whose end he would know, whose end could not be altered because he had seen the end and even sniffed the faint, sweetish horror of the end before it had begun?

"What shall I do, Arrigho? Where shall I go?" Kavanagh asked after he had finished.

Why is he asking me? Ezra thought angrily. Why must I decide? He looked at Kavanagh. He wanted to look at his hands, but out of some perhaps misplaced delicacy he did not let himself.

"Go to your room and wait there. I'm expecting a visitor in a few minutes. I'll come and see you afterwards."

"To my room, eh?" said Kavanagh and Ezra saw the shadow of suspicion in his small eyes.

"He thinks I mean to get him to wait in his room while I go for the police," Ezra reflected.

"What did you mean to do?" Ezra asked.

"I was in two minds, Arrigho, whether to go back to the shop and burn the old raincoat I was wearing. I left it over there just now in the room behind the shop where we gut the fish. There's always a bit of blood and muck about there, and maybe what I got on it wouldn't be taken heed of. And then again I had a mind to go straight to the barracks and be done with it. Or else first to Father Mellowes and make a clean breast of it to him."

"Did you meet no one all the time you were walking with Annie out there beyond the dog-track and no one on your way back alone?" Ezra asked.

"Not a soul."

"Go to your room, now," Ezra said. "I'm expecting Miss Mellowes, and when she's gone I'll come and see you and tell you what to do."

"Right," said Kavanagh. Now he had trust in Ezra. Ezra was a man who had seen much death and destruction, who had seen blood flow, bloody faces, bloody hands.

When the other had gone Ezra sat on where he was. His room was no longer as it had been; the walls no longer made a little haven of tranquil security. What the walls had shut out they now shut him in with. Where could he find help—help for Kavanagh, for Annie lying dead out under the trucks, for himself?

He heard Romilly's footstep in the corridor before she knocked at the door, her quick, eager step and decided knock. She came in with pink cheeks, smiling, with her long, darting strides, quickly greeting him, taking off her coat, settling into a chair. She began to speak in her faulty German, beginning sentences that she could not bring to an end, waiting, leaning forward for him to remind her of the words that did not come to her.

"Ich bin zu Ihnen um sechs Uhr gekommen. Ich bin zu Dir gekommen; Sie sind um fünf Uhr fort gegangen." I am come to you (to thee) at six o'clock. I am come. They went away. It is dark in the street. In the street it is raining. Why doth thou (do you) look so sad, so gay? I am so sore, I have such an ache. This evening I cannot speak good. This evening I am dumb, numb, silent, cold. It rains, it snows, it blows, it bleeds, it blossoms.

"Why were you so late?"

"Am I late? Yes; I am late. Thou art late; they are late. I was late because I had not meant to come after all."

"To-night I cannot teach thee German. It is best thou goest."

"Don't bother to teach me, then. Can I not stay a short time and drink a cup of tea?" she said.

"If you stay I'll speak in our own language and tell you things that you don't want to hear."

She did not answer. She waited. Ezra rang the bell and asked Eileen to bring them a pot of tea.

She wanted to go and she did not want to go. She had come from the visit to the Colonel feeling flat and strangely empty.

92

She had gone at once into the parlour and looked at the holy picture, but for the first time there had been no trace of blood on it. She had been disappointed. Only at this moment had she known how much she had let herself share the excitement of the others, of the children and Mrs. Bamber, over the "miracle." And now just as she had been in some way "relying" on it, it had failed.

Her brother had sat down to his tea with a sigh of relief. She had not dared to show him her disappointment. "Where is Annie?" she asked. She wanted to question the girl, but she knew that neither Annie nor Mrs. Bamber ever wiped the lithograph. It was only her brother who did that.

"I gave her the afternoon off."

She had felt a huge drabness encompassing her.

"Come; aren't you ready for something, Romilly, after the long drive?" Father Mellowes had said. She had shaken her head.

"Surely your faith is not so weak as the others to hang on such silly tricks?" he had said. "They are no more than malicious little ruses of the Devil to excite the nerves."

Her faith. In what could she have faith? Did not he see that the little crowd in the garden had collected drawn by the merest rumour of unknown power and mystery? And she too, she wanted to feel the mystery, to be touched by the breath of the mystery. She could not hear any longer all the small, measured pieties without tangible mystery and darkness. Her days were untouched by the darkness of God or the other darkness. All was lit by the light of day, everything stood four-square in its own small well defined shadow. The Colonel stood up in the light of day, four-square, and took her upstairs to consult her about the decoration of the bedrooms, speaking of curtains and wallpapers and balconies, of all things except the one thing that she wanted to hear and which she couldn't have given a name to. She had been conscious of Ezra at the

93

lunch table and as the Colonel had shown them over the house, not moving in the light of day, but withdrawn a little, withdrawn and with a dark power of his own contradicting the quiet, orderly prosperity. She had not consciously considered all this; it had been present as a tension, as a slight tension and contraction of her nerves and spirit. She had gone upstairs in a' state of expectation; now the Colonel would say or do or be something that would reassure her, that would be like the sweet shadow of her coming marriage falling over her, falling over them both. But it had not happened. Her marriage had remained a pleasant, above-board, daylight arrangement. She had listened and nodded and she had been disappointed and yet not quite disappointed because there was still the slight tension in her, there was Ezra downstairs and there was the bleeding picture. Both these things were below the conscious, bright surface on which she moved from room to room with the Colonel's hand on her arm.

Now she was in the hotel room with Ezra having her German lesson, and in the middle of the lesson he was speaking to her as she wanted and yet did not want.

"The picture," he was saying. "This evening I'll tell you about that too, whether you can bear to hear it or not. This evening is not like the other evenings. Have you felt that? If you would like to go now, go—before I speak words to you that you will not be able to rid yourself of afterwards. They would be a burden that you would take with you to your marriage and that would spoil those quiet and spacious rooms for you."

"No. I don't want to go. Let me hear what you have to say. Tell me about the picture."

"Weren't you disappointed when you came back and there was no new blood on it? Hadn't you wanted to believe in it and even half believed in it?" he said.

"Perhaps. I don't know; I'm not sure."

"And why not want to believe in it? Didn't you want to have something that would touch you and frighten you? What sort of a God do you want? With what do you want Communion? Have you listened to the Sunday sermons, to the pious Sunday words, and seen the people coming back from receiving Holy Communion with small steps and careful, pious faces, full of a desperate, pious pretence that this is the great moment of moments, birth and death and marriage all in one?"

"And if it isn't, whose fault is that?" Romilly said. "Isn't it my lack of faith?"

"Lack of faith in what? All that is no use to you. It's no antidote to all the daylight smugness and security, to the small neatnesses and nicenesses; it's only another sort of neatness and niceness, the folded hands, the downcast eyes, a little piece of pious security."

"Don't you believe in Christ?" she asked him.

"I have heard cries and groans, the groanings of despair and of the tortured, and there have been nights when I've heard my own groans and not recognized them. And in those nights, and in those days, I stretched out my hand and felt the wood of the cross (if it was wood—it doesn't signify, let it be stone, or steel) and I sniffed the blood and I heard the cry, horrible and almost obscene with horror.

"And it wasn't a question of believing or not believing. I was touched by the darkness, by the blood and by the cry. The other day your brother was here," Ezra went on, "and he spoke to me about the two great darknesses—that of the Crucifixion and that in which crawls forever the white Worm. He is right. In a sense he is right—there are these two powers of darkness and nothing else. If the one is taken from you, then you must seek refuge in the other. And they have taken away the first and toned it down and measured it and taken the power out of it and now what is left to set up against the white Worm?"

"What white Worm?" she asked.

"You will know that too. You will know all to-night if you stay here with me, if you do not leave me."

She felt the words like hot coals.

"Why? To what end? Do you want to destroy me too?" she asked. She was pale, her broad face ugly.

"Why do you say 'too'? Whom else have I destroyed?" he asked startled.

"The other girl is dead and your wife deserted. Isn't that enough?"

"You don't know why I ask you, you little fool!"

Were not these the words that she had awaited? Or were they the words that she had dreaded? Not the bleeding of the picture, but these words were the miracle, the miracle of destruction. Behind her was the gentle breath of purity. All the things that she had used and touched had had the shape of order and tranquil innocence. The very typewriter in the Colonel's office had gleamed gently in its black enamel and in her room in Dublin her dresses had hung in their patient, tranquil folds, fragrant with her virginity, with innocence. Around her had been the web of her innocence and all things had been touched by it. Where she had moved it had moved with her, and she had looked on the world through it. She had knelt in churches and felt lightly laid on her heart the gentle hand of Christ, and stood by windows looking out on lakes and gardens with the Colonel's hand laid with almost the same gentle reassurance on her shoulder. Sweet and orderly had been the vision on which her dark eyes had gazed until that day of the picnic, when in the chill cave she had felt a different touch, the grip of Ezra's fingers on her wrist.

Then had come other touches, other darknesses. The *rote Perlen*, the strange German words always mixed with another meaning besides the old meaning that she had learnt in the convent. And she had not turned away from these things, but rather she had thirsted for them.

As Ezra glanced at her sitting there, leaning forward in her chair, he saw her face turn ugly, passing, he thought, from what it had been to what it might be. He was going to tell her about Kavanagh. He was going to touch and outrage her in that way first and then perhaps in the other way too. She had come to him; he hadn't asked her to come. He would wipe some of that look of innocence off her face.

"You want to destroy me," she was saying, looking up at him now. "Very well, destroy me! Spoil me for the Colonel, for my marriage, for everything! Isn't that what you want?"

She was going down into the darkness. She could get up and leave the room and walk up the street out of the town back to her room beside her brother's and sit down in the chair by the window with a book on her knees and repose in her own time, in her own evening. She could turn back to the sure, broad road of all the tranquil evenings that she knew so well and that led her from the sweet pastures of childhood on to-wards marriage and the spacious haven of the house above the lake. On that road the very stones were gentle under her feet and there were no strange and agonised words spoken on it, no dark echoes from cellars or crosses.

But she did not get up and turn back to it. She sat on in the chair because of the new feeling that had come to her in the last weeks in snatches, in touches like thorn-pricks, on the picnic and in this room to the accompaniment of foreign words and in the picture bleeding and now in it not bleeding any more. These were no more than hints and shadows—Ezra's dark, brooding face was a shadow too, a shadow to-day above the gleaming glasses and silver of the lunch table—but they made her reckless, and the passion that had had no gradual and easy unfolding was bursting out in darkness and distortion. The words that she uttered could not contain the outward rush of her feeling. "Destroy me and spoil me" meant also "Save me and keep me," and might even once mean: "My love! My love!"

CHAPTER VIII

THE
VIRGIN

■ WHEN EZRA came back from Kavanagh's room he found Romilly sitting half undressed upon his bed. Kavanagh had been sprawled in a chair with a bottle of whisky beside him. Ezra had taken the bottle away and had told Kavanagh that he would come back later that night to say to him what he had to say and that meanwhile Kavanagh should try to sleep off the effects of the whisky, so that he could listen with a clear mind. Not that he had been drunk, and perhaps had he drunk the whole bottle he would not have got drunk to-night, but Ezra had now decided to bring Kavanagh and Romilly together some time during the night and he wanted to keep Kavanagh sober for the interview.

"What are you doing? Going to bed?" he asked her sharply.
She nodded. "Isn't that right?"

He looked at her. All the neatness, the "niceness," the virgin orderliness were there submitted and waiting. All was exposed and submitted to the white flaming Worm. She was sitting there, bending down and taking off her stockings and he was a tree in the night with that dragon breathing fire in its branches. He was aflame with the white fire of its mouth.

Her hands were trembling and she was fumbling with the strap of her brassière. He went over and pushed her gently on to the pillow and pulled the sheet over her. Her legs were still half out of the bed, her feet hanging just above the floor. He bent and took them in his hands and laid them on the bed. He saw the red mark on the instep made by the shoes. The feet of Romilly, of Margareta, of Annie, of the girl in the cellar, treading their various paths and streets and turning down the last street, the last path.

He thought: "The feet of girls and women, hurrying about bedrooms and parlours and kitchens, down stairs and along pavements, standing, bearing the downward thrust of the body, bearing along the heavy body and the heavy heart of all their errands, supporting them in all their waiting and hanging around." He did not touch her. One thing at a time. He sat down on the bed. He was going to take her down step by step into darkness with him.

He told her of Kavanagh coming to him and of the blood-soaked handkerchief and of the detailed account that Kavanagh had given of his crime. Romilly lay with her head on the pillow, her dark eyes turned up to him in horror and fear. Her breast moved with an occasional soft jerk between the rise and fall of her breathing.

"Is this why you asked me to stay? To load me with horror?" she asked.

"Perhaps."

"What do you want me to do about the murderer?" she asked.

"To see him and speak to him. See something that you have never seen before. Take his hand without showing any sign of repugnance. That will be a good beginning for you."

"I shall try to do what you say, but I shall be afraid when I see him coming in through this door." She glanced at the door as though expecting Kavanagh to appear there.

"What will you do to-morrow?" she went on. "Will you go to the police? Or will you tell him to?"

"I know what it is to be a suspect and a prisoner and I have even had a glimpse of what it must be to await the hour of execution. That is an agony that I have no right to ask anyone to bear."

"But think of Annie," Romilly said. "Ah! I can see her lying out there at this moment with her poor red hands that used to carry in our dishes clenched and stiff. Where did he stab her? Did she take long to die?"

"Under the left breast."

"Oh God, if you would only make things clear!" she exclaimed. "If we should keep his secret it will haunt us all our lives," she went on.

"You can get up and go across to the barracks and make a report. If you can do it, do it," he said.

"And if we say nothing and later he kills someone else, another girl? Is he wearing the same clothes? Wasn't there blood on them?" she asked.

"There's always a lot of blood about at the back of his shop where the fish are cleaned. He left what was bloody there," Ezra said.

"Why did he kill her?" she asked. "Why did he make her smear blood on the holy picture? And why did he kill her? If I knew these things, then all would be clear."

"If you knew these things, you wouldn't be as you are," he said.

"Inexperienced, isn't that what I am?"

"Of course. That's what I dislike in you and blame you for."

"Can't I become experienced and remain innocent?" she asked.

"Don't talk to me of innocence," he said. "When you talk of innocence I am aware of the flame of the white Worm, as your brother named it, burning through my flesh and blood.

That's such an old tale and sometimes I'm so weary of it, Romilly, and I don't want to be reminded of it. I don't mean that I want it to curl up and go into a winter sleep. Oh no; it must crawl too. Only I don't want always to submit to the rhythm of its crawl."

"What are you talking about?" she asked him.

"Well, I suppose you can guess what I'm talking about, can't you?"

"Yes. Only you have a strange way of speaking, Ezra."

"Get up now, girl, and put on your dress and I'll go and fetch Kavanagh."

Kavanagh was sitting as he had left him. He had not moved. His head was thrown back against the greasy upholstery of the armchair and his big hands rested on his knees. Ezra now looked at them. They seemed to rest there so patiently and quietly. "How deceptive hands can be," he thought.

"Come over to my room and we'll have a talk," he said.

Kavanagh got up without a word and went over to the dressing-table to straighten his collar and tie and smooth down his thick, greying hair that stuck out at the back.

Ezra opened the door of his room and Kavanagh preceded him into it. Romilly was sitting in the place where she always sat during her lesson. She was pale, but the ugliness, Ezra thought, had passed from her face and it was strained and fragile.

"Ah, excuse me, your ladyship, I didn't know you were here," Kavanagh said, stopping and staring at her. She was the last person he had expected to see.

"Won't you sit down, Mr. Kavanagh," the girl said. "I come here for German lessons, you know, and to-night Mr. Arrigho told me of the great trouble you were in."

Ezra was astonished at her words. Kavanagh sat down. The presence of the priest's sister and Annie's late mistress—for so she could be considered—struck him as extraordinary and his manner became subtly jaunty, reminding Ezra of how he had been at the picnic.

"I don't know what you have told Miss Mellowes," he said to Ezra.

"I told her the truth.'

"You shouldn't have done that, Ezra. That's no tale for a young lady," Kavanagh said.

There was no remorse in his manner, only a sly cockiness. He had put on his air of man-of-the-world or, rather, man-of-the-little-world, for of the larger world he had no trace.

How Romilly hated and dreaded this man! The night, her night with Ezra, was polluted by his presence. Why did they not hand him over to justice and be rid of him? What was left of Annie was lying thrown down among the dirt in the cutting while he sat there leering at her, Romilly. Loathing and desire and horror had overtaken her. She felt that in stepping out of the shelter of her quiet security she had stepped into a raging flood.

Kavanagh had recovered from the first shock of his crime. In the last hours he had already become a little used to it.

"He isn't pretty, is he?" Ezra said to Romilly in German.

"It's horrible, *ekelhaft,*" she said and the nausea of the strange word *"ekelhaft,"* was almost tangible. Kavanagh shot a sly, suspicious glance at them. He had grown more nervous and listened to every footstep from the corridor as the last lingerers in the bar went up to their rooms.

"Yes; he told me the truth," Romilly said to Kavanagh. *"And* I thought that perhaps I could help you. During the last war I sometimes dreamt of going to the aid of the wounded in one of the foreign cities after the air-raids that we read of, or of appearing among the starving and feeding them or of finding my way into one of the concentration camps and comforting the prisoners. But those were all girlhood dreams, and I have never done anything for anyone. I have never seen a real wound. Not that you are either wounded or starving or a prisoner; but I thought that you might be even more miserable than those. And now I see that I was a fool, as I suppose I'll always be a fool, knowing nothing about human beings. You don't need me. I can't do anything for you, and so I shall go home."

"No; wait a moment, miss," said Kavanagh as she was about to get up. "You knew Annie. You were, I might say, her mistress since she left the shop, and many's the time in the past weeks she's spoken to me of you. You were the only person I ever knew her have respect and admiration for. All the others she was for ever mocking and jeering at in her sly way. Even Father Mellowes with his little basin of water and sponge. But of you, miss, she said, only the other night in the presence of her father: 'She's the only one of them who isn't envious of me. All the gossip and back-chat of the Altamont women about me is more than the half of it envy, because of what they daren't do themselves.'"

"Her father? Do you know her father?" asked Romilly.

"I do, well. He used often to drop in for a chat when she was still in the shop, and he was always pitching in to her. 'You spend your time in ditches, and you'll end in a ditch, me girl,' I remember him saying to her one of the last times he was there.

"'Don't we all end in a ditch? Isn't the grave a ditch with knobs on it?' says Annie.

"'The grave and the marriage bed, Annie, they've the blessing of the priest on them,' says her dad.

"But it was what she said about yourself I was speaking of," Kavanagh went on. "She told me that you had promised to take her with you as your maid when you married and went to live in the big house over at the lake."

"I mentioned it to her. She wasn't very happy at Mrs. Bamber's," said Romilly.

"She was never what you'd call happy. You'd have said she was one of the contented and placid ones, with not a nerve in her whole body," Kavanagh said, "but when you got to know her there was something in her that never gave her rest. At any rate, she has rest now," he added.

"Her spirit may have rest," said Romilly. "But what about her body lying out there like a dead dog?"

"What's the body but clay, your ladyship? Clay to clay," said Kavanagh with a kind of ghoulish pomposity or hypocrisy that made even Ezra shudder. But Romilly remained strangely unperturbed. Ezra was watching her with astonishment.

"How can you say that?" she asked. "Her body was all you cared about."

Kavanagh looked at the girl. For the first time a quite different expression from the cocky, jaunty one he had worn since encountering her in the room passed over his face. Was it fear, remorse, pain? Ezra did not know.

"How could I give it up to every fellow, every damned drover and shop-boy to take his passing pleasure out of?" said Kavanagh. "How could I give up what was holy torment to me, miss, for others to have their fun with?"

Romilly gave him a long regard. Her usually tranquil brows were knit and troubled. She was trying to grasp these words of Kavanagh's. It was very hard for her, and yet she felt that much depended on it. She felt that at this moment she and she alone was his judge. Afterwards he might have other judges, but, if so, theirs would be quite a different sort of judgment, they would represent the law or perhaps the Church. But that was something else and strangely unimportant.

But judgment? Dare she presume to judge? To know, was not that the word that she should have used?

"Had she other men, then?" she asked.

"Other men? She had a horde of them, miss. The last thing

105

she told me was that she was in trouble by that bit of a lad that I had in my shop. If she'd chosen another moment to tell me that, I'd have got over it. But at the very moment of— that is to say, miss, at the very pitch of expectation, she threw that in my face. And even then if it hadn't been for my having forgotten the knife and left it in my pocket and it being laid in my hand—for, by the Mother of God, it was as if it had been slipped into my hand—I wouldn't have touched her. But I know it is hard for you to credit me, because facts speak louder than words and I had the knife in my pocket."

"I believe you," said Romilly. "Besides, if you had premeditated the crime you wouldn't have run back to Ezra and confessed it."

"*They* wouldn't believe me," Kavanagh said.

"Who?" she asked.

"He means the police," Ezra said. The word had another meaning for him to what it had for her. For him there was scarcely a more horrible word than "police." He knew that the Irish police, the Civic Guards, had nothing in common with the secret police and security police of the countries in which he had been. But it had become for him and many others a word that was whispered in nightmares.

"They wouldn't believe me," Kavanagh repeated. "They would think I took the knife with me and lured her to that spot in order to do away with her. And, of course, when it comes out in what state she was, they will come to the conclusion that it was on account of getting her into trouble that I killed her. Especially after the sergeant coming and talking to her that time a couple of weeks ago."

"It doesn't matter what they believe; it is what *you* believe," said Romilly. "Do you believe that what you have done is a great sin?"

"A great sin?" Kavanagh repeated. "If so, then isn't the

world full of great sins, miss? Has Ezra never told of all that went on in that foreign place he was in?"

"No; he hasn't told me. But that was during the war."

"And isn't there always a war somewhere or other? Or isn't it always just before a war or just after a war in some place or other?"

"It may be so," she said. "But I don't have to come to a conclusion about all that. I have no way of knowing the world at large and what goes on in it. I was only trying to understand you and your crime because that is something close to me, that has taken place in our midst. I knew Annie and was fond of her, and I even knew you slightly. When I heard of your crime from Ezra, I'll tell you what I thought, Mr. Kavanagh. I thought: that's the business of the guards. It's nothing to do with me, I don't want to hear about it. To know about it was to be touched by it. I thought Ezra should have gone to the police and then only have told me it afterwards. But that was wrong," she went on to Ezra. "It may be the business of the police, but it's our business too. But I'm so tired now, Ezra. It's too late for me to go home. Will you let me sleep here in your room and you sleep in Mr. Kavanagh's?"

"If you like. But what will you say to your brother?"

"He won't miss me. I often go to my room early and don't see him again, and I can be back for breakfast."

Father Mellowes would not have missed her had it not been for the absence of Annie. When Mrs. Bamber came next morning to tell him that Annie had not returned, he went to Romilly's room to ask her if she knew where the girl might be. But neither was Romilly there. At the same moment he caught sight of Guard Higgins in the garden. Higgins was paying one of his frequent visits to his *Pooideal,* and when the priest went down he found him bending over the bluish, sword-like leaves on to which the drops from the rusty tap were falling.

Father Mellowes knew that Guard Higgins was just the man to send to look for his sister and Annie. For some reason, he supposed that they were together. He himself could not have made enquiries in the town without causing comment and gossip. But Guard Higgins, quite unofficially and, as it were, conversationally, could have a look round for them. Not that the priest was worried. He told Guard Higgins that they had probably gone out for a walk together the evening before, perhaps into the country to visit some relative of Annie, and had been overtaken by the rain. It had rained most of the night.

Guard Higgins got on his bicycle and set off to make a few casual enquiries. As he reached the square at the end of the main street he was aware of a balm in the air of the morning. Whence it came he did not know, from the light perhaps on the hill that he could see at the end of the street, or from a flock of small clouds that were moving tenderly across the sky. These things had power over him and he had no need to stimulate any *grande habitude de voir* in their regard.

He knew that if the priest's sister and Annie, or either of them, had passed through the town last evening they would have come through the square and then probably turned down a narrow street that led directly out to the country. A little way down the street he came on a couple of elderly men leaning up against the wall of a public-house waiting for it to open.

"Good morning, men," he said, stopping and resting his bike against the wall.

"Me bould Patsy," they greeted him. He was well known to them.

"Did either of you lads happen to be around here last evening?"

"We were both of us inside there in the bar till the time it closed," said one of the men whose name was Owen.

"And did you happen to notice anyone pass down the lane, say a stranger, or the like?" The priest's sister was a stranger in

108

the town and in his way Guard Higgins would hear if she had passed without having to mention her directly.

"We did then," said Owen. "A couple of them."

"A couple?" said the guard. "Could you describe them?"

"Why couldn't I?" said Owen. "I'll give you a description of the two of them that will bring them before your eyes the very same as if you had clapped them on the unordinary pair in the solid flesh. And if there's anything I should overlook through weakness of memory, Jim here will put it in."

"Aye; why not?" said the second man.

As the two strangers had been the topic of a long discussion, the first old man was well able to give an account both of their appearance and of his theories as to their business, destination and the place from which they came.

"They were walking down in that direction," he said, "or, as I might say, in the direction of the station. The oldest-looking of the two was wearing a dark-coloured suit and a pair of yellow boots, or it might have been shoes, with a great polish on them, and he had a bit of a bag in his hand with a couple of letters on it, like an N and a W."

"It was not then," said his companion. "It was an M and a W."

"By your leave, Jim," said the first old fellow, "by your leave, me good man, I'll give Guard Higgins the information he asked for."

"Were the two of them men?" asked Guard Higgins.

"And what would they be? It's not straying beasts you're after, is it?" asked Owen.

"Men they were," he went on. He had spent many years watching the passing of all sorts of people along the streets and byways of Altamont, but until this moment no one had ever asked him for any information out of his great store of knowledge.

"The small fellow wasn't carrying any more than a newspaper rolled up in his hand. He had on a smart grey rig-out."

"And a red kind of a necktie," put in the second old man.

"By your leave, Jim," went on the first, "I was coming to that. He was wearing a tie which you wouldn't exactly call red and not exactly what you'd call brown either——"

"It's a woman I'm after," Guard Higgins said.

The old fellow looked slyly at the guard and said no more. He did not believe him. He was convinced that the guard, having come to the conclusion that these were the couple of birds he wanted, was trying to hide this from him for fear that later anything "would get out." Though he could not have given a precise meaning to this phrase.

Guard Higgins had other conversations in side streets and shops, going here and there through the town. He listened to all sorts of tales and gossip. He spoke with topers, shopkeepers, old women and children.

"I happened to look up as I was passing Bulger's public-house last evening and who should I see at the window with Jim Bulger but So-and-so and they appeared to have a bottle of wine on the table between them. He is the very soul of hospitality. . . . As luck would have it I was standing at this very door last night, the same as I'm standing here now talking to you. . . . As luck would have it I saw her as I stepped out into the street, and, as I happened to be going in the same direction, I could not but notice where this person partook herself."

"And hare was that?" asked the guard.

But the tales went on and on. "Well, if you will pardon me, Guard Higgins, in the course of the evening I had occasion to want to wash my hands and, leaving Miss Faring in her private parlour, I went upstairs. On my way to the bathroom—you know the lie of the land at Summers', Guard Higgins—on my way to the bathroom, then, I had to pass, as you know, the room of Summers himself. . . . The fact is it entirely slipped my memory. What I must tell you though is that in the course of our subsequent conversation I did learn . . ."

In one of the narrow streets off the square he came on a group of young ragamuffins well known to him, and these he began to question.

"Listen to me, now," he said, giving them time to gather round and attend to him. "Did any of you notice a strange lady in this part of the town last night or evening?"

A fair little girl stood before him, one bare toe rubbing another with the effort she was making to recall having seen something or somebody so as not to disappoint him. A slightly older child, however, rather than answer questions, was inclined to ask some. She had just begun to enquire what, supposing such a stranger had been seen, was wanted with her when a third child spoke up:

"I did see something just after tea. There was a lady in a big motor-car, just like you say, and there was an ass and cart stopped near the corner and the front part of the car couldn't pass the cart. . . ."

Guard Higgins looked at the grubby, upturned faces. On many of them were smiles. Again he felt a balm in the sweet morning air. These smiles reminded him of the small clouds he had noticed earlier—smiles, which he reflected, are to be found nowhere else but on the faces of children interrupted at play.

One of these smiles, the slowest to fade before the adult scrutiny, lit the face of a little boy called Peter.

"I seen her," he said.

"Where?" asked the guard.

"I seen her down the street."

Guard Higgins felt for the first time since he had entered on his enquiries that he was on the scent.

"We have a picture of her at home," the child added.

Guard Higgins was disappointed. And yet for some reason

he went on questioning the child about the appearance of the stranger he had noticed the previous evening.

"If you'll wait I'll run home and get it," the boy said.

"Is it a holy picture?" the guard asked.

"I don't rightly know whether it's holy or not," said the child as he started off at a run. The guard waited, strolling up and down with his bike. In a few minutes the little boy returned with the rolled-up picture sticking out from inside his vest. He handed it to the guard.

It was a lithograph of several figures against a dark and rocky background. One of these was a woman whose face was lit by a cold light. Under the picture were printed some words in a foreign language.

Guard Higgins studied the lithograph for some moments. *"Le grande habitude de voir"* was demanded of him as much in his duties as civic guard as in his horticultural experiments. Up to the moment of unfolding the picture he had had a quite clear memory of the face of Miss Mellowes, which he had seen at the picnic and on at least one other occasion, but all at once he could scarcely recall it. He stared at the face in the lithograph. Could Miss Mellowes' face have recalled this one to the child? He could not say.

"Where was she going?" he asked.

"I saw her hurrying along and when she came to the main street she was nearly running," said the child. "She crossed it and I didn't see her any more. I think she went into Flood's hotel."

Guard Higgins reached the bar at Flood's hotel soon after it opened. There were already several men, commercial travellers, a cattle-dealer and some locals, drinking at the counter. There was a stir about the place unusual at such an hour, for this was the morning of the day of the Altamont Greyhound Derby, and the names of the half dozen runners printed in heavy type on the sporting page of the Dublin papers were passing from mouth to mouth all over the town. Each of these strange words had its own significance and they were uttered and commented on one after another like the names of a litany. "After the night's rain," one of the men was saying, "the going will be just as Rainbow Cutlet likes it."

From behind an open newspaper came another voice: "Look here, Jack. It says here Pride of Queensborough clocked one minute thirty-eight seconds at Harringay last month."

"The little brindled bitch will take some beating," said a voice in Guard Higgins' ear as he was tasting his glass of Guinness.

"What brindled bitch? Constable Anne, is it? Don't know how she'll relish the heavy going, though. . . . What's that? Heavy going? There'll be no heavy going; the rain has just freshened up the grass, that's all, Jim. . . . Who are you talking about, the Cutlet? No; the Constable. . . ."

Kavanagh came into the bar. He looked around and then limped over to where Guard Higgins was standing.

"Good morning, Guard Higgins. What are you having?"

Guard Higgins started. "I've got a drink, Mr. Kavanagh."

"Come on. Drink it down and have another." Guard Higgins glanced at Kavanagh in surprise. He had not seen him since the day of the picnic, when Kavanagh had shouted abuse at him from the water. Now in Kavanagh's small bright eyes there was quite a different look. He seemed to be waiting for a sign from Guard Higgins that all that was forgotten.

CHAPTER IX

AT
THE
DOG-RACES

■ AMONG THE early arrivals at the dog-track were the two old men whom Guard Higgins had questioned in the morning. They had spent the best part of the day discussing the chances of the six runners in the big race without coming to any final conclusion. In the early part of the day it had seemed to them certain that the race would be won by one of the English "invaders," as they were called, from the Wembley and White City tracks. "They haven't come over here for the air," Owen said, and his companion agreed. But towards noon and after reading the paper they had become impressed by the record of the two dogs from the Dublin tracks of Harold's Cross and Shelbourne Park. Finally, towards evening they had begun to talk more and more about the local champion, Sergeant Grahame's Rainbow Cutlet. The little brindled bitch from the west was the only contender to which they had not given a thought.

As Ezra passed through the gate in the high fence on to the track he felt again for the first time in years the excitement of such a place. The arc-lamps shone down on to the circular track, turning the grass a livid green, and along the railings in front of the stands the bookmakers were chalking up the names of the runners for the first event. Here was another enclosure, another world between walls—the wooden wall of the fence—and he was surprised that in all his brooding and recollection in his room it was one that he had forgotten. He had entered again many rooms, had let the slow horror of prison time touch him again between the narrow white walls of cells, and he had strolled along the paths of gardens, but he had never stepped again through the turnstiles on to racecourses or dog-tracks. Was it because the intense hours spent in these places were lost hours, leaving no trace? Because this was a world neither of joy nor suffering, nor of tranquillity, where, for all the excitement, he had never been really touched?

"In my Father's house there are many mansions," many enclosures. But race-tracks after all did not belong to them. As he moved with the crowd towards the kennels, he saw all the same how easy it was to give himself up to this little world within a world, fenced round from the night and lit up. He felt again the lure of the race-track where time has a different rhythm, welling up to the intolerable tension of the minutes or seconds of each race and then subsiding again and again gathering impetus towards the next race. All other time was left behind—the time of pain, unbearable in its apparent endlessness, the time between sleeping and waking in which dead faces and trees and old letters and all lost things are found again.

He stood with the others waiting to catch a glimpse of the dogs as they arrived at the track. He had the old sense of all being in the balance. But even as he waited, the enclosure with its lights and the shouts of the bookmakers, the gleam of the too-green grass and the white boards of the stands shrunk and dimmed. The shadow closed in on it. Not far beyond the fence, just on the rim of the huge pool of light, the body of Annie was lying. There was the power and not here.

The first dog to appear was the brindled bitch led hurriedly from a car across the few yards of lit concrete to the kennel. The two old men who were standing not far from Ezra recognized both the man leading the hound and the smaller man following with a bag. These were the two strangers whom they had seen pass down the lane the evening before and about whom, as they still supposed, Guard Higgins had made enquiries.

"Look at that, will you?" said Owen.

"The same two boyos!"

"What do you suppose that young Higgins was told to keep an eye on them for?" asked the second old fellow.

"No doubt they've been in the racket out there in the west, and I don't suppose they're here for the air, eh?" the first answered.

"You're bloody right, so you are," said a man standing beside them. Words on the racecourse have effects quite different to words outside it. In these casual words the two men saw a confirmation of their own suspicions. They were now convinced that the little bitch with the strange name of Constable Anne would be the winner. And now the name itself seemed to them to take on a secret significance that only *they* had remarked, as if it was subtly composed of the syllables of victory.

Ezra moved about the bright enclosure. He went up to a bookmaker and put a pound on a greyhound in the first race but he did not stay on the stand to watch the race. He went into the bar under it and stood at the counter with a glass of sherry in front of him. He felt a hand laid gently on his shoulder and saw the big pale face of Father Mellowes, and beyond him Romilly.

"What are you doing here?" Ezra asked in surprise.

"I brought Romilly. I thought it might amuse her. I thought she should see a little more of life," said the priest. He was a strange mixture of *naïveté* and wisdom, Ezra thought. Father Mellowes went on: "I want to go and speak to the sergeant, and meanwhile I'll leave Romilly with you if I may."

116

"What does he want with the sergeant?" Ezra asked her when they were alone together at the bar.

"I think it is to report the disappearance of Annie." She was looking at him fearfully, as she had looked last night as she lay in the bed.

"I could not bear to come here, but my brother got it into his head to bring me, and there was no getting out of it. Is Kavanagh here?" she asked.

"Yes; he's somewhere here."

"Doesn't it frighten you to be here on this side of the fence among the crowd under the lights and know what is lying on the other side of it in the dark?" she asked. "Isn't that knowledge too much to bear alone?"

"I know that you dare not be alone now, and you only came here to meet me. Wasn't it so?" Ezra said.

"Yes. I must be near you, Ezra, until they find the body and arrest Kavanagh."

"Do you think, then, that they'll arrest him?"

But he did not hear what she answered, if she answered at all. For he was considering her words, "I must be near you." If nothing had been around them but the night, then they would have been far apart. He would have been alone in the excitement and pretence of this place, as he had often been before, as all these others were for whom no horror lay just beyond the fence. Yet he knew he would never again be able to mix with the crowd as of old, to feel the tension of the minutes and the peculiar magic of the names of the dogs or the horses. When the first race was over the bar began to fill up again and on each side of him he heard the name of the dog that he had put his pound on spoken. "Late Aroving" it was called, and now these syllables were mixed with orders for sherry and Guinness. A man beside him spoke it, drawing it out as if it had been the words of a song: "Late Aroo-oving."

This initial win revived in Ezra a breath of the old fever. Supposing he could win a certain sum to-night, he would be free. At first he did not regard too closely what freedom this was that had suddenly suggested itself.

> "We'll go no more a-ro-o-ving
> So late into the night,
> Though the heart be still as loving
> and the moon be still as bright,"

the man beside him was singing. "If I could win fifty pounds or so I'd clear off and leave her alone," he was thinking.

"Ah, I can't bear that fellow singing," said Romilly, "because all the time I must think of *her* lying there."

"I remember, during the war, nights after bad air-raids where we drank and sang into the dawn with not just one body but thousands of them lying under the ruins around us," said Ezra. "That was easier than going to bed and thinking about it."

"I left the light burning in your room last night," she said. "I couldn't have borne the dark."

"To-night, when you've said good night to your brother, you can slip out and come to the hotel," he said. "No one will remark you coming in. There'll be such a coming and going there to-night."

Let her come. What right had she to be left alone? If he won enough money to-night he would pay the bill that was owing at Flood's and with the money that was left he would go to England or France. The names of the dogs for the big race were passing from mouth to mouth. Rainbow Cutlet . . . Pride of Queensborough . . . Cheer-boys-Cheer. Let her come to-night, and to-morrow he would clear off. Or let her not come and he would clear off with an even lighter heart.

"Funny names they give the greyhounds, don't they?" she

118

was saying. "What does Rainbow Cutlet mean, or Constable Anne?"

He must win enough money to get away. He began to long to get away, to escape to a place where no shadows lay in wait for him; no dead faces on the other side of fences, not even Margareta's crushed face; and no eyes full of fear and of appeal stared back at him as Romilly's were now doing. No suspicion, no long waiting in uncertainty for a step on the stair, a knock at the door. He could not bear again to feel the shades closing over him. In the past he had been too much involved in many depths and much darkness, in fears and uncertainties, in many, many hours of anguish, of waiting in anguish, of whispered, anguished words, of secrecy. He would never be involved again, neither in death, in love nor in guilt. If to-night he could get the means, he would escape and go his own way; he would take the path that led back to hotel rooms in unknown towns, to bright and anonymous places, to enclosures where he could lose himself in the great pretences again, to race-tracks and beaches and little dark pubs and *bistros*. And when he was tired of being alone there were always those who would give him companionship for a night or a week.

He left Romilly with her brother, who had just returned, and went out into the enclosure in front of the stands. He met an acquaintance, one of the local doctors who also lodged at Flood's hotel, a cantankerous fellow, who was standing at the end of the stand. A light rain had begun to fall and the doctor had turned up the collar of his jacket.

"Damp draught," he commented by way of greeting.

"Where are the dogs? Time they came out, isn't it?" asked Ezra.

"Oh give them a chance. They're still busy framing it," said the doctor.

Let them frame it, thought Ezra, moving on. Let them do

what they liked, and if he won the money that he needed to go away, he would go away, and if not, then he must stay. But he did not think he would stay.

At this moment the most desirable state seemed to him that of immunity. To be in places where walls were really walls and fences were fences, protective, sheltering, shutting out. He must escape back into his walls, into forgetfulness. How he struggled to forget those unforgettable hours when there had been nothing left but waiting and prayer! Ah, that prayer that was prayed in the bones and in the guts! Prayer. To be reduced to prayer as he had been reduced to it—that was doom. The prayer he had been reduced to by the pile of smoking ruins in the fiery night and for many, many subsequent nights, the Margareta-prayer. Always the one prayer, though it might take the shape of other prayers, the street prayer, so many street prayers, walking, waiting in the horror of uncertainty along streets that were always the same, along the one stone street without end, prayer without end. This was the prayer he dreaded and which had nothing to do with the murmuring of rosaries and litanies and Our Fathers that was to be heard mornings and evenings in the churches.

Meanwhile, Kavanagh, who had come alone to the track and had been on the look-out for Ezra without as yet running across him, had wandered off towards the fence at the back of the stands. He was drawn there by a curiosity that he could not smother. He felt an impelling need to have just one look over the fence towards the line of trucks that stood on the siding, and at the same time this was the view that he dreaded. He hoped that the fence would be too high to see over it, as in fact it was. But at one or two points there were cracks in it through which it was possible to peer. He came on one such crack and was just about to look through it when he saw a pale shadow moving on the other side. He straightened and stiffened, drawing in his game leg that had been stuck out at an angle to allow him to bend down.

A white face was staring back at him from the darkness beyond. Sweat gathered in the hair of his chest and armpits. Then the face disappeared and another took its place. He saw that they were the faces of children. He recognised the little girl who had received him when he had called for Father Mellowes on the morning of the picnic.

"It's you is it, mademoiselle?" he said with a glow of gratitude and relief. "Having a squint at puss, eh?"

"I seen it," said a face at another crack.

"You did, did you? What was it you saw?"

"The hare, mister. I seen it running round the first time and sparks were flying out of it."

"And the long dogs after it," said another child with a sudden, short laugh.

"What are the names of them, mister?" the face of the first little boy asked.

Kavanagh looked at his racecard, holding it towards the lights, and began in his hoarse, muffled voice to read out the names to the children. They listened with the greatest attention, their faces pressed to the cracks in the fence, savouring the strange sounds that added mystery and enchantment to their excitement. Pride of Queensborough . . . Constable Anne . . . Rainbow Cutlet. . . .

"Has the hare a name too?"

"The hare! The hare!" shouted the children. The hare had started and was roaring round the track with the noise of a small train.

As Ezra was about to put all his winnings on Rainbow Cutlet two old men pushed up to the bookmaker. He recognised the second of them as Annie's father, whom he had once or

twice noticed with her in the town. He saw them exchange a
nod, and the first old fellow handed a pound-note to the bookmaker, at the same time putting his finger on the name of Constable Anne that was chalked on the board. This dog was one
of the outsiders of the six runners and the price marked up
beside the name was ten to one. Ezra thrust his notes into the
bookie's hand and although the words "Rainbow Cutlet" had
been in his mouth he brought out the other name at the very
last moment.

As Ezra turned from the line of bookmakers he caught sight
of Father Mellowes. The priest was standing in the midst of
the crowd, jostled and now and then greeted by a surprised
parishioner. He had that look on his big face that seemed to
Ezra to hover between a gentle smile and a foolish grin. He
wore no hat and his dark hair that grew in tight curls on his
head was sparkling under the lights with raindrops. His glasses
too gleamed and glistened. With his black, crinkly hair, his
broad face and thick lips, there was something about his appearance which Ezra could now put a name to for the first
time. It was negroid. Father Mellowes liked the soft splash of
the chill rain on his face. It was the only thing in this place
with a touch of sweetness and serenity. Otherwise it was a kind
of inferno. He had come here because Romilly had seemed to
wish it, but from the first he had made a mess of the outing.
The tickets had been more than he had expected; he had not
imagined that the price of entrance to anything in Altamont
could have been more than a shilling. He had gone off to look
for the sergeant, from whom to borrow some money, so that
he could have treated his sister to a drink or two in the bar. But
he had failed to find him. Now he stood looking at the names
chalked up on the row of boards and the numbers against them
that were from time to time being rubbed out and altered. He
had no clear idea as to the procedure or mathematics of betting
and it was a little time before he had the courage to go up to

122

one of the bookmakers and hand him his last two shillings as a wager on the sergeant's dog.

He began to push his way back to the stand on which he had left his sister. But by now it had become completely filled by those taking up their positions to view the big race. Father Mellowes reached a point to the side of the stand out of the main throng and stopped there. He took off and wiped his glasses. He lowered his eyes to the wet concrete at his feet. At the same moment there was a sudden hush over the crowd.

The race into which weeks and months of training, dieting, mustard-baths, massaging and all sorts of other preparation had gone was over in less than a minute. The priest had seen nothing of it, and the first person he asked about the result replied: "Oo won it, is it? The bloody judge, that's oo won if yer ask me!" Father Mellowes realised that he ought not to bother with his question those who had just suffered a disappointment. But the next moment he saw Annie's father, Jim Lee, and another old man and he read on their faces that sly, secret joy that, with its counterpart, disappointment and embitterment, seemed to him the two emotions born in this place.

"Constable Anne got home by a neck, Father," Mr. Lee told him.

"And a fine little bitch she is too," said his companion.

Father Mellowes felt in an awkward predicament. He could not offer either his sister nor these old fellows any refreshment. He had an idea of finding Ezra, of leaving his sister in his care and of then going home. He longed to be back in the quiet of his small room. But by the time he came across Ezra he had lost Romilly. Ezra was by himself at the end of the bar with a handful of notes that he was smoothing out and putting away in his pocket-book.

"Did you win all that money?" asked Father Mellowes. Ezra nodded without looking up. The pile of notes had a fascination for him. It seemed to him that with them all was possible, even to the finding again of the old crab-apple tree, the gates into lost gardens and windows on to landscapes that he had seen in reveries on his bed, or it might have been in the books of his childhood. There was one image of a window high up above a broad river that might have been the St. Lawrence and another that looked out on to a wide, still lake. The water was not dark and ruffled and overshadowed by mountains as here, but this lake shone almost white in a great expanse of view, and there were two islands on it, floating close together on the white water. He knew the shape of these two islands by heart.

"What are you going to do with your winnings?" Father Mellowes was asking him.

"I'm going away," Ezra said.

"Are you going—home?" asked the priest hesitantly.

"No. I'm going away," Ezra repeated.

"Why?"

"Why?" repeated Ezra, and it was he who now hesitated.

"You never come to see me now in the evenings," went on Father Mellowes. "There was a time you came and talked many things over with me."

"I couldn't have talked this over with you, for I've only just decided on it."

"So suddenly? Has anything happened?" asked the priest.

"Yes; a lot has happened."

"And you are seeking peace in flight. Is that it, Ezra? You are going away to be alone again?"

"That is more or less so, Father," said Ezra.

"Yet it is only a few weeks ago, the last time that you came to see me, that you spoke of the duck-pond and the forest. You accused us here of living round our village duck-pond where nothing real ever happened."

"You remember that so clearly?" asked Ezra in surprise.

"Yes; I remember all that you said that evening. And now

you are going away to make your own duck-pond, or isn't it so?" asked the priest.

"What does it matter to you, Father? You may be glad that I'm going."

"No; I'm not glad. If you were going home it might be different. But you are one of my small flock, Ezra, and I hoped to keep you for a time in my fold."

"Was I ever in your fold?" Ezra asked.

"You were given into my fold. All who are here and who come to me are in my fold," said the priest, "and my task is to keep them."

"It is far better for you that you don't keep me," said Ezra.

"No; it is not better. It's another failure," said Father Mellowes.

"Can't you see that it is just for you that it is good that I'm going? Didn't you tell me only yesterday what a fine thing it was that Romilly would marry the Colonel and bear him children and rear up a Catholic family?"

"The shepherd gives his life for his sheep," said Father Mellowes, and again Ezra saw that expression on his face that on anyone else's would have been a foolish grin.

"And does he give his sister too?"

"That evening you spoke of the forest, you had been reading one of Romilly's old books and you said: 'All that happens that is new and fruitful happens in the forest.' Do you still believe that?"

"I didn't know you took my words so seriously," Ezra said.

"And now that you find that the forest, as you called it, is here after all, you don't like it and you want to fly from it," Father Mellowes went on, "but you can't fly from what's in yourself."

"It is strange that you should have taken what I said to heart. I probably spoke a great deal of rubbish," said Ezra.

"There was rubbish and there were pearls all mixed together," said the priest. "We have our duck-pond here too; you were right there. There is the duck-pond and the duck-ponders. But that was all you saw. But to me because of my calling is given to see the other too—the forest. Not only in the confessional, Ezra. I am speaking of my visits to the asylum, the hospital and the prison. It was of these that I wanted to tell you when you came again to visit me; but you didn't come. And now you are fleeing away from my small fold out of a sudden weakness. Not that your weakness is so great as mine. Of course, the blame is to the greatest degree mine. When the wolf comes the sheep shall be scattered. But the good shepherd keeps his sheep."

As at the priest's visit to him during his illness, Ezra was aware of a peculiar, naïve power in Father Mellowes' words. At the same time he struck him as a fool.

"Keep your sheep," he said. "And in order to keep them be glad that I am going. In any case there is great trouble in store for you!"

Father Mellowes looked at Ezra with his broad face—at moments so like his sister's—a little on one side.

"I know what it is, or rather, I fear it. Ever since last night, when there was no more blood on the picture, I have had a great fear."

Ezra looked at Father Mellowes. What could be made of such a face, so unutterably naïve at times in its expression, the eyes so grave behind their glasses, and the thick lips idiotically smiling?

"And my staying wouldn't help you there either; perhaps the contrary," Ezra said.

"Whatever other trouble may be in store for me," said the priest, "and however much I fear it, your going would be a real blow for me, Ezra. It is just you that I know I should not lose yet out of my fold. Ah, how grateful I was when you used to come to me and open your heart to me, and then, too, when

Annie came to me and I thought I could shelter her! Her father is here. I saw him a few minutes ago; and I didn't dare to ask him to come and have some refreshment because I didn't know what to say to him. Though partly, too, I must admit, because I am short of ready money. I stupidly lost the last few shillings I had with me on the sergeant's greyhound."

"Here, Father. Take this," said Ezra, pushing a pound-note towards him.

"I'll borrow it on the condition that you come and see me one evening soon. You hadn't meant to go without coming to see me? Because I still hope to be able to persuade you not to go. What you seek for you won't find by running away. Don't you know that?"

"I had meant to go and pay my bill at Flood's and pack and take the early train to Dublin," Ezra said. "I would have gone yesterday, but I didn't have the money. Getting this money was the miracle I was waiting for," he added.

"Wait just a little longer," Father Mellowes begged him. "Come and see me to-morrow or the next day. Have that much patience, Ezra."

"All right. I'll wait. But you'll be responsible for the consequences."

CHAPTER X

THE
VIOLATION

■ WHEN EZRA got back to Flood's he went up to his room and sat down on his bed. He was still undetermined as to whether or not to begin packing. When he began to think of the last days and of the coming days, he saw and foresaw all in a cold white light without shadows. He might have already been far away and hearing of these things from a great distance. Even the murder did not really affect him, did not rise before him in the shape of a great crime or a great sin. It was a small act of violence, a knife being thrust into flesh and penetrating the heart or some vital artery, and, think of it as he would, he could not be aghast at it. Last night it had overtaken him suddenly and bloodily, and he had looked into its face and recoiled from the violence and distortion. But that vision had vanished; he saw that to grasp evil is as difficult and requires as much imagination and passion as to grasp and be moved by holiness. And now both were indifferent to him. He felt he was in that state when the Crucifixion could take place before his eyes and it would be no more to him than a street accident.

There was a knock at his door. He thought it was Romilly, although he had not expected that she would come. But it was Eileen. For once she was roused out of her soft, measured movements; she almost ran into the room, and was standing breathless by the bed.

"You remember Annie Lee, Mr. Arrigho? She was working for Father Mellowes latterly and before that was in Kavanagh's fish-shop. Well, her murdered body's been found out on the commons. Some of the boys coming back from the dog-races found her, and the sergeant and two guards have gone out there and no one is allowed near the spot. Nothing must be touched till daylight, they say."

Ezra sat on where he was when the girl had gone. Now Romilly is sure to come, he thought. It was only a matter of waiting and she would come, driven to him by the buzz of excitement and speculation that was now let loose in the town and from which even at Mrs. Bamber's she would not be safe. She would come in as soon as she could slip away. Out of fear, she would be driven to come, hurrying down the ill-lit street with her long, rather heavy strides, bent forward in that top-heavy gait that was like her brother's.

The white Worm had only to lie in wait. No rendezvous was more certain to be kept than this one. *"Auf wiederschen bis später,"* she had said in the crowded bar under the stand. Until later. Let it be later and even later. This waiting was easy and sure and it made up for some of all the other waiting in police anti-rooms, in air-raid shelters, in the waiting-rooms of partly demolished stations. And not only there, not only in war and in foreign places, but here too, as Father Mellowes had said. On other beds not far away, on hospital beds and prison cots others were lying, and time was taking on for them that monstrous shape.

Let the Worm have its day, or its night. Let it lurk in waiting, consuming time with its fiery breath. Let there be this to put over against the other waiting, to balance it and make up for it. Below in the public rooms he could hear voices and music. How long had he waited for Margareta that last night? For three hours or four, and then he had gone out and made his way through the burning streets to her street. Waiting for Margareta had always, even before that night, been an anxious waiting. Now he was done with that, with the waiting of the heart, and never again would he be involved in that doom. Let Father Mellowes say what he liked, let him bring up his own words and use them against him; he would seek immunity wherever he could find it.

He would go and find another room with solid, protective walls and a pleasant view on to a beach or a broad, leafy avenue. He would write his insect book, putting into shape and order all the notes of his long observations of ants and bees and gnats. In the mornings he would work on it and in the afternoons there would be little cafés and *bistros* and occasionally racecourses, all sorts of enclosures where time would pass smoothly and sweetly. What was this fold that Father Mellowes offered him? What sort of fold or enclosure was that? He got up and began to pack away his manuscript and note-books into a suitcase, kneeling on the carpet, opening them and reading a note here or there. Ants. "Ant time." "Sideral Time and Biological Time." "Insect Rhythm." "The Time of Baccillae." "The Forest beyond the Forest," he thought, "Forests beyond Forests, Forests within Forests. Father Mellowes offers me his fold. And what I really want," he reflected, "is not a fold that shuts out the forest, but one that includes the forest."

Romilly was standing behind him in her mackintosh. She had crept in without knocking to avoid calling attention to herself. She laid the wet coat over a chair with her quick, precise movement and sat down by the fire that he had kept burning.

"I thought I'd never get away," she said, "from all their ghoulish chatter and turning over and over of every wretched detail they had been able to gather—or is it I who am ghoulish, knowing, knowing and keeping silent? Ah, Ezra, I thought there would be no end to it. Mrs. Bamber and another woman

who had seen the electric torches of the guards and had listened
to the whispers on the fringe of the little crowd that had collected in the rain. And then a man who came in later with
more details, and the children gaping in through the open door
till my brother chased them off to bed. Dinah and Joey and the
others; and it seemed to be me they were staring at with their
big eyes waiting for me to confess. 'Her waterproof had been
thrown over her almost naked body,' the man said."

"Now they've something to revel in, to roll themselves in,
like dogs in a dead dog," said Ezra.

"And Mrs. Bamber said to my brother: 'The picture didn't
bleed for nothing, Father.' The picture will be raked up all
over again too," Romilly went on.

"Let them enjoy their murder," Ezra said, "as they enjoyed
the war. As they enjoy every disaster from which they're spared.
And not only them; we're nearly all the same. When I said to
you at the dog-track that after a bad raid we used to stay up
talking and drinking because we couldn't bear to go to bed and
think, that wasn't true. We were glad of the raid as soon as it
was over because it made the lives of those who escaped more
precious. And here, during the war, weren't they glad to read
of all the death and horror, and glad to be able to say: 'How
frightful!' and go on living their own lives with an added zest?
You were here and you must have seen it, Romilly. Was there
ever a real tear shed, or even a sigh? And it's the same with
Annie. They are all glad, and that the gladness is secret makes
it all the better."

"For God's sake, don't go on like that, Ezra. I've heard
enough for one night. For two nights I've heard and seen
nothing but a nightmare."

"You were never touched before and now you're being
touched. The touch of truth isn't a pretty touch," he said.

"That's not the whole truth, what you were saying."

"No. There are one or two who have no need to revel in disaster," he said. "Your brother, for instance. A few people whose own hearts are full enough or peaceful enough not to need the stimulus of the disaster of others."

"What were you packing for?" she asked, looking round at the half-filled suitcase.

"I had thought of clearing off," he said.

"Then, if you're clearing off——" She broke off, and went on: "What's to become of me?"

"You will marry your colonel and dine to the light of candles in silver candlesticks."

"After these last two nights, how could I go and live there and be as you saw me be the other day, and as he wants me to be?" she said. "No; I can't go back. I've begun to go astray and I must go on."

"You haven't yet gone far astray, as you call it," he said.

"To deceive my brother? To say good night to him and slip out of the house and run here through the streets like a mad one, isn't that far? Ah, Ezra, a week ago I couldn't have dreamed of it. But I don't regret it. Not for a moment do I regret it. Remorse? Not me." And she shook her head vigorously, but her dark eyes were bright with fear. "And even if you go, I won't regret it. There'll always be somewhere for me to run to."

"You'll run back to the Colonel. You see if you don't."

"I won't. That's one thing certain. Never, never." And she pulled down her mouth and shook her head, but the light in her eyes was strained and her brows tense.

"And what about Kavanagh, if they don't arrest him? Will you tell them?"

She shook her head again, with her full lips pinched together. She was tense, on the verge of breaking down, but she held herself together.

"A raincoat thrown over her naked corpse." What passion had that been to make her strip off her clothes on a damp, chill

132

evening like that and in such a place, on an evening when she, Romilly, had slipped on a pullover before going out again.

Tiger, tiger burning bright
In the forests of the night.

Whither was she going? At the end of it, what fires, what forests awaited her too? And then to be found by the beam of police torches. To the light of silver candles; Ezra's words, always mocking, wounding. Never would she now reign with the Colonel over that small kingdom of gleaming, opulent quietude. She had been asleep—asleep and adream with the bloom of the dream on her lips and the dark bloom in her eyes. Until in the chill cellar of a cave he had caught her wrist and she had begun to wake, to stumble. Stumbling out over the loose stones and rocks, through the German words, *"ich bin zu müde, zu dumm, zu wund,"* the first steps, astray steps, waking steps and then the beam of police torches focused on her shameful, bloody secret.

No more the evenings in her room in which her heart bloomed gently in the dusky quiet of faith, kneeling in prayer, in faith. And the mornings, faith in the morning air she breathed, in the scent of her soaped breast. To move in faith, in faith to type, the keys jumping under the tips of her fingers to the tune of faith in her heart, in her hands.

Faith in the God of innocence and security, in peace on earth, and goodwill and in "With my body I thee wed."

And now to run like a mad one down the ill-lit street in the rain to this room with the packed suitcase on the floor, to give herself up. This is my body. As perhaps Kavanagh was at this moment giving himself up. Take it, this is my blood. These are my tears. This is—what is this?

To be given up, to justice, to love, to destruction.

"They might come and take him any minute," she said. "Is he in his room?"

"I don't know," Ezra said.

He was watching her, her face, her clothes, her muddy shoes that she had not had time to change since coming back from the greyhound track. And even the mud on her shoes was to his taste.

"They might come in here looking for him," she said.

"Let them come."

The white, heartless Worm. They talked and the words were his words, but the breath in them was the breath of the Worm. And mixed with her words was the one word: "Take!"

"Why should he give himself up?" Ezra was saying. "Out of a sense of justice? But to what justice? Is the law just? The makers of the law, don't they kill and kill when it suits them, not one or two, but thousands and thousands? Is it possible to make a law that life is of all things the cheapest at one moment and a law that life is sacred at the next?"

"Of course you are right," she said. "I don't mean that he should give himself up out of a sense of justice, but out of love."

"Out of love? What love? Love for whom?"

But of course she could not say. She hardly knew what she was saying. She was mixing up Kavanagh with herself, judging him by herself. Putting ridiculously into the heart of Kavanagh what she dare not admit in her own.

The moment came and their talk faded out. The moment came without tenderness or any softening of it by him. He had hardly touched her, nor spoken one word of endearment. With beating heart, she was stooping down and undoing her shoes. Like a street-girl, he thought.

"Do it quickly, quickly," she was thinking. "Let it be done and finished."

From below came the sound of music.

"They didn't postpone the dance," Ezra said. "Lose too much money. The sergeant has shares in the hotel, you know."

She laid her shoes on the hearth. One of them fell on its side, and he saw it had a hole in the centre of the sole. Is she really poor, then? he wondered. What did she earn as a secretary, a typist, or whatever she was? He now remembered hearing from her brother that they had a mother to support. He saw what a great piece of fortune her marriage to the Colonel would have been for her.

She nodded. There was an awkward moment when her shoes were off and this awkwardness he liked and did not hurry to help her out of.

Where was the bottle of wine, the whispers, the sweet and easy descent from one awareness to the other? Crossing to the bed, she stumbled over some books by the open suitcase, her naked foot flipping open one of the ledgers in which he had written his notes on the behaviour of his ants.

There was a knock on the door. Ezra went over to it.

"It's me, Moss," said Kavanagh's voice through it.

Ezra opened it a crack and saw Kavanagh's face with his slant eyes and red complexion thrust into the opening. He smelt the drink on his breath.

"What is it? I'm just turning in," Ezra said. He was in his trousers and stockinged feet.

"Turn in, is it, Ezra? Well, if that's the case I won't . . . I thought we might have knocked one back together. But another time, eh?" He stood with his face in the chink, leaning over on his stick; after a moment he said in a lower voice: "You've heard the news?"

"Yes."

"I don't know what chance you have of sleeping with the bloody racket they're making downstairs," Kavanagh said. Ezra stood waiting. "She was just as I left her with her hands crossed on her breast and her feet laid side by side," Kavanagh went on.

"Who told you?"

"I saw her with my own eyes. I was there with the others;

135

that's where I've been till an hour ago. The guards took possession then and let no one near."

"What did you want to go there for?" asked Ezra in astonishment.

Kavanagh looked at him, with his face thrust in at the crack, and did not answer at once.

"I couldn't keep away from her," he said after a moment. "Living or dead." He withdrew from the door. "Good night to you." He turned towards his own room.

Ezra went over to the bed and took the girl in his arms.

"Who was it?" she asked.

"Kavanagh."

He felt her shivering, stretched newly naked in his arms. He took her with a despairing malevolent pleasure, quickly and contemptuously, with his head turned away from her breast. What right had she to be as she was, without the knowledge that Margareta had not been spared? He would disarrange her neatness and spoil her niceness for her! Let her be a rose, but a rose in whose very centre was the Worm!

With this body I thee enclose . . . with this blood, with these tears . . . with this maidenhood I thee wed.

He violated her, but she did not know it. Yet she was conscious of the horror too.

She was Annie in the dark and the mud, and the knife going into her. And the light was the lights of the police torches shining on her, exposing her, illuminating her secret and bloody shame. She lay in his arms between living and dying, in that space of a quarter of an hour, in that little space of time and silence in which tides turn and cities are taken and the bright, virgin moon turns to blood.

She was shuddering as Margareta had gone on shuddering beside him even after the earth had ceased to heave and shudder under the bombs. With this flesh I thee enclose. . . . When they pulled away the raincoat in the light of the torches, was

136

there much blood on Annie's body? Or mud? Or what? she wondered.

In his room, Kavanagh was lying on his bed with a tumbler of whisky on the table beside him. He stretched up his arm, feeling for the bell behind the bed. His hand felt over the wall, fumbling and at last his thick finger came on the nipple of the bell and pressed it. When the door opened and Eileen looked in Kavanagh called out to her: "Come here!" She saw that he was far gone in drink and did not venture closer.

"Come on in, little chicken. I won't pluck you," he murmured in his hoarse, muffled voice.

"Try to get some sleep, Mr. Kavanagh," she said, and closed the door after her with her careful precision.

"This bloody place! This gimcrack town!" murmured Kavanagh. He took up the glass of whisky and drank it down. Then he slowly slipped his legs off the bed, moving his stiff one with difficulty, until his stockinged feet were resting on the carpet. He got to his feet, balancing himself with a hand on the bed-rail and reached for his stick where it lay against a chair. He limped heavily to the fireplace and began to poke the fire with the stick. He stood leaning forward on it and its point remained thrust into the glowing coals. He stared into the red cavern of the fire. Then, straightening himself, he withdrew the stick. Its varnished tip had caught fire and was burning with a small bluish flame. He limped and staggered about the room, bulky and heavy-swaying on his fiery crutch. He stopped and stood, listening heavily, drunkenly to the music coming from below. The flame flickered out and a little curl of blackish smoke rose from the stick-end against the worn, red carpet.

He saw for a moment the plump white hands folded over the wound and from under them the trickle of black, dried blood.

137

Ezra and Romilly heard the station clock strike one. *Ein Uhr*. She lay there, under his hand; the fear was no longer in her eyes. They were heavy with thought or with sleep or with some kind of half-drunken well-being that comes after crises, after air-raids and narrow escapes from accidents. She was thirsty and he got up and filled a glass of water for her at the tap and poured in a few drops of whisky to take away the flat taste of the water.

"Perhaps nothing can justify us," she was saying, "but if there is anything, then it's only that we help Kavanagh to bear his crime and to expiate it."

"Why do you go on talking of Kavanagh, last thing before and first thing after?"

He drew her into the dark aftermath, the warm, tumbled disorder of the bed in which the Worm had been stilled. Here again was another time, meandering, unhurried, wafted along on the breath of warm, relaxed limbs. And the words were different words to all the others, to those at lunch or dinner, on tracks, in pubs or cellars or between man and man or woman and woman. Words now were dark and ill-defined, not having the clear-cut shape and meaning of words from the head, but rather, coming nebulous and darkly glowing as though from the belly. Yet is was horrible to be lying here with her, to feel her body beside him.

A hush had descended on him, and on the world, on the hotel and on the street, on the trees and on the mountains and the seas. It was like the hush after the air-raids, when he remembered standing at the broken window of his room and looking out at the pall of smoke and the pale, broken walls and hearing the sound of the ambulance bells. The great aftermath, the warm, sickly smell, the fury not stilled, but hidden, and her breast pale and gently breathing under his hot hand.

"Did you see those children at the track?" she asked him.

"No; what children?"

138

"Dinah, and Joey and the others. They were at the fence. I heard them shouting and I went over. They had loosened one of the boards and one of them had squeezed through. He had something gripped in his fist and he thrust it into my hand. Such a dirty little urchin as you never saw," she said, making a face with her face close to Ezra's on the pillow. "He gave me a whole fistful of pennies that they'd been begging around the town all day. Two shillings in pennies and halfpence. They wanted me to put it on a dog for them. 'Be an angel, miss, and put it on that big, black brute of a dog of Mr. Bulger's,' he said. God knows where they pick up these expressions."

"Be an angel and just move your leg a little bit, miss; yes, that's fine," he said, but she did not catch the mocking and cruelty in his voice.

She was telling him about the children, and they moved for him through the great hush, their voices gentle and their movements tender as they passed before him lying with one heavy arm encircling her.

"Jimmy or Joey—I get their names mixed," she was saying, "said he had a picture at home the spitting image of me, and some story or other about showing it to Guard Higgins when he was looking for me. I asked my brother afterwards, and he said he'd spoken to the guard about Annie and me this morning. 'Annie and you,' he said, as though we were in the same boat, Ezra. And so we are, in a way."

"In what way, for God's sake?"

"They were all coaxing and wheedling: 'Be an angel, miss. . . . Do . . . miss. . . . If you please, ma'am.'"

"Aren't you safe and sound in my arms, Miss Angel? What's that for a tune they're playing below?" he asked, mocking.

They lay listening. And he kissed her, kissing her without tenderness, to the sound of the wheedling voices of the children, to the music coming up soft and drunkenly and to his own tormenting thoughts.

139

"And did you put it on for them?"

"I did, and, of course, it lost, and now I shan't have the heart to tell them. I'll have to fork out a few shillings of my own."

"Out of the goodness of your heart. 'She gave him her hand and heart.' Do you give me your hand and heart, Romilly, my love?" he said.

"Ah, why do you jeer at me?" she said, growing suddenly afraid.

The voices of the children, as she recalled them, reached her from far away, across the gulf that now lay between. Dinah, Jimmy, Joey and herself as a child, inviolate, their grubby little, blue-veined bodies slipping, sleeping, running untouched through the days and nights. The pure childblood, flowing sweet and inviolate and blue in the veins, knees scratched and bleeding and dusty, arms scratched by the thorny hedges, but, all the same, untouched, unshadowed.

Her arms that had been plunged into hedges in search of birds' nests and blackberries, her brown, scratched, dusty legs that had run the roads and the fields, had now encompassed and enclosed him.

"Those kids are holy terrors," she said. "Do you know where they got most of the pennies? Out of the collection plate. Joey serves Mass and hands round the plate with the other server and on Sunday he pinched as many pennies as he could slip into the sleeve of his surplice."

But pinch pennies as they might, fib and pilfer and squabble as they might, they remained untouched and could kneel before the altar as they played in the grey streets or on the muddy commons, light-hearted, whole-hearted, pure-hearted.

She and Annie had been children only yesterday; almost nothing, a breath of a few swift years, divided them from childhood.

"My angel, my kid, my sweet," he was murmuring to her. "*Mädchen, schönes Kind.*"

140

"Is that what you used to call Margareta?" she asked.

"Do you think I would call you what I called her?"

"Call me what you like and do to me what you like. Didn't I run here to give myself up to you? Beggars can't be choosers and I'm less than a beggar. I'm lost and I'm ready to be lost, Ezra."

"You're not lost; you're all right," he said.

"I'll come whenever you want me, to do what you like with from now till you go," she told him.

"Get up and go home," he said. "I've had enough."

CHAPTER XI

PAST
AND
PRESENT

■ NEXT MORNING, after a late breakfast, Ezra strolled across the street to the pub on the corner opposite for a glass of Guinness. Not for the sake of the drink, but because this leaning on the counter in the glass-partitioned bar with the drink by his hand was a breathing space, some sort of indifferent space between himself and the others, Romilly, Father Mellowes, Kavanagh, Annie, and between himself and himself.

There was some quiet talk going on at the counter about the murder and about the dog-races. Nothing loud or excited, but damped down by plenty of good stout and plenty of good time. Those who came here in the mornings had a leisurely way with them. Ezra knew them by the exchange of a word and a nod on other occasions. They left you alone; even when they talked to you, they left you alone. That was the great thing about pubs: you came and went, had your drink, got into all sorts of discussions and arguments, but always between you and them there flowed the cool, black, stouty waters, or watery stout, and there blew the beery, tobacco-y breeze.

Wish-wash, wish-wash, went the bar-tender, giving the glasses a rinse in the basin under the bar, then drying and polishing them with a circular, rhythmic motion of his hand and elbow. The clink and chink of the glasses put back under the bar and the soft plop of the corks drawn out of the Guinness bottles. Sweet to his ear were these gentle, indifferent noises, saying nothing, begging nothing, communicating no sorrow, no secret.

"Everything must be looked at in proportion," a fellow with a glass of Guinness in his hand was saying to his companion. "This murder, for instance. What is it when you look at it against the panorama of history? History puts things in their proper places. The man who has studied history is a man with a broad grip."

"Aye; a broad grip. I bet there are some queer things to be learnt from history," said his listener.

"And what is history itself," went on the talker, "against all the times that have no history? Twenty great civilisations there have been in the world and each one of them has disappeared off the face of the earth. Ours will go too as sure as we're standing here."

"And when it does go there's bound to be something left, isn't there? The downfall of civilisation is only a manner of speaking," said the listener; "there's a lower standard of life for a time, I suppose. That's about as much as it amounts to."

"A lower standard of life, is it?" said the historian. "I tell you, man, the time's coming when we won't be standing here with glasses in our hands and our elbows resting on the polished wood of a counter. There'll be no more glasses and no more wood except what's rotting on the ground or standing in the forests."

"There'll always be men and women. You don't deny that, do you?" said the other.

"There'll be creatures. Men you might call them and women you might call them. But what kind of women will they be without their nylons and cellophanes, with ne'er a comb or a looking-glass or a piece of soap? They'll stink like the cattle

143

out there in the street," said the first man with a nod through the window towards a herd of cattle that was snorting and slithering by in the rain with mud and excrement caked on their tufty rumps.

"Is it the Atim or the Rooshins you have at the back of your mind?" asked the listener.

"There's a great gap coming in the course of history; that's all I can tell you."

"A great what?"

"A great gap," repeated the historian.

"Aye; a gap. For a moment I thought it was the Japs you said were coming."

At the other side of Ezra there was a man investigating the crime before a jury of two.

"What do we find?" he was saying. "A girl who goes with her paramour to a secluded spot and strips off her clothes. For there was no suggestion of them having been taken off her by force, mind you. She is willing and accommodating; mark that. Any suggestion of rape is ruled out from the start. She's with a friend, whom she met by appointment on the commons or with whom she strolled out from the town. Yet we know it was a wet evening, mind that. From a little before six it had set in to rain."

"But maybe they were out there before six," put in one of the two jurors.

"I was coming to that. The man came out with a knife in his pocket. With the intention of murder. He had laid his plans. Keep that in mind. Therefore we cannot suppose that he came out to meet her in daylight when they could have been seen and remarked by anyone who happened to be about. They must have met or come out together after dark; that is to say after it had begun to rain. But who in their senses would stroll out to the siding and strip off their clothes on a pouring wet evening?"

144

"Aye, that's a poser," said the second juror.

"We have three clues," went on the investigator. He spoke slowly and gravely, relishing the part of world-renowned private detective Brady, public prosecutor Brady and judge Brady all in one. "Number one: the bleeding picture. Mark that! The picture bleeds in the house where Annie Lee is employed. Number two: the knife. The murderer came out with the knife in his pocket. Number three: the rain. Now where do these clues lead us, in what direction do they point?"

The two jurors were hanging on his words.

"Drink up, lads, and we'll have one more apiece," said the detective, on the crest of the wave.

"Let us reconstruct the scene," he went on, when the drinks were slid across the counter one way and the wet coins the other. "Who put the blood on the picture and for what purpose? What made the murderer go out to meet his victim with a knife in his pocket and why did she strip herself in the rain? Consider all possible motives. Robbery? Ruled out. Rape? Also ruled out." The judge raised his glass of Guinness to his lips and the two jurors did likewise. They were trying to recall the other words that went with robbery and rape. Arson? No. Blackmail? No.

"The previous character of the victim and her habits," went on the investigator, "what do we know of them?"

"Well," said the first juror, "not wishing to speak bad of the dead, and may she rest in peace, but she was known as light in her ways."

Investigator Brady nodded.

Further along the bar-counter a couple of stalwarts were deep in talk. Neither murder nor the possible collapse of civilisation was their subject, but the great race of the night before.

"They kept her very quiet, running her now and again at out-of-the-way country tracks in the west," the first gambler was saying; "then they bring her up to Dublin and let her

145

loose at Harold's Cross after giving her a big feed of porridge a couple of hours before. Porridge and all, she came within a nick of winning. Good. What do the boyos do then? They bring her back to the west and lie low for a bit after entering her in the Altamont Derby."

"Downy birds," commented the second greyhound-fancier.

"What's their next move?" asked the judge of form. "They bring her here in a ten-year-old Ford with a cracked windscreen, and a couple of days' growth of beard on their two innocent-looking mugs. They came driving into Leahy's garage and put up the rattletrap of a car and asked where they'd find a doss-down for the night. When Leahy had given them the bit of information with one eye on the brindled bitch, he asked them: 'Excuse me, boss, is that Constable Anne that's running in the big race to-morrow evening?'

" 'Aye; that's right,' says the boyo addressed.

" 'And do you fancy her chance at all, if you don't mind my asking?' says Leahy.

" 'Well,' says the boyo, wagging his head and letting on to be calculating and weighing up this way and the other way. 'Well,' he says, 'we've some smart dogs against us. There are the two fellows from across the water and your own local champion, what's-his-name?'

" 'The Cutlet,' says Leahy.

" 'Aye, to be sure. I don't say the little bitch here'—and he gives her a prod with his toe—'has the class in her to come home in front of the likes of them. But never say die, eh, mister?' And all the time he was letting all this gab out of him the little bitch was shivering at his heel with her tail tucked in between her legs.

" 'You wouldn't have given a fiver for the three of them, with the car thrown in,' was what Leahy said to me when I called in to see him later in the day."

146

Tom, the Boots from Flood's, coming up from behind, touched Ezra on the elbow.

"Excuse me, Mr. Arrigho, there's a lady enquiring for you over at the hotel. I caught a glimpse of you crossing the street in this direction a little while ago and I thought I'd just dodge over and let you know, Mr. Arrigho."

"Well, now that you're here what'll you have?" Ezra asked. "What sort of lady?" he added.

"Thanks, Mr. Arrigho. I'll take a bottle of stout. Dark and in the middle years," said Tom.

"How do we know that the clothes were not removed after death had taken place?" Ezra heard one of the two jurors asking.

"Because there were no bloodstains found on them," detective Brady said.

"Hark at them," said Tom, after he had inclined his big ear to the medley of talk, "sleuthing and prophesying and bloody running the race all over again backwards. D'you mark Mr. Byrne on my left," he went on, lowering his voice, "lecturing the little fellow about a gap in history, and he one of the last to leave the bar over at the hotel in the early hours of this morning? I'd back him to drink his way through any gap in history."

Ezra left Tom with his second glass of stout and went back to the hotel and into the coffee-room, where the Boots had told him he had asked the lady to wait. He pushed open the glass door and met a breath of stale sour air, and there on a chair in the middle of the stink and broken glass of the night's revelry sat his wife.

"Hello," he said, taken aback at the sudden contact with the past. She sat there before him, small and dark, smaller than he had remembered her and with that deceptive air of frailty about her. He kissed her on the cheek.

147

"What on earth are you doing in such a sordid place, Raz?" she said. The old pet name leapt at him, to greet or to accuse or to mock him? He did not know.

"Come up to my room, Nancy," he said. "It's not so stuffy there."

He led her to number eighteen and she followed him with that deceptive timidity of hers, and when they entered the room she hesitated, not knowing what to do, where to sit.

"Why did you hide from me? Was that necessary?" she asked.

"The same old Nancy having a name ready for everything," he said with a smile. Arson, blackmail, robbery and rape, hiding, abandoning.

"Why prevaricate?" she said. "You were hiding."

"Must we begin judging everything all over again and giving a name to everything?" he asked. "There are so many actions and situations that have no names."

"All right, Raz. Let it be. I don't want to judge you."

"I am come not to judge the sinner, but to call him to repentance," said Ezra. Why was he speaking like this? He was looking at her feet in their very small, high-heeled shoes. He had kissed Margareta's feet and the feet of a prostitute in Paris, but never the feet of his wife. They were proud feet with their high arches, haughty feet.

"I only came to see how you were getting on, and I thought you'd like to hear about me too."

He nodded.

"I've been getting on as I always got on, running all the risks that I needn't have run, for no prize or good reason, nourishing myself on husks and swill and thriving on them. And I suppose you remained looking out from your ivory tower, too proud or too fastidious to come down out of it," Ezra said.

"I don't know about the ivory tower. But I've remained

148

alone, if that's what you mean," she said. "Not out of pride, though. Simply out of indifference. Is that girl here too?" she added.

"No."

"No? That's funny. I thought she was with you and that was why you hadn't let me know you were back."

There was a pause and then she went on.

"Was that only an *affaire,* then, too?"

"Ah, Nancy, all these names for things!"

"Don't be cross, Raz. I'm only trying to understand it all."

"What is there to understand?" he said. "Me? You? There are so many mes and many yous. Sometimes you are there before me in one way, on the edge of sleep or when I'm alone in a pub, and I see you walking away down that glen road after a quarrel we had had; I see you walking away with your head held high and I suddenly grasp you, grasp the misery and hurt pride and despair in you at that moment. And then at other times I see you as someone quite different, someone I hide from, as you call it. And me, I'm a creature of more and worse extremes. I'm this, that and again the other.

"Do you know a few hours ago I seduced a young girl, a virgin, for whom neither before, nor during it, nor after had I any feeling whatsoever. As I lay in bed with her in the early hours of this morning I felt such a disgust as I think you must often have felt. She asked me for a glass of water and when I handed it to her I wished it would poison her."

A look of pain appeared on Nancy Arrigho's small, pale face. She looked at him through the smoke of her cigarette with the vague incomprehension and distaste with which she looked at beetles and spiders.

"Sex," she said with that weary distaste. "How nasty it is and how sick I am of it all around me."

"Yes, I remember the scorn you always had for it," said Ezra, "and how you used to speak with disgust of glands and membranes. We never had the same instincts. That is the first thing that a man and a woman must have to live together. It doesn't matter so much about their thoughts, but they must have the same instincts."

"And they'll usually be low ones, won't they?" she said.

Ezra laughed. "Do you still dream of intellectual companionship and the knight in shining armour?" But he put out his hand and laid it on her knee. "Oh, I know the story that you tell yourself, and perhaps others. 'I gave my youth and my faithfulness to whom? To a blind, egoistic boy, who later turned into an adventurer and gambler, leaving me to my loneliness and waiting.'

"And, of course, that's true on one level. But there are so many levels, each with its own true story, contradicting all the others. If you could have shared with me in my adventures and gambling and in all my stupid or worthless passions, then we would have been close. Because it's not sharing hardships together that binds two people so much as sharing what seem to others to be follies. But you couldn't share my follies and irrational enthusiasms; you could only look on in tolerance and patience and sometimes in irritation and anger. You were always so aloof from and contemptuous of the circus, Nancy, and the market-place. You buried your talent in the earth. What are the words? 'I know my lord is a jealous lord, reaping where he did not sow.' "

"And you, Raz? What have you done with your talent?"

"I lost it. At least I risked it and lost it," Ezra said, looking at her with an unaccustomed, tender smile on his dark, bony face.

"Did you try very hard to make me share your follies as you call them? Didn't you go off running round the country with your drunken friends and leave me for weeks. And wasn't I always faithful to you?" she said.

"Yes, you were faithful to me, but you had no faith in me.

Better you'd been less technically faithful and had more real faith. Do you know there are tiny things harder to forget than infidelity?"

"What sort of things?" she asked.

"One day when we were driving to a race-meeting in the car and I took the wrong turning and went some miles astray before finding out, and you told me you had known all the time and hadn't said anything because you were afraid we might arrive too early at the course. Do you remember?"

"Well, what of that?" she said.

"Only that I still remember it and the chill of it," he said. "All the chills with which we damped each other, instead of dampening each other with the sticky sweat of desire and the secretions and exudations of those glands of yours!"

She blew cigarette smoke out of her finely shaped nostrils.

"But I didn't mean to rake up all this old tale, Nancy," he said. "That's so useless. And I haven't offered you a thing. What would you like? A drop of whisky? I've got a bottle up here. Or a cup of tea?"

"The whisky that you gave your virgin before seducing her, I suppose?" his wife said.

"I'll tell you how it was if you like," he said. "She came to me the night before last and said: 'Take me. Destroy me.' She was engaged to a wealthy country gentleman, ready to become his intellectual companion. But I didn't take her then. I let her go."

"Why?" asked his wife.

"I don't know. A whim. Because perhaps she was capable of such folly, and then last night she came again," Ezra said.

When he handed her the drink the past came back to him. Through something in the way she held the glass or sipped from it the nine years were rolled away. He was back and the world was back at that point in time and space before the last nine revolutions around the sun. A place lost, swept back into the wake and sucked away into the outer darkness, to be remembered and mentally weighed, but never till now re-breathed and re-tasted and re-touched. The knowledge was in his blood again, in his hands. He knew the feel again of the heavy loose bolt in the back door of their house and the way it slid into the hole in the whitewashed stone of the inner wall. He knew the pressure of the knob of the bolt against his palm as though he had left the house with Nancy only a few hours before. He knew it, the very touch of its doors and walls and windows. And he knew himself as he had lived there, un-touched by hunger, catastrophe, flight, death, loss.

He knew the feel of the wheelbarrow as he wheeled it along the passage to the room where the wood was stored for winter; his arms and shoulders knew the twist that they must give at the door and his ears knew the dull thud of the logs as he threw them and his nose knew the wood-smell and the dusty lime-smell that rose from the corner where the logs hit the wall and the plaster crumbled dustily off. Sweet and sad was this knowl-edge.

"What are you thinking, Raz?" she said. Her body he had not known and did not know. Not as he knew the house, not in his blood, in his shoulders and arms, palms and nose and mouth. In six years he had not known her as he had known Margareta after six weeks so that he could still feel. . . .

"I was thinking of the house, of Mostrevor."

"Haven't you missed it? Your room and the garden?" Nancy asked.

"Yes; I have missed it. I have missed it till I nearly died of missing it. As I imagine the dead missing the accustomed day, with the new death-time turning their hands to clods," he said.

She was sitting there and she knew by the sound of his voice that he would not come back and the old bitterness was cur-dling in her breast. Not that she was not well rid of him. She knew that.

"What have you been doing besides seducing girls and drinking?" she asked.

But he was not going to be irritated any more, no matter what she said. She had come to him and he knew it had not been merely out of curiosity or to indulge that old scorn of hers. A little of these things might have been mixed in the impulse, but it had come from the heart. She had come down out of her tower, overcome her touchy pride and driven all this way to find him out. How sordid Flood's must seem to her, he reflected, with the smell of drink still in the stale air and the still unswept floors and his own ugly room! She sat there small and dark and vaguely remote with that vague, remote smile on her lips that he knew. He thought: She has lived so long in a tower of idealism that she cannot escape from it. She is trapped behind the wall of her own judgments. She has judged the world and most of its activity to be evil and foolish and has been proved right, but what satisfaction is there finally in being right? To prove oneself morally right and to get no pleasure out of being so, is not that bitter?

There was a time when he should have taken her in his arms and wooed her out of all her prejudices and disgusts and judgments. If he had gathered together all the passion that he had spent and squandered elsewhere might he not have done so?

"That was hurtful, Raz, that I should find out you were here by chance through a stranger. Through a doctor, as a matter of fact, who was spending his holidays with some neighbours and whom I met one day at tea. When he heard my name he asked me if I was not a relation to an Ezra Arrigho who was staying at the same hotel where he lived in Altamont."

"Yes; I should have let you know. I began letters to you several times and tore them up."

"Was I so hard to approach, Raz? Your own wife?"

"Ah, Nancy, what does that mean, wife? Wasn't any girl I

might have picked up in the ruined, starving cities where I was more of a wife to me than you?"

"All the same, you might have sent me a few words. I did not know where you were or if you were alive," she said.

"I didn't want to hurt you, neither now nor in the old days," he said.

"Yet if you had long ago stuck a knife into me and thrown me into a ditch you'd have hurt me less than you have done," Nancy said.

There were some moments of silence between them. The noise of bicycle bells came up from the street.

Did he know the anguish of waiting, of hoping, of waiting? Of waiting for letters, for a word, and when the letter came reading it with a beating heart, scanning it over and over for some sign that is not there? Did he know what nine years of patient hope were? And then in as many minutes to have that hope mocked, and, instead of the words she had dreamed of once, having to listen to tales of callous seductions, did he know that?

She got up. "Look Raz," she said, in that tone that plunged him back, back into that other time. "It's no good us talking any more now. I'm going on to Aunt Nuala. It's only about two hours' drive from here. And I'll call back on my way home either to-morrow or the next day. Let's see, what day of the week is to-day?"

She still never knew the day of the week or the date, he reflected, nor had probably any more idea of doing accounts or not being cheated by the tradespeople. He told her what day it was.

"Unless you would rather I didn't," she said.

"I would like you to," he said. "But you'd better stay for lunch now. I'll order some salmon for us and chicken and a bottle of wine." But he remembered that she was not interested in food. She had looked down with her remote contempt on those who weren't satisfied with a boiled egg and some bread and butter on a tray.

"No thanks, Raz. If I start now, I'll be at Aunt Nuala's for a late lunch."

The car was standing in the street outside the hotel and he put his head in through the window to say goodbye when she was in the driving-seat. Talk about enclosures! He was for a moment enclosed and embalmed and buried with her back, back, back. A packet of "Sweet Afton" cigarettes with the flap torn off (why do you always open the packet like that so that it can never be properly shut again?) and the blue leather dressing-case with the bits of half-torn-off labels (who knew if there was not still that one from their honeymoon?) a fur coat with a torn lining all lay together on the floor of the car among the burnt matches. For a moment he breathed in the air of the car interior, the faint smell of leather, spilt powder and tepid oil. His feet were on the post-war pavement of Alta-mont, but his head was in another world and time. His eyes were on the leather case to see if there was still that stain on the corner it had got when he had brought back the Sunday joint in it from an afternoon's shopping in the local town. He reached in and picked up her coat and threw it on the rear seat. Under it was her leather hand-bag. (Could it be the same one? All her handbags had always looked alike, had looked like her.) It was lying open on its side and he had a glimpse of a flap-jack oozing powder, another packet of "Sweet Aftons" and a rosary beads (or was it a necklace of some kind?).

"We'll have that lunch to-morrow, Nancy, or the next day," he was saying.

"Don't bother ordering anything special, Raz. I don't know when I'll get here."

Through the wind-screen he saw the Civic Guard sergeant

and Guard Higgins crossing the street and entering Flood's. "Going to interview Kavanagh," Ezra thought. "To arrest him?" There were two of them.

Nancy was smiling at him with her small, full mouth and looking at him out of her grey eyes, at whose corners he saw the creases, with that half-critical, half-appealing glance.

"Well then, Raz, goodbye till to-morrow or Saturday."

"Friday," he corrected her.

He went back into the hotel and up to the desk, where he spoke to Miss Casey. He asked for his bill.

"You're not leaving us, I hope, Mr. Arrigho," she said.

"No. I don't think so. Not just yet."

Then he ordered a lunch of salmon and chicken for two at one o'clock. He had money now and even if Nancy had not been tempted there were others who would be. The principal guest had refused the invitation to the feast, not the marriage feast and not even the re-marriage feast, simply a little quiet luncheon with a bottle of the best, but he was not going to forgo it. He was going out into the highways and see who he would find.

"The sergeant and Guard Higgins were asking for Mr. Kavanagh just now," Miss Casey was saying. "They've gone up to his room. I suppose they want to take a statement from him about that poor girl, seeing she worked in his shop before going to Father Mellowes."

Father Mellowes, that was who he would ask to have lunch with him.

CHAPTER XII

LUNCH
AT
FLOOD'S

■ "Well, here we are," said
Father Mellowes seating himself opposite Ezra. "It took us a
long time, several thousand years, from the cave to a white-
clothed table like this."

Ezra smiled at the priest. When the plate of salmon was put
in front of him he bent over it with knife and fork with naïve
relish. Ezra had gone to the church and waited for him coming out after hearing confessions at midday, as he did twice
a week.

"I'm glad you could come. I was afraid you might have been
too busy," Ezra said.

"Oh no, I'm never busy. If I was busy I would be sure to miss
doing just those things that I'm here for," Father Mellowes
said. "To be busy would be to put a wall between myself and
my little flock."

This morning he had got up, as usual, soon after it was light.
As he had strolled in the garden before going into the town to
say Mass he had met Guard Higgins. The guard, in expectation of a day of much work at the barracks, was making an
early visit to his weed. The priest had watched him as he tenderly bent over his bluish shoots. The sun was rising into a
clear sky after all the rain; under the ilexes the air was dim

and smelt of damp leaf-mould, but the guard was sniffing the early morning breeze. "Do you get the whiff of the sea off it, Father?" he said. "When the wind's in that quarter at this time of the year there's often a smell of the sea on it in the early mornings."

When talking to the priest he had little or no difficulty with his articulation. He had gone on to speak of the crime, but not with the avid curiosity of the others last night. He had let the breath of the sea-breeze, real or imaginary, into the conversation and it never took on that air of dog rolling in dead-dog, as Ezra had expressed it to Romilly.

"A disobliging poor creature," Guard Higgins said, "and one that the polite word wouldn't get you very far with." He was thinking of the day he had gone to her for a piece of ice. "A violent man like Mr. Kavanagh would have been likely enough the one for her."

"A violent man," repeated the priest. "Would you say that?"

Guard Higgins was thinking of how he had gone on that scorching day to the lake and of the abuse that Kavanagh had shouted at him from the water. But Father Mellowes, watching the round, red face of the guard as he examined his weed, had recalled the sentence in the letter that he had been unable to translate for him: *"La grande habitude de voir."* Among his flock there was not one who seemed to the priest so innocent as the guard. For the innocence of the children was something different and far more precarious.

On his way back from saying Mass, Father Mellowes had called in to see Annie's father. His talk with the old man was only one of several which on this day required to the full whatever qualities of shepherd he might have. And how incompetent he found himself when the test came! He had returned home, and although he was later than usual Romilly had not yet been up. There had only been Ginger to greet him, waiting patiently under the breakfast table. He had drunk a couple of cups of tea before his sister had appeared and sat down opposite him.

"I had a long talk with Romilly this morning," Father Mellowes said to Ezra as he began to eat his salmon. Ezra waited.

"She has written a letter breaking off her engagement to the Colonel."

Ezra met the priest's grave brown eyes and felt his own face going pale and shut. The priest's placid countenance with its thick lips had lost all its glee of a few moments before. Is he a complete fool? What is he? thought Ezra.

"My sister told me all that passed between you and her these last two nights," Father Mellowes went on.

"All?" repeated Ezra.

"All that she could speak of with propriety, that is."

"Yet in spite of that you came to lunch with me?" said Ezra. What astonished him was not merely the fact of Father Mellowes' accepting the invitation, but having been so simply delighted with the menu on glancing at it as he had sat down. Here was something that he could not fathom. Unknown depths of humility, or greed, or idiocy, or a mixture of all these?

"I was coming to see you in any case, Ezra," he said, "if you hadn't invited me. It was since your arrival here and the talks that we used to have in the evenings that I was shown my own weakness. The sin of complacency is soft-footed, Ezra, it creeps in upon us with such an air of peace and quiet. And even my visits to the asylum and the prison were not enough to protect me from it. I didn't take sufficient account of what was occasionally whispered to me in those places. I put that from me, Ezra. It was only when you came from abroad and brought tidings that were in some peculiar way horribly reminiscent of those other voices that I listened. Listening, I heard what I was afraid to hear. And I began to be shown the truth of these warnings. God permitted the false peace and

159

quiet in which I had been living to be broken. From the moment the blood began to appear upon the picture I could half foresee what must come—that those nearest to me, those most in my care, would be stricken."

"That day we went to visit the Colonel and you spoke with such pleasure of the good Catholic marriage Romilly was making it struck me as strange," said Ezra. "A strange way of looking at things for someone who is a preacher of the Gospels."

"I was thinking too much of her security," said Father Mellowes.

"That's what they all want in their hearts, your good Christians," said Ezra. "And when they don't want it for themselves, then for their children or husbands or wives or sisters. Have you ever watched certain mothers feeding their offspring? Have you noticed the animal lust with which they stuff the spoonfuls into the child's mouth? And when it's full to bursting they coax it into taking another for Mamma and still one more for Pappa and each extra mouthful that they cram in is a satisfaction for themselves. And it's not even the grunting of the sow with the litter at her tits. Or the groaning of a street-girl up against a dark wall with a man. It's something far nastier than these. It's the lust of the flesh for the sake of the flesh, family flesh and blood. It's the beginning of the lust for security."

The priest smiled slightly. "We come from poor people, Romilly and I," he said, "and she had a hard time before she got the job as the Colonel's secretary."

"And is it really necessary that she break off her engagement because of last night?" asked Ezra.

"Yes. And she wishes to do so. She has written breaking it off and giving up her job. She will stay on here with me, but not at Mrs. Bamber's. I shall find a small flat for us. I had thought perhaps that Mr. Kavanagh would let us his flat now that he is not using it any more. I shall go and have a talk with him after lunch."

"About his flat?" asked Ezra.

"Yes; about that. And if he wants to speak to me about the other thing it will be an opportunity."

"You know about that?"

"Romilly told me of that too," said Father Mellowes. "As I said, she told me everything, because she could not tell me one thing without the others. It was nearly ten before she came down to breakfast. She drank some tea, but she would not eat anything. At first I thought it was the shock of hearing about the finding of Annie that had affected her and I tried to comfort her, but she said: 'Annie is lucky. She is luckier than I.' And she put down her head among the cups and plates and wept. For a time she would not speak. I wanted her to tell me and she wouldn't.

" 'All things you can tell me, whatever it may be,' I said to her. 'Have I not just come back from the church where I took the bread and wine in my hands and said the words over them: "Take, this is my body, this is my blood." Saying those words and knowing them, only in my small measure, my ridiculous fashion,' went on the priest, 'knowing what wrung them from what heart, do you think, Romilly, there can be any other words that could surprise or shock me? On a day begun with those words, as all my days begin, all the other words are answered. And yours,' I said to her, 'Romilly, whatever they are, give them to me, tell me them, and whatever they are they will be swallowed up in the words I must take in my own mouth and pronounce each morning.' "

"You have a strange way of speaking to her, Father," said Ezra.

"I know how to speak to her. I know one way as you may know another," said Father Mellowes. "And then she lifted her face and told me of her coming here the evening before last, of your telling her of Kavanagh's confession to you and then of what passed between you that night and last night, all the shapes that the night took on for her and the vilest were the bloody handkerchief and your packed suitcase."

"She didn't see the handkerchief," Ezra said.

"Then you must have told her of it."

"I suppose so. I don't remember."

There was a pause as they ate and then Ezra said: "If you really believe in those words of the consecration, then I can see that no other words are likely to be too much for you. But to believe in them, even fifty or sixty per cent., isn't that to reject all this mode of life and all this morality?"

"Our Lord appears as He will. In many guises to many people, revealing Himself most to those who are most ready to follow Him. To you also He has appeared, has he not, Ezra?" the priest asked.

"I haven't given Him so very much thought," said Ezra. He did not wish to be drawn into this discussion, but the priest said:

"It is just because you haven't given Him any special or studied thought that I would like you to tell me how He has appeared to you."

"He has appeared to me, as you put it, Father, to some extent as you appear to me," said Ezra. "As a man who would have accepted my invitation to lunch to-day just as you have accepted it. And not come picking and sipping at the food or drink either. And just such a girl as Annie would have been ready to serve Him, would have come running with bowls of water for His feet and dried them on her hair. He liked any-one who let themselves be carried away, especially if they were carried away in His direction, of course. But better be carried away in any direction and become a prodigal son or a lost sheep than not be carried away at all, that seems to have been

162

His point of view. And like you, Father, He sought the mad, the possessed, and the sick and dying, they being in a sense nearest Him and most likely not to be appalled and scandalized by the extravagance of what He was going to do and be at the end, when His hour came. Anything to get away from the calculators, the adders-up and subtractors, the moralists for whom the ordinary fleshy communion was already a little suspect and for whom therefore what He meant to offer would be an outrage.

"While I was waiting for you to come out of the confessional in the church this morning, Father," Ezra went on, "I saw how such a man would listen to the sins of the penitents, His face a little like yours, as of another race. And the sins that He would reprove would be the sins of those who were never carried away. As for the sins of the flesh there would be no: 'How often, my child?' or 'Did you do this, that or the other?' On the contrary, the best excuse would be that what had been done had been done with abandon. There was no moral disgust of the flesh, but simply an impatience with it, with the old fleshy communion. Because He had something else up His sleeve. That was probably what fascinated a woman like Mary Magdalene; his outrageous, not-yet-revealed passion and the stored-up abandon. It was not hers, but it touched hers in the blood.

"Or the woman at the well in Samaria," Ezra went on. "He opened his heart to her because she too had been carried away by the flesh, apparently, to the tune of having had six or seven men. He went around among the mad, the incurables, street-girls and children. If He had a room, it was probably as full of children as yours is half the time. He went around with His stumbling-block of a secret, with His life secret, as a murderer goes round with his death secret, obsessed and absorbed by it. Up till then the great abandon had been in sex. But sex wasn't enough for Him. Far from being too much or too abandoned,

163

it wasn't abandoned or bottomless enough. In the last two or three days and nights of His life, He revealed in His body what was to be the final secret of flesh and blood, the new secret beyond sex that had weighed on Him like a guilty secret. From the Last Supper to the Crucifixion, He plunged to the last depths of flesh and blood and tried to pull His disciples down with Him, but they couldn't go very far. If when you take those words of His into your mouth and repeat them, Father, you really believe in them, then you go down too into that pit of abandon, into those two nights. And I can see that when Romilly comes and tells you of her two nights you set the others over against hers as you set them over against everything."

"Go on, Ezra," said Father Mellowes. "Go on to the end."

"That is the end, as far as I'm concerned. Two days and two nights in which bloody handkerchiefs, packed suitcases and wild outcries like 'Take me. Destroy me!' would be simply nowhere and nothing. And then hung up between the two thieves or murderers or whoever they were. With someone like Kavanagh on one side of Him."

Father Mellowes had been listening with his head slightly tilted and that half-smile, half-grin on his thick lips that disconcerted Ezra. The salmon had been finished and the roast chicken had been brought and the priest was cutting the last crisp pieces of wing from the bone.

"And there endeth the gospel according to St. Ezra," Ezra said with a smile. He poured Father Mellowes and himself out some more wine.

The dining-room at Flood's was a large, ugly room with a cold, uncarpeted floor and frosted-glass windows that gave out on to a narrow lane behind the hotel. But the food and drink were good and there were always many people there, cattle-dealers, commercial travellers, local bookmakers with their women, and one or two of the more prosperous businessmen of the town.

"When you speak of the two last nights of our Lord, I follow you," said Father Mellowes, "but when you speak of the other night, the night of sex, it is harder for me. I don't know it."

"Who knows it?" asked Ezra. "And who if he does know it could tell it?"

Ezra had drunk two or three bottles of Guinness over at the pub and then a glass of whisky with Nancy, and now the wine had the effect of bringing certain thoughts and feelings, that were usually hidden and hard to get at, to the surface.

Ezra had scarcely noticed the taste of the food, the chicken going into his mouth and his words about Christ coming out of it. He had been aware only of the small white-clothed table and of the priest leaning over it opposite, negroid, listening as his mouth moved in eating, listening with his whole bent body. And all the time Ezra had never forgotten that upstairs in Kavanagh's room they were asking him about Annie and that perhaps it had even come to the point of saying to him: Where were you at six o'clock on the night of——? In the midst of his own words he had heard these words or other questions, and behind the questions still far away on the horizon a little cloud of suspicion no bigger than a fist.

"The women I know best," Father Mellowes was saying, "are those you have spoken of. Women like Mary Magdalene and the woman of Samaria and the two sisters of Bethany, because, you see, I have read and re-read the Gospel account of them. These women, and then my sister."

"And in the end perhaps you know more about women than I do," Ezra said. "You love them with the love that Christ loved them with, and therefore you know them."

"Are you mocking me, Ezra?" Father Mellowes asked. "Well, you can mock me, too. I speak in a way that deserves mockery, but at the same time I am serious."

165

"I'm not mocking you, Father. I believe in your knowing these women, these Marthas and Marys of yours. What else do you do in your room but brood over them?"

Father Mellowes' smile lengthened for a moment. "And *your* Marthas and Marys, Ezra," he said, "were they very different?"

Ezra said: "One evening I was sitting on a bench in the park of a city, reading. A few people were strolling past, not many. When someone went by alone I lifted my eyes from the book just enough to see if it was a man or woman. My thoughts were on what I was reading, but below the thoughts was the instinct to take a quick look. I saw a pair of dusty, worn shoes, bare legs and a bandaged ankle. The shoes had that shapelessness about them that very old shoes get. They went by slowly. At the very top edge of my field of vision I had seen an edge of skirt, a hem. I went on reading and after a bit I glanced up again and I saw the shoes and the bandaged leg a little way away where they had stopped. I turned back to my book and the hem of a faded summer dress was imprinted between the lines. I closed the book and looked round. On the slope of the bank at the other side of the path a girl had sat down with her back to me. Below the dusty slope of grass there was a pond with some children playing by it. I saw the ugly blue dress stretched over the broad back of the girl and her hair with a ribbon tied round it in front and cut too short, with the ends sticking out from the neck. I couldn't see her face, but I didn't want to see it, not at once. All that I had seen was what I wanted, even to the bandaged leg."

"You must try to make that a little clearer," the priest said. "I am easily mystified in these ways. As you say, I can sit in my room and glean much out of the old stories, and especially out of the Gospel, but with the more modern realities I'm often at sea."

"I don't know about modern realities," said Ezra, "but I'm

trying to tell you how one day in a foreign city during the war, after years of reading and culture and responsibility, I saw this woman with no face; I saw a pair of old shoes and a bandaged leg and the dress stretched over her back as she leant forward with her elbows in her hands, leaning over heavily, with a kind of heavy, dusty grace as she sat on the parched bank with a cheap, paper-backed book in her lap. If I had begun to consider it I would never have gone over to her; if I had thought about her and about myself and what there could be to say to her. But I didn't think. I was heartily weary of thinking and considering and talking in general, and of reading the great masters and the philosophers in particular. I saw her gazing around her with the same slow heaviness with which her feet had shuffled past and I caught a glimpse of her young face, tawny-coloured and the eyes rather small. I would have gone over to her even without seeing her face, but seeing it I was reassured.

"I sat down beside her and said something to her. She could speak very little German and at that time my own German was very bad, so that we hadn't even a common language. With her dumbness and dusty, tawny weariness she annulled all that I had known and been used to. She was like the night to the day. I sat beside her and we smoked cigarettes mostly in silence, and I made an appointment for the following evening. We repeated the time over and over, getting it right in the language that we weren't quite sure of. *Acht Uhr*."

"Mary and Margareta and Martha and the woman by the well," said the priest. The woman in the park, the woman by the well, the woman taken in adultery. Ezra knew that the priest saw things against that background with which he was so at home. Over the lunch itself the Gospels shed their pervading shadow which came partly perhaps from something in Father Mellowes himself, partly from Ezra's earlier monologue.

But now Ezra interrupted himself to say what he had meant to say all along: "I saw the police come in and go to Kavanagh's room an hour or so ago."

Ezra wondered if the word "police" had anything of the same sinister sound for the priest as it had for him. But he thought not. He was immune, seeing everywhere the hand of God, Ezra supposed.

"Do you think they are there still?" Father Mellowes asked. "I must go to him as soon as they have gone."

"We can ask Miss Casey. And then, if you like, I'll order coffee up in my room."

They heard from Miss Casey that the sergeant and Guard Higgins had left some time before. They went upstairs to Ezra's room, where Father Mellowes left his hat and coat. But he did not then go direct to Kavanagh's room, but down the passage to the bathroom, into which he shut himself. He wished to be alone a few minutes before going to Kavanagh. He sat down on the chair by the side of the bath. The small room had not yet been cleaned; there was so much to be done after the revels that had dragged on into the early morning that Eileen had not yet got as far as the bathroom. Dirty towels smeared with lipstick hung across the side of the bath and in it lay dissolved cigarette ends and a sour smell of vomit lingered in the air.

Father Mellowes leant forward with his chin in his hand; he began to hear the familiar voice again, the voice that always had the last word. At lunch he had not said all to Ezra. Nor to Romilly, to no one. So much as he had said to them was true. But there was more. When his penitents came to him, or when Romilly had come to him with her confession, it was true that in the light of the other words he could comfort them and her. Against her words he had these others to put, as day against night. But the horror was that these words were not the last words; beyond them were others. He did not know exactly

168

what they were, for he never heard them distinctly. They were as a grunting and a growling into which the sound of the holy words slipped. "Ah, Christ," prayed Father Mellowes but the name was meaningless in his mouth, like the other names, Rainbow Cutlet, Constable Anne. A dog in the valley of dogs.

This is the end, thought the priest, the night of the dog. The words of life turning into a canine howl in the night. He lifted his face to the mirror which had been scrawled over with soap and saw his listening countenance, listening, listening to the last, unintelligible howling.

This was then the hell that lay in wait for him, this polluted bathroom, this kennel in which to be shut up for eternity. This was what lay beyond the Last Supper. He had gone round sniffing into all the kennels with the holy name and the holy words in his muzzle and he had always, at the back of the other smells, smelt his own smell, the cur-smell. He knew now the blasphemies that had been scribbled on the dirty walls of the cells and the words cried, mumbled and whispered in the asylum. Now he knew them and sniffed them and tasted them.

He leant forward and covered his big face in his hands. The electric light—there was no window in the place—shone on to the tight curls of his black hair.

"Amen, Amen, Amen," he repeated in what sounded to himself a senseless growling.

CHAPTER XIII

COME!

■ FATHER MELLOWES had remained so long with Kavanagh that Ezra had not waited for him. He had drunk his coffee and gone out again to the Corner House where he had been in the morning. He could not return to drinking Guinness after the Burgundy at lunch, but he ordered a bottle of red wine and sat down with it in a corner. He drank slowly, not getting drunk, but remaining in that state in which the world moves by to a different rhythm, the touch of life on the senses is subtly altered and becomes almost caressing. The shape of the bottle caressed his hand as he lifted it to refill his glass. Things and people lost their sharp contours and distinctions. What weariness there was in the endless looking on the world through the bright, discerning eye that reflected differences, distinctions, contradictions! It was a relief sometimes to close that watchful eye with wine or Guinness. Or though a woman. With Margareta it was so, as he had tried to tell Father Mellowes. He had not picked her out with his eye or discerned her with his mind, and all the time he had been with her there had been this rest and blessing of instinctive contact. Why had the bandage on her bare, rather thick leg been more moving than the nylons on the

170

legs of other women? That is what he had begun to explain to Father Mellowes and had not been able to.

How she would have entered into a day like this with him, moving from pub to pub, or back to the same pub until a point came when she would have said: "Let's go to the cinema —*wollen wir nicht ins Kino gehen?*" so that they didn't reach the point of drunkenness. And they would sit in the dark cinema not seeing the film with the bright, discerning eye, her hand in his, and afterwards she would never be able to say much about what they had seen.

Ezra went out and wandered for a bit along the streets past the lit shops. He was in the streets for a bit and then up in his room and then down having dinner in the restaurant, moving from place to place without really noticing them or how long he was in one place or the other. After dinner he came into the hall of the hotel and stood there undecided whether to return to the pub across the street or go up and look for Kavanagh in his room. As he stood there he saw a car at the door of the hotel and someone who seemed to be a long time getting out of it. Another drunk, he thought. There was a shuffling of figures across the pavement toward the lit doorway. The driver seemed to be supporting someone. Ezra saw a contracted movement beneath an overcoat. Not the loose swayings and balancings of drunkenness, but the rhythmic contortions of a cripple. The figures passed through the door out of darkness into the light. He saw the face above the flapping overcoat, tilting over sideways above the supporting arm of the driver, at each heavy gyration of the leg. The face of horror and joy, now straightened and motionless to stare at him, and he before it, bearing up the unwieldy weight beneath the overcoat in his arms. Both staring and dumb and the driver stooping and putting down the small, broken suitcase. Still dumb, he turned and slowly climbed the stairs, lifting with one arm the clumsily moving weight from stair to stair with tears running down his face. Slowly along the corridor and into his room and the weight slipping from his arm on to the bed.

"Feel me, touch me. It's me! Turn on the light."

"No; wait, wait." Her tears wet and hot on his hand.

"See, I'm here, I'm alive, *nicht?*" she said. "Here's my paw," and she put her hand to his face. He pressed his nose and mouth into her palm, and then his mouth against hers that was a warm, salty tasting well of life.

She began to speak, still in a whisper; they had been whispering in the dark of the room.

"All this time I've been trying to get here. I was in a camp with other of my people. I was lying for years in a bunk in the camp only writing letters and filling out forms to be allowed to come to Ireland. If it hadn't been for a friend who helped me, Bogusky, running all over the place, I'd never have been able to get here. Only I had to let him have me; I'd nothing else to repay him with. It doesn't matter, eh? Not tragic, is it?"

"No, no. Ah, little Hare," Ezra said, calling her by his old name for her, "how can anything matter any more except this. You were dead and now you're here. What else is there—only these two things."

"It is so, *nicht?* I wasn't dead, though. I hadn't got home that night when the raid came. I was in another cellar and we were buried and something was broken in me. I was brought to a hospital outside the city, then to another far away and they told me there was no post any more. You see how I am, I am all out of joint and hideous. I can only crawl and hop. I'm not nice to sleep with now; it's like sleeping with an old carthorse."

"My God, sleeping, what's that?" he said. "We don't need it, Hare. Nothing do I need but your dirty little paw like this. That's consummation and salvation."

172

"What long words! Anyhow, you can have other girls; only let me stay near you."

"Little fool," he said, "don't you know that this is a new day? This is a new life, a kind of resurrection!"

"Let it be what you like, only give me some soup. I hadn't any money to eat anything on the journey."

"Then you want something more solid than soup."

"What there is. In the camp there was soup and stew. I don't know how it is here in Ireland. I have seen nothing—a few streets and a river and a tavern. I asked a policeman where Mooney's pub was on the quays, because that was the one name I had always kept in my head from the time you had told me of the nights you had had there. I had kept those names always: 'Mooney's,' the 'Quays,' though I'd no idea what the Quays were. I went there and asked for Mr. Mooney. I had waited so long and crawled so far that I didn't give a damn any more what anyone thought of me. I just said to him: 'Ezra Arrigho.' Perhaps you weren't in Ireland at all, perhaps you were dead."

"And if I hadn't been in Ireland or been dead?"

"There was the river and there were some steps down to it just near Mooney's and I would have tried to walk down them, and I can't walk down stairs without a rail to hold on to. I would have fallen. I had thought that out too. Mr. Mooney couldn't make out what I wanted. I went on repeating your name and in the end it dawned on him. He scribbled your name on a piece of paper and I nodded, and then he wrote down this address."

She went on telling of how the publican had given her a drink and later brought her to the station and put her on the train for Altamont.

"God save him," said Ezra, "and blessed is the evening that I spent drinking in his pub, the only one of all the old haunts that I've ever put my nose in."

He had turned on the light and was staring at her again as he had stared in the hall. She had come back to him from the dead. Of course, there was the explanation, being evacuated to a distant hospital: the letters that they did not bother or could not have posted for her, and then the war ending. But no explanation could diminish the mystery. He rang the bell and when Tom came, asked him to bring up something to eat and a pot of tea.

"Ach, God! Who was that? Will he turn me out?" she asked.

"That was the waiter to bring you something to eat. No one will turn you out."

"Then I can stay here, in some corner?"

He reassured her.

"Bogusky couldn't understand me wanting to go to you," she went on. "He used to say that you wouldn't want me. 'There'll be plenty of girls where he is,' he said, 'with sound legs.' 'That's very right,' I said to him, 'but there'll still be an hour sometimes in the evening when he'll be glad to sit in the corner of some room or café silent with me as perhaps he can't be with the others.' Then Bogusky would laugh and say: 'All this sweat and trouble, so that at the end of it you can sit and say nothing.'"

The station clock struck. On the wintry corner of that street she had said: *"Bis acht Uhr."* And now it was eight, or it might be nine, or ten, he was not sure, and she was here.

There was a knock at the door and Father Mellowes came in, accompanied by Kavanagh. The priest had been in Kavanagh's room ever since lunch. Kavanagh had begged him to remain, not wanting to be left alone, and they had spent the afternoon playing cards together. They had looked for Ezra once or twice, but had not found him. When they saw that Ezra had a visitor they were about to withdraw again, but Ezra said: "This is Margareta, and she has come to stay, so we have

174

time enough." He was glad that Kavanagh had come in. After half avoiding him all the last day or two, not wanting to be involved, he now felt a strength in him to stand by twenty Kavanaghs. He had no more qualms or doubts.

The priest and Kavanagh shook hands with Margareta and Ezra said to her in German: "These are good people. The priest is a good priest, not like the others, and this man with him has committed a serious crime and the police are after him."

"Ach, God. Poor fellow," said Margareta. "Is there no end to the police?"

"I thought she was dead," said Father Mellowes.

"She died and I sat by her smoking grave," said Ezra. "For me it was her death. I saw her dead under the pile of ruins and now I see her alive again, but the other dead face will always be there too. I have lived with it too long."

"How precious she must be to you now, being doubly precious," said the priest.

"That's a queer thing for you to say—especially queer after last night," said Ezra.

"Last night? Ah, that! There have been so many nights of darkness and despair lately, even in the middle of the day! But we can still turn them to good; it isn't too late. See, Ezra, she has been given back to you, not just for your sake, though, but for the sake of the new life."

"What new life?" asked Ezra.

But before the priest could answer, Kavanagh broke in: "Aye, it's all very well for you—a new life. But with me it's all up. The sergeant was over an hour with me. 'Where were you at five o'clock on the afternoon of the fourth? When did you last see Annie Lee? At what time and in what place,' and Guard Higgins taking down everything in shorthand."

Kavanagh was slumped in a chair, his big hands dangling between his thick thighs. There was something repulsive to

Ezra in his present attitude of fear and despondency. But stronger than this repulsion was another feeling; he no longer regarded Kavanagh as a stranger, as a completely separate being from himself. He saw in Kavanagh his own image, a little altered or distorted perhaps, but there was no final wall between his blood and Kavanagh's blood, his flesh and Kavanagh's flesh.

"You know I can't be alone," Kavanagh was saying. "I get the creeps when I'm alone."

"You won't be alone," Father Mellowes said to him. He added to Ezra: "Romilly and I are going to live in Mr. Kavanagh's flat and he is going to live there too and look after the business here in Altamont. That is what I was saying about a new life. That will be our new life, and now there must be yours. You won't be going away now, will you?"

"No. Or at least not far. You see, Margareta's a cripple. Her hip was broken that night of the raid and it wasn't set for days."

"Then you should come with her to us, too," said Father Mellowes, "where she can be looked after by Romilly. It would be better than being in a hotel." Father Mellowes now proposed that they take both floors of the house above the fish-shop and that they all should live there together.

Margareta had not been able to follow any of the conversation. But she did not want to. She was filled with a deep peace, although her back and limbs ached as though the long journey had set every bone in her body out of joint again.

"The priest suggests that we should go and live with him and his sister and Kavanagh here in a house further up the street. There it would be quieter and you could stay in bed as much as you have to without ever being disturbed or having strangers about."

"Ach, Ezra," she said, "why do you ask me? Give me a

corner somewhere near you and don't ask me anything or I'll begin to howl all over again."

"What does she say?" asked Father Mellowes.

"She says queer things. Everyone is saying queer things this evening."

"Isn't it time that we stopped saying the common and careful things?" said Father Mellowes. "As you yourself first pointed out to me, that hasn't got anyone very far. Isn't it time too that we forgave each other? Perhaps this is our last chance to lead a new life and if we don't take it there won't be another. And your wife, Ezra, let her take her place in it too. Let her forgive you and Margareta and come and live with us too.

"Do you really think that would work?"

"Of course, I'm not sure," said Father Mellowes. "But don't you begin to feel it might? Isn't there already here in this room this evening a beginning? Don't you feel it too, Ezra? As if we were only waiting for a word, for one of us to speak the word."

The Boots brought in a tray and laid it on the table. Ezra arranged it at the bed for Margareta and poured out tea for her and the others.

"Do they disturb you being here, the others?" he asked her.

"How could they disturb me? To be in this room with you and your friends after living always in a hut with twenty strangers and even Bogusky a stranger, good as he was to me, that is heaven, " she said.

"What does she say?" asked Father Mellowes.

"She says this is heaven!"

Father Mellowes got up and went over and sat down beside Margareta on the bed. He laid his hand on hers. His negroid features took on a further gravity.

"Through my blindness, one of the souls under my care has been taken from me, and you have been given to me instead," he told her.

"She doesn't understand a word you say, Father," said Ezra.

"No matter," said Father Mellowes. "She does not understand and she understands, because it is easy to understand what I want to tell her."

"All the same, it wouldn't work," said Ezra, who had been thinking over the priest's proposal. "And, anyhow, what's the point of it? Why should we all go and live together as though we had anything in common, when we haven't? In brotherly love with prayers morning and evening, is that it?"

"It would be a great thing all the same if yourself and the foreign young lady would come and live above the shop, too," said Kavanagh, unexpectedly breaking in. He was regarding Ezra anxiously out of his small eyes.

"Why a great thing?" asked Ezra. "On the principle of the more the merrier?"

"What does he want?" asked Margareta from the bed.

"He wants us to go and live with them."

"Let us go, then."

"Though I shouldn't expect you to care to live in the one house with me, Ezra," Kavanagh said. "It's a queer thing, but I keep forgetting what I've done and that I'm no fit company for decent people." He passed his big hand over his face and then leant forward to spit into the fire.

"Do you know," he went on, "I kept Father Mellowes talking to me and playing cards with me the whole damn afternoon because I hadn't the spunk to sit there alone and wait for them to come back for me."

"I was glad of your company too," said Father Mellowes. "When I came to your room I was in as much need of help as you were."

Kavanagh's scared face had helped to dispel the face of despair and madness that he had looked on in the bathroom. It often haunted him these days, tempting and mocking him.

"The sergeant asked me not to leave the hotel as the superintendent had come down and there might be more information that they'd need in a hurry," Kavanagh said. "You don't know, Ezra, none of you know that the greatest blessing on this earth is to be able to sit in your own room and say to yourself: 'Here I am and here I can sit as long as I like and there's no one coming to take me away or even to as much as ask me a question.' Or maybe you do know it, Ezra; from what you've told me if there's anyone else in this hole knows it but me, it's you, Ezra. Not that I'm trying to make out any similarity. I am guilty. My hands are bloody and yours were not."

Though Ezra did not contradict him, he had again that feeling, not of pity, but of something more direct and instinctive, as if there was no final and protective wall between his flesh and Kavanagh's.

"I said to Father Mellowes," Kavanagh went on to Ezra, "I said: 'You've only got to go across the street to the barrack and tell them that I killed her and I won't raise a finger to stop you.' Didn't I, Father? Weren't those my words?"

"Yes," said Father Mellowes. He was sitting on the bed beside Margareta, who was greedily eating the cold meat and bread and butter.

"Ach, God. All what you've got here!" she said with a full mouth and in even worse German than usual.

"And why didn't you do it? Why don't you do it now, Father?" went on Kavanagh with a miserable bravado.

"That is not my task. That is not part of the work I have to do," said Father Mellowes. There was a complete simplicity in his work as he understood it. All here in his parish, but more especially those in sin and pain, were the flock that he must keep. There had been nothing said about handing any of them over to earthly justice, and with his simplicity bordering on *naïveté* he had no doubts at all about his duty in face of the crime.

"I still don't believe it's any use," Ezra said, looking across at the priest, "this taking literally of some words in the Gospels and trying to make them work. This 'love one another,' and 'Feed my sheep' or lambs or whatever it is."

"Didn't we agree before that there were only two sources of real power, of heart-power? Two dark powers that can overthrow all the daylight powers, the money powers and the State powers?" said the priest. "Didn't we say that there were the two nights against the great grey worldly day, the night of Christ and the night of sex? It was you who called them nights. And that is the truth, Ezra."

"I'm not denying that," said Ezra, "but I say that neither your Christ nor your white Worm can be followed directly and literally. I saw some conquering troops trying to follow the one for a few weeks in a sacked city, and I see you trying to follow the other and I don't shrink from either, or perhaps I do shrink from them both in my flesh, but my soul, if I have one, doesn't shrink as it does when I find myself in the midst of one of our respected Altamont families or as it did at the Colonel's. My spirit isn't nauseated by you and your activity as it is by almost everyone else's including my own, but I still say that it won't achieve peace on earth, not even peace on a little bit of earth, not even in one flat above a fish-shop."

Yet he did not want to argue and he was ready to try living there, to come and live there with Margareta. He did not much mind where they lived and, as Father Mellowes had said, it would be simpler for her as a cripple than living in a hotel. That was the main reason for going there. That, and Nancy. He thought he saw at last a solution to the problem of his marriage. And it was not, as he had known for long now, to go back and submit to all the outward trappings of marriage, to being husband and wife in a house together, preying on and slowly destroying each other. But in a small community, not held tightly together, without bonds and rights and duties, then if there was still that heart-power in them, something by which they could touch and move each other, it would have a chance.

But would Nancy ever accept such a thing, the presence of Margareta, not to speak of the others? Could she ever leave her ivory tower to come down and live among them?

"Peace above the fish-shop," repeated Father Mellowes with his stupid grin. "I didn't promise that. I only say: Come! For my sake and for Kavanagh's. Let us try living together and being patient with each other and putting up with each other for a little. Bring your joy in a new life, that you have in you to-night, with you, you and Margareta, and share it in the measure that you can with us. Give it to us and we will try to shelter it and give it back to you. Like that perhaps it will endure, while hidden and stored up between you alone it will diminish and grow stale. Come for a little time and then if you don't like it you have only to pack your bags and cross the street again." Ezra knew that they would go. When things began to take a new shape there was no stopping them. And before that there was no use in trying to force them. There had been no use in his packing his bag last night, there would have been no use in his going off even to the other end of the earth. That would only have been a scratching on the outermost skin of the nebulous, onion-like globe of life. He saw his life as a core wrapped in many layers of membrane, the outer membranes of space and time and the inner ones, near the quick, of heart and nerves and senses. Each membrane or web touched lightly and mysteriously on the others, there was this touch quivering through the globe from web to web, reshaping it. But whence came this ripple, from within or without, he did not know.

Father Mellowes was addressing himself to Margareta again. He was slow to accept the fact of her not understanding him, or perhaps it was just because she did not understand more than a word here and there that he liked to speak to her; it was a communing with himself in the presence of the girl while Kavanagh was telling Ezra about the lay-out of the top story of his house, the one above the flat, which had for long been untenanted.

"You know, it's strange that our Lord never said a word about the police," the priest began.

At the word "police" she stopped eating and looked round at him anxiously.

"No, no," he said, laying his hand on hers. "You are safe here. You are safe and sheltered here with us. Do you understand, Margareta?" She was looking across at Ezra, but at the priest's words, at the unfeigned gentleness of the tone of the words, she looked back at him satisfied.

"I was thinking of Kavanagh. The police are a machine and that is the trouble. Perhaps there must be police, but let them only not be a machine, even a machine for justice. It's the same with the priesthood. We too, Margareta, run the same danger of becoming a machine."

"Machine?" repeated Margareta, smiling at him in the middle of her eating. "As for machines," she said in German, "this little machine has stuffed itself so full of food and drink that it's got to disappear a moment. I used to be able to run out of the room and be back again so quickly that Ezra couldn't believe it. All went with me quickly, like the Orient Express, we used to say."

The fire went out, the street was silent, only in the Civic Guard barracks lights burned as Sergeant Graham and the superintendent examined the mass of notes that Guard Higgins was still busy typing out from the sergeant's notebook and his own shorthand reports of interrogations made during the day.

Margareta lay in the darkness of this night at the end of her journey. Ezra had settled her with pillows to relieve the ache in her body. She took his hand and laid it on her side. He felt the contortion of flesh and bone under his palm and he knew what it was that she wanted to say by this. She could not have put it into words, certainly not into a language not her own.

Women like Margareta, he thought, say all without words and say what words can't say. How far they are from being capable of "intellectual companionship" or of philosophising. He thought of her limping slowly and painfully along the Quays to Mooney's, seeing out of the corner of her eye the river and the steep steps leading down to it. She had gone into the public-house and said his name, nothing else; she had not been able to say anything else. And now too that they were alone in the middle of the night she could not say much more. No fine phrases, no poetry, almost no endearments, nothing. Darkness and silence, the dim reflection of the street-lamp on the ceiling, and a mute gesture.

CHAPTER XIV

THE
UNRETURNED

■ NANCY ARRIGHO lay in bed after awakening and listened to the sounds from the yard. She heard Aunt Nuala up and about in the yard, giving instructions to her man in her deep, vibrating voice. This voice, the clanking of the pump and the cackling of hens coming up through the open window and the drawn-down blind into the dim room gave the mornings here their repose. She lay in bed in a world where the worst that could happen was a goat breaking through a hedge into a wrong field or a rat slipping into the chicken-coop through a hole in the wire. Then she would hear the voice of Aunt Nuala raised to a high, vibrating resonance which seemed to come up out of her very heart.

Nancy got up and began to dress slowly and absent-mindedly raising her thin arms as though there were weights on her wrists. As though her meeting with Ezra yesterday had hung a further weight on them. She must decide whether to leave her aunt's to-day and drive back to Altamont or to wait until to-morrow. Or not to stop at Altamont at all; to drive straight home.

There was a fire burning brightly in the small sitting-room, its flames reflected in the glass-faced bookcases. Nancy stood by the window looking out on to the garden, the two dark cypress trees and beyond them the crab-apple tree which Ezra had seen glowing with its red fruit against so much foreign darkness. There was sometimes a long wait until breakfast when the early-morning chores in the farmyard had not gone smoothly. She had often sat here on winter mornings with Ezra, one on each side of the fire, and been closer here than when they were at home. She thought of him sitting in that dingy room with his dark face cupped in the palm of his hand and heard him speak about his dirty adulteries. There was this dirt in him, this revelling in dirt and commonness. She had told Aunt Nuala about her meeting with him, but nothing about what they had talked of.

"Nothing is sacred to him," Aunt Nuala had said. "He's no reverence for anything except his own skin."

"Not even for that," Nancy had said. "He's quite ready to go and risk it stupidly and uselessly." The rich vibration came into Aunt Nuala's voice when she spoke of Ezra. She had once been fond and proud of him with his scientific books. He had sometimes come to stay with her alone, without Nancy, and he had had a way of getting on with her. Ezra had been happy for a few days here now and then. He had found repose and shelter here in the small, cosy sitting-room with its old-fashioned books and pictures and in the thick-hedged garden. He had spent many hours watching the bees as they came laden over the hedge out of the wide, clear evening into which the smoke from the distant village rose. Never at home had there been such hours of peace. The still air, the tiny hum of the bees, the scent of mignonette, the crab-apples glowing like a cluster of small red lamps and the wide, tender light in which the whole sky was bathed from the far misty hedges to the north to the low hills in the south. The earth and fruit and sky of his own land. And then at eight he would go up to his room where a can of hot water covered with a towel had been placed by the wash-stand, and tidy himself for supper. As he changed his shoes and brushed his hair he could see from the window the brown cattle grazing in the fields. *Acht Uhr*. He would not have even known what the words meant. He would hear the supper-bell tinkle downstairs, rung by Aunt Nuala's dark little maid.

Nancy was still standing by the window when Aunt Nuala came in from the yard. Nancy kissed her on her cold, yellowish cheek on which there grew a soft down. They went into the small dining-room full of heavy antique furniture, with engravings of Ireland's national heroes on the walls. Aunt Nuala sat with her back to the window in the place that she had sat for as long as Nancy could remember, small, stocky and dominant. Nancy sat on her right, with her chin slightly raised, "looking down her nose" as Ezra used to tell her. His place had always been opposite Aunt Nuala, and Nancy was conscious of his absence as she never was at home now. It was as if his ghost or daemon, because she could not imagine something so unsubstantial about Ezra as a ghost, was there beside them. She felt its presence, seeing it darkly with the eyes of her breast. Instinctively, she knew that Aunt Nuala would speak about him. She would speak of him with a little rage of bitterness and into her voice would come that strange musical, almost sensual note.

She lifted the silver cover and helped out the fried eggs and bacon and Nancy suddenly recalled the taste of a piece of bread dipped into bacon-fat that Aunt Nuala had put into her mouth when she had been a small child. Nothing had ever since tasted so delicious and food was now more or less of a disappointment, like so many things.

"But what you haven't told me, Nancy, is what he's doing there living in a hotel in Altamont?" Aunt Nuala began.

"I don't know what he's doing," Nancy told her for the second or third time.

186

"That's a good one, by the hoaky! When we all think he's dead, killed in an air-raid or something, my lordship comes cooly back and settles himself at an expensive hotel without as much as a word to you or anyone. He doesn't give a tinker's curse for any of us as long as he can sit back in a good hotel where he's waited on hand and foot. Upon my word, he always was an impudent pup!"

Her voice rose on the last words to that vibrating note and Nancy sensed the pent-up bitter rage behind the apparently no more than slightly contemptuous dismissal of Ezra.

"He's got a girl there," said Nancy. She hadn't meant to tell Aunt Nuala this, but there she was saying it, giving outlet to her own sense of hurt and betrayal.

"Wait a bit, Ezra, my fine fellow! Oh, I tell you, my lad, you'li be singing a different song soon. You were always a mean, selfish little devil, anyhow. But just wait a bit, you'll find yourself on the street with not a brass farthing between yourself and starvation if I know anything about you!"

By now Aunt Nuala's voice had risen to a strange, musical note of bitter passion.

She leant over her plate of bacon and eggs, her square little body tense and her face gone yellowish, and Nancy watched her mouth moving as she ate with protruding lips in an angry enjoyment. She looked down her nose at the little spinster and agreed with her, but with the eyes of her breast she was conscious of Ezra and of his silence. It seemed to her that he answered her and Aunt Nuala with his silence. Behind the empty chair on her right a patch of sunlight lay on the wall, and this light striking into the little room was the silent answer of the absent. She knew that there was a considerable grain of truth in every word that the old woman uttered, and she found herself agreeing with her and adding some observations of her own in her cool voice, but all the time she was aware of the sunlight on the wall behind what was Ezra's chair, and a silence. "Ah, how much wiser is your silence, Raz, than your words," she thought.

"Whose money is he squandering this time?" Aunt Nuala was asking. "I suppose he's got some damned fool of a woman to pay for him!"

"Probably," said Nancy.

She sensed that her aunt's rage was the rage of disillusion and frustration and remorse of the ingrowing thorn. A whole life she had spent in thriftiness, and a careful righteousness. She had kept her lamp trimmed and full of the oil of righteousness and waited, but the bridegroom had never come. In none of all the chaste nights of well-earned rest had there ever been the cry: "Lo! the bridegroom cometh!" She had been cheated. Somehow in the end she had been cheated, but she dare not admit it.

"Ah, Raz," thought Nancy, "why wouldn't you bother to buy and keep her affection? It wouldn't have cost you much: a few more visits, an occasional confidence or some little harmless confession, a few more letters. You bought your girls with your airs and your fine talk, and they had no need of you or you of them. And you could so easily have sweetened the last years of this old woman."

But aloud to her aunt she said: "And not a word about how I had been getting on, about the place or anything. He brought out a bottle of whisky and began talking about the lunch that he would give me."

Silence, and the sun on the wall. The silence of the absent.

Aunt Nuala was slowly stirring the strong tea in her cup. She liked to linger over breakfast.

"He seems to have cut himself off from all his former boon companions too," she said. "I met that Geraghty fellow, a couple of weeks ago. He's one of the racing and drinking crowd that Ezra used to be so thick with, and he was asking me if we'd had any word of him. 'Not as much as a penny postcard,' I said, and by the look he gave me I saw that he had formed his own opinion of Ezra long ago."

"I don't suppose he's kept in touch with any of his old friends," said Nancy. "There was always a kind of heartlessness about him. He'd use people and then drop them."

"Like he used you," said the old woman, looking out of the corner of her eye at her niece with a commiserating leer.

"Ah, Raz, why did you get us into this impasse," thought Nancy. "You with your silence, answering all with your silence that you could never answer with words. Must this old woman go down to her grave in her bitterness, as she will soon go, when you could so easily have given her a little warmth and comfort? And me, Raz, do you know sometimes I'm afraid of becoming such an old woman too, disillusioned and embittered. Perhaps you think that wouldn't be your fault, but I'm not so sure. You could have saved that too, at least the humiliation. Ah, you can sit there so quietly. I know that strange silence and patience of yours, watching your bees or your ants for hours on hours and I half-know what you want to say with it. But let me have my say too; let me speak out all my hurt."

"He used you," went on Aunt Nuala, "when it suited him. He had a house to come back to after his trips and lie low in when he was short of cash and do a bit of writing in, though, upon my word, I don't think he ever knew what a hard day's work was in the whole of his life."

"Is there any use me calling in to see you again on my way back, Raz? For you to throw your filthy seductions in my face?"

But she knew she would call in. She would even leave to-day after lunch if she could find an easy way of breaking the news to Aunt Nuala, who was certainly expecting her to stay another day or two.

"He used me too, when it suited him, coming down here

when he'd nothing better to do." Latterly he had come without Nancy and usually by train, by the local train that arrived at the small country station at eight o'clock. And she would put on one of her old mannish felt hats, take a stick and, in winter, light the stable lantern and sally forth to meet him. She would be standing there on the strip of platform when he got out, a small figure planted squarely in the dark, the feeble light of the lantern flickering on her old tweeds. Ezra would stoop down and kiss her quickly on the cheek and walk beside her up the road towards the one or two lights glimmering through the trees. Those had always been precious moments for her, this welcoming of him to her little house at the end of his journey. Sometimes she thought that he depended a little on her, on the knowledge that at the end of all his journeys there would always be the lantern on the small, dark platform and her hand in his and the lights at the end of the lane.

But now what was left to her but disillusion and bitterness? He had gone his own way without a thought for her evening welcomes in which she had put her heart. He had gone his own way in strange places with strange men and women who reaped and did not sow, squandered and did not save, scattered and did not gather. He had left Nancy, and perhaps if he had done so in another manner with much forethought and consultation and a taking of her, Aunt Nuala, into his confidence, an asking of her advice, she might have forgiven even that. But he had just gone off, or not bothered to come back, casually, nonchalantly, without an explanation to anyone. And that was what she could not forgive him for: his nonchalance, his immunity to all his duties and responsibilities. Instinctively, she felt that that was the deathly insult he had offered her, not insulting or denying her personally, but the gods in whose image her life was shaped.

"He never had the slightest sense of responsibility. My lordship simply followed his own pleasure whenever it happened to take him," she said aloud.

Nancy nodded, glancing down at the mannish little old woman munching bread and bacon-fat. It was all quite true what her aunt was saying, and why then did it seem so pointless, and why on earth was she more conscious of the silence and the sunlight on the wall over the empty chair?

Aunt Nuala grunted and wiped her mouth on her napkin and poured out another cup of tea. Nancy remembered something that Ezra had said to her long ago. He had been watching one of his horrible spiders. "The texture of life is strangely loose," he had said, "as loosely woven as that web. And there's no good trying to pull it tighter."

She had not known what he meant, but funnily enough his words had remained. The words other people said, like those Aunt Nuala said, though she knew very well what they meant and agreed with them, soon dissolved and were gone.

"But if I call in to see you on my way home, Raz," she thought, "will what you say to me have the wisdom of this silence of yours here at the breakfast table? Oh no, of course it won't. You will go on in the same old way, casual and cruel and, as this old woman says, selfishly. Why did you tell me about your seduction of some wretched girl? Was that true? The queer thing is, and that is what is so horrible, that I believe it is true. You can revel in all sorts of common nastiness. You like lowness for the sake of lowness. Cheap and common things or people can draw you as I with all my years of patience and faithfulness apparently could not draw you."

After breakfast her aunt took Nancy round the farm. She was glad to get out of the little dining-room into the sweet autumn morning. As Aunt Nuala plodded stockily beside her through the thick, dewy grass Nancy saw more clearly how frail she had become. Her square little figure and mannish walk hid a frailty that was painful to Nancy. Not out of love for the old woman, because she did not love her, but because it threw the shadow of death so close to her, right at her feet. As Aunt Nuala showed her the cattle and called to her favourite calves with a musical tenderness in her voice, calling them by pet names, letting them nuzzle her hand, Nancy thought: "How lonely she is and how lonely am I! What is the cure for loneliness, what is the secret? Not to store and take care and fulfil all one's duties or she would have found it."

"Dais-y, Dais-y, here lass, here lass, come-a, come-a," Aunt Nuala was calling across the field to a calf that stood straddle-legged, its ears like heavy velvet leaves sprouting, pricked, from its raised, dark head. It was a deep red, almost violet in the morning sun, beautiful, and for these moments the bitterness with life was hushed in the old woman by the ungainly, loosed-legged gallop of the calf as it came to her, swishing its tail, and swinging its slobbering calf-head. And when it came to her, nuzzling her, its long, pale tongue dropping saliva on her dry, yellow hand, she fondled it and coaxed it in a tender language of her own.

Supposing she had let go all her pride, her reasonable pride and had written to Ezra that time when she had had the note from him saying he and the girl were in prison—supposing she had written: "I will stand by you and her, whoever she is, in the face of all other people, of all the officials of all the countries of ours and hers and the one where you now are, and no matter what she is or isn't to you. Whatever you want from me, whatever I can do write and tell me, now and in the future. . . ."

But how write like that and lose her self-respect and the respect of her friends when they got to know of it? Why add folly to all the other follies? And to what end? She had done more than most wives: she had accepted more neglect and nothing had come of it.

The calf was nearly knocking Aunt Nuala over, butting its dark, knobbly head into her chest.

"Steady, Daisy. Steady, girlie. Upon my word, she's as strong as a bull!" said the old woman, laughing and staggering backwards.

At one side of the field a row of beech trees grew along the bank of the ditch and Nancy recalled a day when she had sat there with Ezra. They had lain side by side in the dry ditch under the shade of the trees and he had put out his hand and touched her. She did not remember what they had been speaking of or whether it had been morning or evening, but only looking up into the heart of the tree above her and the shock of his hand on her. She had not wanted that, certainly not then and there, not in a ditch with all the rather furtive and premeditated pulling up and pulling down of clothes. He wouldn't mind that, perhaps even like it, losing so easily all self-consciousness in his lusts of the moment. But she had gone on looking up into the pale, shining leaves of the beech tree, enclosing herself with them, and his hand had dropped away from her.

They escaped from the calf and walked back toward the yard.

"I suppose you'll auction off all the cattle and all my old furniture as soon as I'm under the sod," Aunt Nuala said.

"For heaven's sake don't speak of death, Aunt Nuala. I can't bear people speaking of death and dying," said Nancy. But there was nothing in her slowly iterated words that gave the old woman much comfort.

"Why not speak of it? It's a fact that's got to be faced, isn't it?" went on her aunt. How she longed to hear something that would in some way sweeten and soften the hard, dread outlines of the fact. But instinctively she knew that she would not hear it.

The word "death" struck a chill in Nancy's heart a little bit

in the same way as Ezra's hand had chilled her that day long
ago. She experienced the same shrinking. And the old woman
felt this and that now all those around her would turn from
the fact of death and leave her alone with it. If some other
great misfortune threatened, if she lost all her money or if she
suddenly fell under some grave suspicion with the police (she
thought of even such an absurd contingency in her effort to
try to grasp what was behind her great loneliness), Nancy and
her little maid Jenny, and even others less near to her, would
stand by her and be a comfort to her. But when they saw the
hand of death they were struck with an uneasy silence, a kind
of coolness towards her. As though she were herself guilty of
something with which they did not want to be mixed up.

"I've left you the house and the furniture and the livestock,
Nancy," she said. "Most of the money, as you know, is in trust
and will revert back to my brother's children. And may it do
them no good," she added, for she had cut herself off from that
side of her family and hated the thought of her death benefit-
ing them.

She stopped on a little rise of ground to look back at her
cattle. The light lay on the red-and-white backs of the grazing
cows with its bright, unending tranquillity and twinkled along
the flanks of the calves. Nancy saw the line of pale-trunked
beeches and the dry ditch full of leaves and twigs and shadows.
The two women, the older and the young, stood there each
with a loneliness in her breast that neither could assuage for
the other.

"By the hoaky, there's a chill like a knife in the air," said
Aunt Nuala, turning and clumping on. "I hope to heavens
Jenny's kept up a good fire for us. I wouldn't be surprised if
there's a bit of frost this evening."

"I must be leaving after lunch," Nancy said.

Aunt Nuala turned her yellowish face to her and gave her
a long, shrewd glance from under the brim of her battered

felt hat. Her nose and cheeks were a mottled pink and her eyes seemed to have become smaller in the fresh wind.

"Ah, she's going to run back to him, the damn little fool!" she said to herself. "They're all the same. All women are fools, fools! But let her go. I can't stop her. They will all be taken from me."

"Do you ever pray?" she asked Nancy.

"Pray? Well——"

"I know it's a queer question to spring on you, but I was wondering what people are thinking, the sort of people you come across up in the city. I was wondering if praying has gone out of fashion since the war," Aunt Nuala said. "And the people abroad, those who were in the war as soldiers or those who went through it all as civilians, the people where Ezra was, for example, did they pray?"

"I don't know. We didn't speak about his experiences," Nancy said.

The old woman would have liked to have known that. It might have been the only thing that would have made her less lonely, if she could have felt some contact with all those who had been swallowed up in the horrors of the war. If only Ezra had come back to talk to her and tell her something about how it had been. If he had sent her a card: "Coming down by evening train," and she would have taken the stable lamp, for the days were drawing in, and gone to the station to meet him. She would have felt his lips brush her cheek and they would have started back together up the dark road. She had now the feeling that he alone might have brought her that word of comfort.

"I suppose you'll see him on your way through Altamont. I suppose you'll make another call on his lordship," she said.

CHAPTER XV

KAVANAGH

■ EZRA LEFT Margareta in the room that he had chosen for her in the house above Kavanagh's fish-shop. They had met Father Mellowes there early in the morning and all had gone quickly and simply, the choosing of rooms and settling of other details. Margareta had a small room at the back and Ezra one next to her, and on the other side of the passage were Kavanagh's room and the sitting-room. The kitchen was at the end of the passage. Father Mellowes and Romilly were to have two rooms on the top floor.

Ezra went back to Flood's to collect a first load of belongings. There were things, too, to be bought in the town for the little community. Was not his winning at the dog-races part of the whole turn and shaping of events in this unexpected direction?

The door-bell rang and Kavanagh limped to open it with darkness in his breast. They had come for him. Ezra had a key and Father Mellowes was not to return until the afternoon. He had been kneeling down in front of the fireplace in Margareta's room trying to kindle a fire. He got heavily to his feet, slowly swinging round his stiff leg under his body.

"Wonder who that is," he remarked to Margareta, putting only casualness into his tone which she could grasp, if not the words. To her he showed nothing, partly out of an instinct to shelter her from anxiety and partly because of an instinct to keep his fear secret.

If they had come and it was the end, then there was nothing to do but to give himself up to the despair that was lurking in him like a numbness, creeping over him, stilling and numbing his heart and senses. Then goodbye to lighting fires, to coal-dust on his hands, to the smell of fish, to the settling of rugs as he had just now tucked one around the foreign young lady's feet. Her feet had been icy cold. That came from being a cripple, he supposed. As now his heart had gone cold. Goodbye to the winter evenings when the lights came on along the street, the light of his own shop and of the other shops. Formerly he had felt contemptuous of Altamont and its activities, but now he longed only to be able to spend here the coming winter in the midst of people and lights and business.

He opened the door. At it was a messenger boy with a large brown-paper parcel. Kavanagh stood for a moment peering at the boy, his head thrust forward from his heavy shoulders. Then he reached out his big, coal-blackened hands and took the parcel with a kind of reverence. He carried it back and laid it on the table in Margareta's room.

"Better wipe your hands before opening it," she said to him. "What's that, miss?"

She pointed at his hands. He looked at them and went and washed them obediently and came back and opened the parcel. It contained the blankets and sheets that Ezra had bought.

All that Ezra saw in the streets and in the shops had the lineaments of joy. When he stood at the counter of the iron-monger's and there were hands stretched across it with wrapped-up purchases and hands taking them, these minutes and insignificant gestures were sweet and new. He was seeing many things for the first time. Even the drab bricks of the houses seemed tenderly laid. He returned to the flat with his parcels. Margareta's small room had already an air of peace. Was this not a more possible peace than that of his old home, of all the other rooms and houses? For here there was not the sense of that precarious peace, of a security created by shutting out the rest of the world. Not the false ease and spaciousness of the Colonel's house, nor the cosy homeliness of Aunt Nuala's. The air of this room was sweet and fresh in his heart.

He showed Margareta and Kavanagh the things he had been buying. Kavanagh examined everything with a childlike interest as though he was seeing them for the first or the last time. And after all had been unpacked he still stayed in the room, tidying away the paper, sweeping up the grate, bringing coal for the fire, limping slowly here and there, lingering in their company.

"You don't mind me leaving you alone with him?" Ezra asked Margareta.

"What is there to mind? He's as gentle as a lamb. If only they don't get him!" she said.

"And if he's guilty of a great crime?" asked Ezra.

"Ach, haven't you and I and all the others gone through enough in prisons and camps and God knows where? Haven't enough innocent been condemned for it to be time for a few guilty to go free?"

Ezra made several journeys from Flood's with his belongings. Coming back to the hotel in the afternoon, he found Nancy waiting for him. They sat in his room and they spoke at first with constraint. He felt the suspicion in her and the resentment. But he wanted to open his heart to her, to speak as he had not been able to yesterday.

"There's no good us trying to begin all over again, in the old way, Nancy," he said. "If we were to shut ourselves up together like all the couples, we'd soon explode apart, and this time violently. Isn't there something horrible about the thought of all the married couples shut up together in houses and flats everywhere, all the watertight little families bound together more by fear and suspicion of the rest of the world than by love of each other? And even if there is love of each other, it ends by turning stale and sour in the close and heavy atmosphere of such an existence. Ah, Nancy, there's only one thing for us to do, and that is to renounce our marriage and all its works, and to approach each other as two people might who have been shut up in prison together, sharing the same cell, and are now meeting again outside, in freedom. We know each other like two fellow prisoners get to know each other, with that half-knowledge."

"All these words, Raz," she said wearily. "And what do they mean? Simply that you want to be free to have a good time in your own way and leave me to mine."

"What I was going to say," Ezra went on, "is that if we now make up our minds to stand by each other, not out of some duty or rights, not because we're married, but because we're neighbours (it may sound a queer word to use, Nancy, but you'll know what I mean by it, we always knew what the other meant), if we now stand by each other, then we'll have begun something better than we ever had before."

"To stand by each other," she repeated. "That's a funny thing to say. Have you stood by me?"

"No; I haven't. And as a husband I never shall. There's no good you coming to me and saying: 'I'm your wife. What are you going to do about it?' Because that's a dead relationship and it can't touch me. But if only you would stretch out your hand to me, Nancy, and say: 'I'm not your wife any more, but your neighbour. We have eaten from the same table and slept in the same bed. Therefore help me,' then all would be simple again and true between us."

He saw in her eyes the struggle, the fear, the hurt, the hope and the fear of more hurt. She lowered her chin from its faintly disdainful tilt and regarded him with a flicker of her old smile.

"Listen, Nancy. I'm going to go and live in a house here with four or five other people, and if you wish you can come and live there too. There we shall try to live together in peace and gratitude. In gratitude for being alive and for being together, after having been in a sense dead and alone."

"What sort of people?" she asked suspiciously. "Some of your girls too, I suppose?"

"Simply come and stay with us a little without judging," he said. "Come without prejudices and suspicions and the old angers, Nancy, and we shall try and make together a little corner of tangible peace. I don't know if it is possible. And yet, do you know, Nancy, at this moment I believe all is possible. I believe if you will only leave everything, all that seems to you just and becoming, your pride too, and come and live with us, with Margareta, the priest and his sister and Kavanagh the fishmonger, with us poor, needy and, if you like, sinners, you, too, as one of the poor and needy, then, who knows, the days may be sweet again and the nights tranquil."

At the name "Margareta" an expression of disdain passed over Nancy's mouth. The line of her lips hardened and she said:

"I thought you told me she wasn't here."

"Nor was she. I thought she was dead; but she came back. Ah, Nancy, don't let that torment you. She can do you no harm. Perhaps dead she could have done you harm, for when, as yesterday, I thought she was dead, I could never have come to you as I do now. She won't rob you or cheat you of anything. She asks for very little. From me she asks for very little, and I too, Nancy, I've learnt to ask for very little. In the face of death one wants only a few things, the things that there are plenty of for everyone."

200

Nancy had lit a cigarette and was absently letting the last of a mouthful of smoke trickle out between her lips. He remembered her so often like that as they had talked, sitting there listening with a kind of absent-mindedness as though his words never really reached her, as though she heard them behind a veil of cigarette smoke.

"When I was at Aunt Nuala's and she was going on in her rather malicious way about you, and I imagined you there in your old place, Raz, sitting there in silence, that silence was beautiful. But what you say isn't beautiful; it's muddy and common," she said.

"Come and I'll show you where we live," he said. "And if you like you can bring your things from the car. There are still one or two empty rooms. You can choose one of them and we'll go and buy what is needed for it. Wouldn't you like that, Nancy? Wouldn't that be like the old days, the early days?"

"And what about Mostrevor, Raz? Do you think I can just abandon it and let it go to ruin?"

"Yes. That's what I think. Abandon it, abandon everything, and come out with me now and we'll find a corner for you and get a basin and hang up a mirror—there are beds enough. And later, if you want, you can bring a few more things from Mostrevor, but not too many; we don't want to clutter up our lives again with belongings."

He saw her hesitate. She had been touched through the veil of cigarette smoke, through the ivory gates of her tower. For a moment the very affront and unreason of his proposal had moved her in spite of herself. She was touched and angry, moved and hurt.

In the street it was beginning to grow dusk. Ezra and Nancy entered the house through the side door and he went in front of her up the dim staircase. There was a salty, clammy smell of fish that came from the shop. Ezra looked into the sitting-room, which was empty, and then led her down the narrow passage to Margareta's room. The door was ajar and he pushed it open and went in. The room was lit only by the fire that was blazing brightly and Kavanagh was sitting at it. On the bed Margareta was sleeping with a blanket, on which fell the flickering light and shadow, covering her.

Kavanagh got to his feet and shook hands with Nancy. For a moment as he had entered the room, Ezra had had an impulse to tiptoe out again before he had been seen.

"The young lady's sleeping," said Kavanagh in his low, muffled voice. "She's a long and tiring journey behind her.

"Father Mellowes was here and left some things and he'll be back again later," he added.

"Good." And Ezra laid his hand on Kavanagh's shoulder. He was not free with his gestures and he was surprised at himself. As his hand rested on it awkwardly for a moment, he saw over Kavanagh's shoulder the slim figure of his wife standing by the shadowy bundle on the bed looking down at Margareta.

"Come," he said. "I'll show you the other rooms."

He showed her the flat, the sitting-room with all its varnished and heavily upholstered furniture, the big table in the centre covered by a stained, red-plush cloth; then the other rooms, bare and drab and not yet lived in.

"Who was that man?" Nancy asked.

"That was Kavanagh, the fishmonger. He owns the flat."

They were standing in the room to which Ezra had brought some of his things.

"Will this be your room?" she asked.

"Yes; but if you come you can have it and I'll take one of those on the top floor with the priest and his sister. It's all the same to me what room I have," Ezra said.

"Do you really want me to come, Raz?" she asked.

"Yes."

It was the first thing that he had wanted of her for a long time, and that was more than all words to her. But why here to this horrible little house on the main street of a provincial town? To leave the garden and woods of Mostrevor, the gentle, wooded hills that she looked on from her window and that had been her one joy in a world of mostly hateful people.

The face of the sleeping girl that, without asking, she had known was Margareta had touched her with a pang of pity. Like that, asleep, people had another aspect than when they were awake and active. Awake, she was probably that designing little creature that she had expected, but there, looking on her asleep in the shadows, there had been a moment of recognition. Nancy had, in spite of all her sense of wrong, seen in the sleeping face, not the feared stranger, but something almost familiar—a defencelessness, was it?—like her own.

But no, he couldn't really expect her to come here and give up the one thing that was left her.

"That's something I couldn't do. It would be no good, Raz. I'd go mad in a place like this."

"Then what would you have done in other places, in the places where I've been?" he was going to ask, but he did not. Argument was no good.

"Well, then, I suppose there's no point in your seeing the rest of the house," he said.

They climbed down the dark stairs and went out again into the street. Nancy's car was standing outside Flood's hotel.

"Then goodbye, Raz," she said to him, turning to him as they reached it and holding out her hand. When she was already in the car she said: "You should go and see Aunt Nuala. She's a lonely old woman, and in spite of all she says about you she'd be glad to see you."

Ezra did not answer. He saw his wife's small face turned to the instrument board with a delicate, set expression.

Ezra stood and watched the car drive away down the dusky street. He turned into the hotel, put the last of his things into a suitcase and returned to the flat.

Father Mellowes and Romilly were also there, and Ezra helped with the arranging of the scanty furniture in their rooms. When he was alone with Romilly in her room, hanging curtains at the window, she said: "Why are you coming to live here, you and your Margareta?"

He turned from the window. She was bending over a cheap chest-of-drawers with the drawers pulled out. He saw from the traces around her eyes that she had been weeping.

"Your brother asked us to. You know he has faith in us being able to help each other."

"Isn't it more likely that we'll go on tormenting and destroying each other like wild beasts shut up in a cage together? My brother looks on it as a fold, but he doesn't know, he doesn't know."

"What doesn't he know?"

"What we others know. The devils. The devils that made me run like a mad one through the streets the other night to you, that made Kavanagh kill Annie, that made Annie put the blood on the picture; and they're in you too, I've seen them in you when you came over to the bed to me after talking to Kavanagh at the door." She was kneeling on the floor in front of the open drawer, her head bowed.

"Yet I've the feeling that it's just he who does know them," Ezra said; "these and the others by which men are possessed."

"He came in here just now," Romilly said, "to hang a crucifix over my bed. But I told him I didn't want it. I daren't have it any more. And what did he say? 'Till now you have never known what it was. It's only now that you can appreciate it.' What did he mean by that? Is it necessary to go through such a nightmare? Or to drag oneself through filth as we have done? I can't believe that. And then he looks at me with such a peculiar smile, as though he had grasped nothing, like an idiot. I don't know what to make of him lately; and all these visits he makes to the asylum and the prison. He comes back sometimes with such a strange expression and that smile on his face. I wonder if he really knows what he's doing in bringing us here? I certainly don't know what we're doing here, Ezra, or what can come of it except more horror and torment. I see nothing, nothing but darkness and madness everywhere I look, as though the whole world is full of shame and violence."

Father Mellowes was standing in the open door with a large picture in a heavy, old-fashioned frame in his hands.

"Would you care for this in your room?" he said to Ezra. "Romilly and I have had it since we were children." Ezra took it from the priest and they went down to Ezra's room with it, and Father Mellowes began hammering and hanging and adjusting as if he had no other care but to get the Christmas-number lithograph hung exactly over the mantelpiece. Ezra watched him with the same doubt that he had so often had. Where did wisdom end and idiocy begin?

"My wife was here this afternoon and I showed her the flat," Ezra said.

"And what did she say when you asked her to come and live here?" Father Mellowes said, fiddling with the picture.

"She didn't want to leave Mostrevor."

"Ah! How hard it is for those who have possessions!" said Father Mellowes.

"And then it was hard for her to accept the presence of Margareta," Ezra went on. "Marriage may be holy, but it is also apt to be heartless as far as the rest of the world is concerned. The heartlessness of marriage to all that seems to threaten it is really shocking," he said. "I don't mean only in this case, because that is perhaps understandable. But in general, what a horrible egoism family egoism is, and your Catholic family egoism is the nastiest of all!"

"Then let us try to live here together in another spirit. Let us bring our heart and soul to this new life, Ezra," said the priest, turning from the wall and looking at Ezra with the light glinting on his glasses, so that Ezra saw nothing but the black, curly hair and the thick, smiling lips.

"Do you begin to have faith in it?" he added.

"I don't know that I have," said Ezra. "I really don't know. But I've a peculiar faith in you, Father. That's what I've got. I don't know how I've come by it and I even fought against it for a bit, but there it is. Not in you as a priest, Father, not in what you stand for in your priestly office, but simply in you."

CHAPTER XVI

THE
ANOINTING

■ IT WAS in the evenings as they sat round the table at supper that Ezra had for the first time the sense of being part of a daring and delicate experiment. These first evenings, with the autumn wind smelling of smoke and the rain blowing down the main street and the boy putting up the shutters of the shop below, he knew that all was in the balance as they gathered at the table. It would have been easy for one and then another to have failed to appear, for him and Margareta to have gone over and had supper alone together at Flood's, or for Kavanagh to have been kept by one of his cronies somewhere in the town. But this did not happen. There was something that drew them together. They came into the room from their own rooms or from the town, and when they were gathered round the table together there was a faint, flickering fusion between them, less charged and intense than that between two people, a melting of the core of self-consciousness. The little group felt the first stir of a life of its own, a tenuous ripple around the table that touched and laved the remotest corners of each single heart. This life, after its first stirrings, would have wavered and flickered out in the great counter-stream of darkness that flowed against it from the very stones and bricks of the town had it not had Father

Mellowes to shield and re-kindle it. Though how he did so was not apparent. Nothing of this was really apparent. The first days passed in a settling down and a settling into the various modes of living that each of them had chosen or accepted.

Romilly did the cooking and the marketing and had a girl to help her with the house-work. Kavanagh worked in the shop. Father Mellowes was as usual much of the time out in the town on his visits or in the church. Margareta was happy in her room darning the socks and stockings, mending what had to be mended, while Ezra spent the mornings working on his book. Sometimes he took her out in Kavanagh's car or he came and sat with her in her room or they went across to the hotel and drank wine or whisky until Margareta said, "Come, let's go home," and they returned to the flat. And it was not drab or dull, the return there; it did not cease to keep something of a refuge for them about it.

They felt the unexpected life of the little group encompass them. There was a dark and subtle field of power set up between those living in the house. Ezra was more conscious of it than the others. There opened before him vast and strange vistas. He saw that, after all, there were other modes of communion beside the old and played-out ones, other cults beside the marriage-cult and the family-cult. He said nothing, even to Father Mellowes. He was still by no means sure whether in this particular case the sense of release that they had sometimes when they were together in the evening—release from the various prisons of each self into a fleeting experience of communion—could last or grow.

Coming home the third or fourth evening after their move into Kavanagh's house, Father Mellowes was greeted by Guard Higgins just outside the fish-shop.

"Can I speak to you a moment, Father?"

"Come on in with me," said the priest. "You haven't seen our new home."

"Not now, Father. I'm on duty." They stopped in the dark side street opposite the house entrance. A misty rain was falling and the guard drew Father Mellowes into the shelter of the wall.

"Do you know why I'm here, Father?" said Guard Higgins, with his face close to the priest's in the dark.

"Yes," said Father Mellowes.

The guard was surprised at this answer. "Ah, Father, you can't know that, and I dread telling you, for it'll be a great shock to you."

"You needn't tell me, my child," said the priest. It came quite naturally to him to call the other thus. All were his children, but Guard Higgins always struck him as one of the most childlike. The wind blew round the corner from the main street in gusts and the street lamps cast a dim light on to the wet pavement, the very stones of which were dear to the priest.

"I, too, in my own way have a little of 'la grande habitude de voir,'" Father Mellowes went on, and in the darkness of the doorway in which they stood, his thick lips parted gently in that grin that appeared so disconcertingly on them. "You are here to watch our house," he added.

"Has the sergeant spoken to you, then?"

"No one has spoken to me. But I dare not sleep, either. I must watch and wake too, not as you watch, but for my own."

"The sergeant is only waiting for the report on bloodstains that were on a coat that we got from the shop," said Guard Higgins.

"How long must you stand here?" the priest asked.

"Till midnight, Father. Then Guard Casey relieves me."

"And what do you think about while you wait here alone in the dark?"

"What do I think about?" repeated the guard. The priest always asked such irrelevant questions. Higgins reflected a moment and said: "As I saw you turn the corner, I was thinking about the *Pooideal*."

"Yes?"

"It has weathered all the tests and now I have planted a plot with it and one day soon I'm going to let in Mrs. Bamber's goats on it and see if they eat it."

They were both silent as someone passed by close to them. The station clock was slowly chiming the hour, the strokes sliding up out of the night and ebbing back into it like waves from a hidden ocean of time.

The priest saw the profound darkness and felt the wind blowing out of it and that nothing could more than ruffle its surface. The street lights were no more than one facet of the manifold breast of darkness, scratches that glimmered on its surface, and the occasional passers-by were but clottings and stirrings of darkness within darkness. And in the midst of this travail of wind and darkness stood the house opposite as though alone. He regarded it from across the street and saw it standing there alone, built of darkness, and shut within it, as though buried in the bowels of darkness, those who had been given to him.

"Let me watch and wake, then," he prayed. "Let my watching and waking be as sound and as perfect as the sleep of the dead."

"When will you come for him?" Father Mellowes asked.

"I don't rightly know. Some time to-morrow the sergeant should have finished fitting together the proofs. I only wish that yourself and your sister weren't there in the house, Father. Maybe you could take her off somewhere for the day, that you might both be spared the shock of it," said Guard Higgins.

"It's not of us I'm thinking," said the priest.

"Don't waste your pity over him, Father. It's only justice that's being dealt out to him. What did he deal out to Annie but the cold knife into her heart?"

210

"That knife was not so cold as your justice," said the priest. "And it struck quickly. Agony is a mysterious concoction of many things, of fear and of time in the first place. In Annie's agony there was very little time. But in his there will be weeks and months of which each hour will be endless."

"Isn't it the law, Father? And there must be the law and the police."

They drew closer into their shallow shelter as a gust of wind and rain whirled from between the dim lamps of the main street and broke with a spatter against the wall. In the kitchen window above the dark door opposite a light burned where Romilly was preparing supper.

"You and I," said Father Mellowes, "have we an authority and a law that outweighs the word that God has traced with His finger on our blood?"

"What word is that?" asked the guard, uneasily.

"What word? Listen to it, listen to it. It does not sound like our word, 'Justice,' does it?" said the priest.

"Maybe if I was to listen I wouldn't hear what you hear, Father. While I was standing here alone, before I began thinking of the *Pooideal,* like I told you, I was wondering what he was doing in the house over there. Was he sitting down to supper? Or was he perhaps out with another girl somewhere? I thought to myself, Father: Supposing it had been my sister instead of Annie? Or, if you'll not take it badly, Father, suppose it had been your own sister had been found out there in the ditch with her breast all bloody? You remember how it was that the two of them, Miss Mellowes and Annie, had both disappeared that same evening, this very day week it was that I was making my enquiries, and couldn't your sister have been the one who never came back, Father, if you'll allow me the manner of speaking."

"I have thought of that too," said Father Mellowes.

"One of her hands was cut across the palm," said Guard Higgins, "as she must have tried to ward off the knife."

Occasionally a car passed up or down the main street, but the fleeting imprint of light was as quickly and silently filled up again with the wet darkness as it was made.

"That man's a wild beast when the rage takes him," Guard Higgins went on. "I've had a glimpse of it myself and I've heard of it from others. If I stand here on a night like this, it's so that others may sleep safely in their beds."

"Then God be with you, watching," said Father Mellowes, "and with him too, waking, and with Annie, sleeping."

He crossed the street and went into the house. Supper had been laid and they had only been awaiting his return to sit down to it. During the meal Ezra kept glancing at the face of the priest, at the glistening forehead with the tight crown of black hair, and the big mouth that smiled so easily. It was smiling now and Ezra thought of what Romilly had said of his expression when he returned sometimes from his visit to the asylum or the prison. To-night Ezra thought he began to grasp it: it was the smile of someone on whom a difficult piece of knowledge begins to dawn, the smile of recognition given to the unbelievable simplicity of a long-sought solution suddenly stumbled on. But his forehead was still in the profound darkness and in his brows were gathered insoluble shadows.

Father Mellowes was speaking to Kavanagh, who sat beside him. Ezra saw Kavanagh lay down his knife and fork and his dark face turned white without losing its swarthiness, turning white underneath. There was silence in the room; not that the talk between the others immediately stopped, it went on, but in the presence of silence approaching, coming up behind them, and standing behind their chairs.

"That's the end of me, that's good night," said Kavanagh. His face was dark-white and as though he had been flayed. He spoke out of the silence, already from far away. He felt he was slipping away from them out of the circle of the table, of these who were now his friends. But now that the hour had come there was in this letting go of all that he had been holding on to in itself a kind of strength. All in a moment he had let go and was carried down to where the other road began, the straight, empty road where he would have to walk alone, short and yet long—long as a lifetime.

"If I only knew I'd have a visit from one of you afterwards, at the end," he said after a silence. "But none of you being a close relative, I don't suppose they'd allow you near me."

Romilly turned to him. Her face was like that of someone in a trance, the eyes burning dark, the mouth in a kind of brooding, musing reverie and the words came out of it like the words of an old song that she might have been murmuring to herself: "You won't have to be alone. I'll be with you. At the end, too."

Kavanagh was looking at her still with that flayed look on his heavy face. "They won't let you, miss. I know how it is. You, not being a close relative, can't visit a condemned man."

"I will marry you and I will be with you," she went on in the strange murmur. "My brother will marry us in the early morning."

She looked at Father Mellowes and he was smiling that smile that Ezra had just begun to think he had got a little clear.

"That's right. I will marry you. Do you hear, Kavanagh?" He inclined his glasses towards Kavanagh, regarding him intently as though he had been a child who had perhaps not caught the sense of something told him.

"You can't do that, miss. There's got to be measure to everything, and you can't go saddling yourself with a bloody name. You with your brother's fair name, miss, can't bind yourself with crime in the bonds of matrimony."

Her mouth, like the blossoming of her strange desire in her

face, was softly set in determination, long and ugly. She had no longer the untouched look that had aroused Ezra's contempt; she sat there in her neat blouse, but beneath it her breast was no longer immured in its white immunity.

"Let me marry you, Kavanagh," she said, "for I'll never again have a chance of being a wife, so simply and fully. That is what I've wanted to be, though I didn't know it. This is really the miracle I wanted when I saw the picture bleeding. I wanted someone to come and say to me: 'Save me and help me and be to me wife and mother and sister against all the world and the devils.' I didn't know it, but I wanted some miracle like that. And when I ran to you, Ezra," she went on, "it was because I thought perhaps I could find it with you. But you didn't need me. You only needed me to pretend I was Margareta, and I couldn't even help you to do that."

"Will you stop, for the love of God, miss," said Kavanagh, "or I'll be taking you at your word, and that would be a nice scandal to let you and your brother in for."

She went on speaking to him out of her trance, convincing him of he himself scarcely knew what. That he would marry her, and while anguish and death were being given him with one hand, the very opposite—of which he had not dreamed—was being given with the other.

Father Mellowes supported Romilly in her singular wooing. He tilted his glasses towards Kavanagh and said to him:

"Let it be as she asks. I will marry you in the early morning, and when they come for you you will have a legal wife who can go to you when no one else can go. And for those weeks and months Romilly will have a husband for whom to live in the bonds of charity and peace. That is true marriage, children," he went on, looking round the table. "I didn't know it before, but in a marriage like this the sacrament is purified of all the misuse that has been made of it. It was you, Ezra, who opened my eyes when I was blind. Do you remem-

ber what you said to me that day at the Colonel's a week ago
—can it really only be a week ago?—when I spoke so com-
placently?"

Kavanagh did not follow more than half of what was being
said to him. But the fact of this young lady wanting to marry
him was in itself more than enough to try to grasp. No explanation that she or the priest might give made it any clearer.
Women were queer. He left it at that. There was nothing of
which they were not capable. He felt a new breath of life in
him in the very face of death. He stretched his hand across
the table and took hers. He held it, looking out of his haunted
little eyes into her musing face. He felt his blood, that had
been cold and as though dead in him since the night of the
murder, stir. He said:

"By God, then, miss, if you're so sure of yourself and if your
brother's willing, let us be married and be damned to the lot
of them!"

The night was still long, and none of them thought of sleeping. Father Mellowes suggested they play cards and a table
was drawn up to Margareta's bed and the fire made up in her
room. Margareta, settled with cushions in her bed, played too.
She had not followed the events that had been spoken of, but
she sensed the tension and the waiting. It reminded her of the
waiting for the coming of the bombers in the war, when she
and Ezra would huddle together in the cellar with the others.
But she did not ask him what it was. She was content to lie
there with the cards in her hands and Ezra sitting on the bed
beside her.

Kavanagh fetched some bottles of Guinness from the kitchen
and poured glasses for Father Mellowes, Ezra and himself.
His face had regained some of its smouldering potency. The
shadow of death had faded from it again and the small eyes
perused the cards in his hand at each new deal with an absorbed eagerness that astonished Ezra. How easily distracted,

how shallow is the heart, he thought. And yet in the very midst of the shallowness were caverns opening into eerie depths.

He had been drinking Guinness here with Kavanagh and Annie on a night in that other time in which he had groped and wandered, moving in the narrow circle of the Altamont main street, and his room at Flood's, and, in the circle of time, groping around to that other street, always coming back to it, wandering down it, waiting along it, drinking it with his drink and tasting it with his meat. Now he was delivered from it, and, sitting on Margareta's bed dealing the cards, he knew himself delivered from the irremediable horror of time.

Towards morning Father Mellowes went up to his room and came back with his black, shabby missal. He sat down at the card-table again and opened it, turning the thumb-eared pages with hands that were at home again among the thin leaves. He began to read aloud from the Psalms. Through the sombre flow of the verses passed and repassed the night-wind in the chimney, lending its shape to the words and the words lending their shape to the night-wind. Out of the mouth of the priest came the words still moulded by the fear and faith and pride of the old Israelites; even in a strange language the rank, dark smell of the blood and the dark, lustrous bodies still clung to them. Kavanagh listened, gathering up the cards slowly and tidying them into a pack. He did not follow the words except here and there when he seemed to catch some cry of despair or fear or longing.

"Although I must wander in the shadow of death I fear no evil because Thou, Lord, art with me. . . . In Thee our fathers trusted; they trusted and Thou set them free," Father Mellowes read. "I am poured out like water, my heart is as wax melted within me. . . ."

Looking at Romilly, Ezra thought: A short time ago she

216

was not "poured out like water"; she was like water saved up and stored in a glass jar.

"Sad is my soul in me, O God, when I brood upon Thee here,
Here on Jordan's bank, on mount Hermon, singular moun-
tain!
Depths call to depths, Thy waterfalls roar,
Thy waves, Thy floods all break over me!"

When the others had gone, the priest and Kavanagh into the sitting-room and Romilly up to her room, Ezra opened the window. A grey spume of light lay on the wet roofs, though the sky was still black. He brought a basin of warm water from the bathroom.

"Come. I'll help you to dress," he said to Margareta. "You must put on clean things."

"What for?"

He told her. She showed no surprise. She sat up, and he drew off her stockings and washed her feet. Then he found a new pair of stockings that he had bought for her and a pair of black satin shoes that he had bought that first morning when he had gone from shop to shop still in a trance at her resurrection, buying whatever caught his eye in which to clothe her living body, useless finery like the shoes among other things. Now he put them on her feet, kneeling by the bed, and she watched, stiff with the pain in her hip that was always there like a hot coal against her flank after lying a long time in the same position.

"You'd think it was me was the bride," she said.

"Don't keep your leg so stiff," he said, trying to force her heel into the shoe. When he pulled on her foot it was as though he were pulling her apart.

"But that is not pain," she was thinking. "I mustn't forget what pain is. That is only pain where I am alone and lost."

The rhythm of the Psalms lingered in his blood like the beat of a distant ocean. He brought her the new dress that he had bought for her and which she had not yet worn. He began to help her taking off the old garments that she had worn on the journey and in the camp. Although she could have managed alone, she let him undress her and then bring fresh water. All belonged to the ceremony of this night that she was conscious of without understanding. He took her old and much-mended clothes and folded them and put them away. He spread a towel on the bed and put the basin on it and began to lave her as she lay there. He passed the sponge, that lay like a living thing between his hand and her flesh, over her breasts and her belly, her loins and flanks, slipping over the gleaming planes of her body and into the folded shadows, his hand moving heavy and brooding and yet light on the sponge in whose web the water had turned to balm.

She lay and let the pain and the warm, clinging touch of the sponge mingle over her. She did not know what he was doing, and yet again she knew. She lifted her arms as he sponged them, and her hands as he took them into his and they lay, one after the other, in his.

Then he took one of the towels that he had bought and had never yet been used and which still smelt of the loom, and spread it over her, pressing it softly to her with his hands, drawing up the damp from her flesh, drawing the towel down, moulding it with his hand to her body and, when it was wet, taking another.

There was nothing said between them. There was the intermittent moan of the wind in the chimney and the sombre, glowing lamentation of the Psalms echoing in his blood, determining his movements as he leant over her, purifying them of awkwardness or self-consciousness or a limited, impatient desire.

218

He took the new underclothes that she had put back in the tissue paper after having looked at them that first morning when the parcel had been delivered. He drew them on to her and then the evening dress that was of some black, heavy material and would reach to her feet. As he was fastening it at the back and she was leaning over, supported on his arm, but all the same this movement causing her great pain, he heard a whistle from outside the street. He recognised it as a police whistle; perhaps Kavanagh had gone out and this was the sign that the Civic Guard watching the house was to give.

"What was that?" she asked. For her too there was a familiar fearfulness in the short, shrill sound that nevertheless had come to them softly through the shut window that gave out on to the back.

"It's probably nothing," he said. But he went to the sitting-room door and, opening it, looked in. He had a glimpse of the heavy form of Kavanagh kneeling by the table on one knee, his other leg stuck out stiffly behind him. Although he did not see Father Mellowes, the priest had apparently been hearing Kavanagh's confession and he was now repeating his penance. Ezra closed the door softly and went back to Margareta.

"He is there," he told her. "The priest has been hearing his confession before the marriage ceremony."

Ezra washed his own hands and face and then switched out the light and lay down beside her on the bed to wait. As the fire died down, he saw the window panes lose their brilliant blackness and take on a deathly, greyish hue. Margareta had fallen asleep, and he dozed off too into a restless slumber in which there were voices and a soft eerie whistle, neither man's nor bird's.

He woke to see an apparition standing in the greyish light that now filled the room like fumes. Paler than the dawn in the room was the crowned figure in ghostly white, though the whiteness of the garment he could only conjecture by its contrast to the other objects in the room.

He sat up and switched on the light. Romilly sprang out of the vanished shadows in all her dazzling whiteness. She had put on the wedding dress that she had had made in preparation for her marriage to the Colonel. She had gone up to her room and spent an hour or two in putting it on and adjusting it, in altering a detail here and there.

"Come! All is ready," she said.

CHAPTER XVII

THE
MARRIAGE

■ FATHER MELLOWES read the words in a low voice, as though to himself, over the wreathed head of his sister and the murderer's head. He stood in his shapeless and stained black suit in front of the empty fireplace on which two candles burned. There was no other light in the sitting-room. Ezra and Margareta sat a little behind the other two. Kavanagh had a cheap ring that he had once given to Annie to wear when he had taken her for a week-end to a seaside hotel.

It was quieter in this room as the wind was on the back of the house. The station clock struck and Margareta asked in a whisper what time it was.

"*Sieben Uhr,*" he told her.

"It was the hour of rising in the prison," she reminded him. He knew by her voice and expression that she had been going to say: "Isn't it the hour of prison executions?" but at the last moment had not said it.

She had no pain any more. She felt her body purified and healed from the long years of dust and dirt and straw mattresses, from fear and anguish. She could not help looking down with pride at her black, high-heeled shoes which looked so smart when she was sitting. It did not matter that she could not walk in them.

Father Mellowes had closed the book and was addressing them. The words had a weightlessness and *naïveté* about them and seemed to be borne away and vanish as soon as they were spoken.

"Love one another, little children. Bear with each other, forgive each other. Never be indifferent. Indifference is the beginning of hell. Hunger and loneliness, prison cells and even prison yards are not hell, little children, but indifference and complacency are the beginning of hell.

"Therefore love each other; and let there be no wall of indifference between you; break down the walls of indifference because you are one blood and one flesh. . . ."

They signed the church register of marriages which Father Mellowes had gone over to the church to fetch along with some other things he had needed for performing the ceremony. It had been his exit from the house in the early hours of the morning that had caused the Civic Guard at the other side of the street to blow his whistle. That had been the order he had received from the sergeant, to give this signal that could be heard in the barracks should Kavanagh leave the house during the night. He was then to be followed. In the darkness, the guard who had relieved Guard Higgins at midnight had not been able to determine immediately whether the figure was Kavanagh or not.

Romilly put on an overall over her white gown and went to prepare breakfast. Kavanagh limped from the sitting-room to his bedroom and back to the kitchen, at a loss to know with what to busy himself. Fear and desire and a third more obscure emotion mingled within him. He was driven distracted by the thought that there would be no opportunity to get his teeth into the ripe plum that had so unexpectedly fallen into his lap. Who knew, though, what might not yet be done, if only behind the door of a prison cell or in the visiting room if there happened to be one of the guards he was well in with on duty? Even to get his hand on to her was a thought that quickened his heart-beat. His heart that was at the same time listening—listening like an animal in a thicket for the hunters. Each early morning step along the pavement outside might herald their coming.

He smoothed the clean white table-cloth over the table and began pulling up the chairs. Lust and fear and between them, like a small pale blossom between two thorns, a movement of unfocused gratitude. For he did not know nor pause to try to find out on whom to focus it. Father Mellowes? His sister? Rather, he was inclined to credit Ezra for the faint and confused sense of being cared for that he had in the midst of the violence of other feeling.

He addressed Ezra with a spark of his old vulgar playfulness from which Ezra had still a struggle not to wince.

"What say to that, boy? Not a bad start for an old sinner like me, eh?" And he went out to the kitchen where the priest was holding the tray while Romilly laid it with the bacon and eggs and tea-pot.

They gathered around the breakfast table, the women in their finery, Kavanagh going from place to place with a bottle of whisky and pouring a few drops in each cup of tea. Father Mellowes looked as though the very life had been drained out of him. His big face was blank and white, lit only by the two circles of glass before his eyes. Romilly was still in that state of musing trance in which she had passed the whole night. Kavanagh could not take his eyes off her. He wanted to address her, but he did not know how to begin. The meal passed for the most part in silence, and afterwards it was time for Kavanagh to go down to the shop. He shook hands with them one after another, and when he came to Romilly she went out of the room with him. He stood beside her in the dim passage that smelt of bacon and eggs, close to her, with the blood burning in him, but he still had not quite the courage to disarrange the gleaming gown. His face was before her face and his lips and tongue were burning for her. His mouth opened and in a whisper he uttered a quick litany of shameful epithets. She stood against the wall, her wreathed head raised to him, her mouth musing.

She went up to her room and took off her wedding-dress. When she had changed, she cleared away the breakfast things, avoiding her brother and the others, avoiding being with them in quiet in which there would be an opportunity of speaking beyond the few casual words. Then she left the flat and went .downstairs and entered the small room behind the fish-shop through the door in the back. She stood there near the big white-tiled sink that was used for the cleaning of the fish. Both Kavanagh and the boy were in the shop and she could hear their voices through the open door. She could hear the bell on the outer door of the shop ringing when a customer entered and the muffled voice of Kavanagh behind the counter.

About her lay the heads and tails and guts of fish. The tiles were covered with the cold, slimy blood of fish and the flaky, opalescent scales. The boy had not yet cleaned up and the little room stank of the cold, salty blood. There was nowhere to sit, so she stood leaning against the wall by the corner of the sink from where she could see a narrow angle of the shop.

The boy came in carrying a fish in the white basin of the automatic scales. He started at the sight of her, but said nothing, turning his back to her and busying himself gutting the fish over the sink.

She was waiting there a long time, leaning against the white-tiled corner of the wall, and the trance had not yet left her. Through it she was aware of the splashing of the tap and the swish of the broom as the boy began to sweep up the fish offal.

It was a Friday, a busy day in the shop, and Kavanagh did

224

not leave it to come into the back room. She heard the constant jingle of the shop-bell and the tearing of the roll of brown paper each time that Kavanagh wrapped up a parcel of fish.

"Sprawled out on my belly like a rat in a trap," Margareta was saying to Ezra in the room above, "with the teeth of the trap into my back and side, and my face in dust and plaster." She had not before spoken of the two nights in the cellar. "There I was spreadeagled like one crucified, with my arms out and wedged down, and the blood running down between my buttocks and turning cold on the concrete under my belly. I was fainting and coming back, fainting and coming back and, when I was back, pulled back by the pain, I had to wait till the pain set in in the opposite direction pushing me away again."

"Could you recall me then?" he asked. "Could you recall anyone?"

"Yes; there was a way in which I could recall you, but it wasn't in love. There is no more love left in the body then, no longing except for death. It went on and on until it was a life in itself there on the cross. I know now that it was only two nights and the day between, but I knew then that it was a life. I can't tell you this, Ezra; in words it is nothing. There were no words there. There was the pain pulling me back and then pushing me down again to the brink of death and then the not going over the brink. I was struggling and struggling to go over the brink. In the swoons I knew that I was trying to go over and not quite going.

"Afterwards in the hospital it was neither one thing nor the other. I mean, neither death nor life. I still couldn't really long for you. I wrote to you; I think I wrote to you twice, but I hadn't the power to long for you. It wasn't only that you had been taken from me, but more than that had been taken.

225

"It only came back gradually. It began to come back in the camp. Then I could still not believe in life, but I began without real belief to try to find you, to come to you. I wanted to crawl to you. I felt still like one taken down from a cross and it had been too much there on the cross, too long a lifetime and too much. Then there was nothing left but perhaps to crawl a little way along the ground. All my limbs were aching, and I used to lie in my bunk, turning first one way and then the other. There was Bogusky, and I sent him there and everywhere to make the applications for me and to fill out the forms, and I only had to put my name to them.

"When I wanted to go out to the shed where the buckets were I had to get one of the girls to help me. I couldn't manage alone, because of the primitive arrangement without proper seats. When Bogusky saw me once hobbling back out of the shed with the girl he said laughing: 'What there's a way out of there must be a way into, no matter how much of a cripple you are!' Something like that. He didn't mean it badly. That was his way. Only I was taken aback. I didn't know he wanted that of me. My whole body was so full of pain that I couldn't imagine how it could have left in it any pleasure for anyone. But in the evening he came to me and I said: 'Be a bit gentle, that's all!' Because I couldn't bear being turned about, this way or that. Otherwise it was nothing to me. He got me the papers and the money and he would have done it for nothing, but when I knew that it needn't be for nothing it was all the same. A little more pain or a little less, that was what it was, nothing else."

"All that is over," said Ezra; he was sitting with her, his hand resting on her knee. "Didn't you feel all being laved away, all the horror and the dirt?"

"Yes, yes," she said. "At first I didn't know what you were doing. I didn't know what it meant; but afterwards I felt

226

what it was and you don't have to tell me. You don't have to say anything."

She had always this dislike of speaking, of things being said. Her instinct was to leave them in darkness. It was very much for her to tell him what she had told him, and it had taken the several days that had passed since her return for her to do so.

Romilly waited and waited.

"Do you want to speak to the boss?" the boy asked her once.

"No."

He looked at her with a shining, gutted mackerel in his hand and went on with what he was doing.

It was horrible and at the same time in the very centre of the sense of horror and humiliation there was a breath of something else in this patient waiting. She had no sense of how long she had already been there in the gleam of the white tiles and the fish-smell. She heard another tone in one of the voices from the shop, a word or two pronounced at a lower more insistent pitch than those of the customers. Across the narrow angle of the open door she saw pass the dark blue of a Civic Guard uniform.

She left her retreat and came into the shop. The Civic Guard superintendent, whom she did not know, was holding open the outer door of the shop, ushering out a woman with a shopping-bag, and a second guard had come round behind the counter and was standing before Kavanagh.

She heard the words and saw the gestures; all that she had waited for she saw take place, but in a subtly different way to the way that she had foreseen in her long reverie of waiting. Kavanagh was stretching his hands out in front of him with the palms together in a gesture that reminded her of that day of the picnic when he had stood in his striped bathing-suit on

227

the little stone pier about to dive. The gleam of the handcuffs passed softly into her, like a pale, deathly arrow of soft light.

"I arrest you for the murder of . . ." She untied the strings of Kavanagh's apron for him and pulled it off. He looked at her, seeing her for the first time, with an entirely different look to that with which he had leant towards her in the passage. It was now a different face, with all the lust drained away out of it, dark-white and as though flayed by invisible lashes.

"Shall I go and pack up some things for you? I'm Mrs. Kavanagh," she added to the superintendent.

"Mrs. Kavanagh?" he repeated. The sergeant had never mentioned anything about Kavanagh having a wife.

"You can bring what he needs along later, some time this evening," he told her.

"And can I see him then too?"

"Certainly."

Kavanagh walked out of his shop with one wrist handcuffed to the wrist of the guard, followed by the superintendent. As he was about to go through the door, the superintendent turned back and said to Romilly: "How long have you been married to him?"

"I have only just been married," she said.

She went back up to the flat. There were four or five children waiting for her to whom she had been in the habit of giving religious instruction every Friday. They were the children she had talked to at the dog-races, and among them were Dinah and Joey Bamber and the little boy who had worshipped her since her coming to Altamont. He began now to confess to her what had been lying on his conscience and worrying him.

"I meant no harm, miss," he said. "I only brought the guard that picture when he was enquiring about you because I thought it was only that he had a message for you from the priest."

228

"What picture?" she asked, looking round at the children, not knowing what they wanted of her.

"Don't mind him, miss," said Dinah. "That's all an old tale, gone and done with."

She had gone over to the window and was looking out of it up the street. She heard the voices of the children behind her, arguing and shrill. She saw her husband and the guard walking side by side up the street on the opposite pavement and the people turning to look at them. She felt an arm laid around her waist. She looked down at Margareta. She had taken off her shoes and was much smaller than the other woman, of a smaller and broader build. Speaking slowly in her faulty German so that the other, whose German was even worse, might understand, Margareta said: "They have taken him, haven't they?" Romilly nodded. "And now you love him, don't you, in the last five minutes?"

Romilly was looking into Margareta's broad, upturned face. "Oh no, no!" she said.

They stood together at the window until Kavanagh and the guard passed out of sight.

"Shall we send away the kids? You don't want a lot of kids hanging around," Margareta said.

"I can't disappoint them."

"Ezra will look after them," Margareta said.

So Ezra was left with the children and the two girls went up to Romilly's room, Romilly helping Margareta up the narrow stairs. It was a chill, drab little attic, but neither of them noticed that. The wedding dress was spread on the bed with the veil and wreath. Margareta took up the wreath and turned it in her hands.

They sat down and Margareta took out a packet of cigarettes and offered it to Romilly.

"I don't smoke."

Margareta lit one for herself and sat smoking for a while in silence.

"What was the crime that he committed?" she asked.

"Don't you know?"

"No. I never asked," Margareta said.

"He killed a girl with a knife."

Margareta sat with the cigarette between her lips, her eyes on the bare wooden floor, reflective and quiet. Romilly was conscious of the great quietude of the other and was comforted by it.

"Who needs us most we will love most. It can never be otherwise," Margareta said.

"It's someone like you, a woman like you, who will always be greatly needed," said Romilly. "I think all men would need you. As for Ezra, he would never forgive me because I wasn't you. I would have liked to have been you; I was jealous of you. I kept thinking about you and hating you because you had lived and died and, in a sense, I had neither lived nor died. I went to him in his room at the hotel, and in the end in a kind of despair he told me to undress. I undressed and got into his bed. I had never been with a man before. He came over to me and I knew that he was trying to pretend it was you. Ah, it was something that I cannot forget, how he looked at me, trying not to see me, to see someone else. All was hopeless, hopeless. You don't know what sort of hopelessness that is, Margareta, and if you did you wouldn't be angry."

Margareta had not been able to follow all of what the other girl said. Romilly's small amount of German deteriorated in the stress under which she was and Margareta was often at a loss to know what she was saying. But it did not matter. She grasped that the other was making some sort of confession to her, and all she had to do was to forgive her which was no trouble at all.

"I, angry?" she asked.

230

"All the same I hated you once because you were a woman and I was a virgin. I lived in a strange world where all is arranged in care and order and the mornings smell of purity. Do you know what I mean, Margareta? To live as a virgin, isn't that to live in another world where everything is smaller and neater and self-contained? All is small and delicate and closed in to itself and not writhing out at you in longing and torment as now. How easy and sweet it was then, but oh, Margareta, what a horrible prig I was. You don't know! I had never been touched, never as much as breathed on by anyone or anything. The first time was in a cave by a lake near here, when Ezra took my arm and dug his fingers into it out of pure anger and irritation with me."

Margareta sat not trying very hard to understand what Romilly was saying. She knew from experience that it was good for the other to talk to her, to say all the things to her that she couldn't to anyone else, not even to her brother. What these things might be did not much matter, Margareta was not very curious about them.

Towards evening Romilly packed Kavanagh's washing and shaving things and a pair of pyjamas into a bag, and went round to the Civic Guard barracks with Father Mellowes. There they saw the sergeant, who was sitting at his desk with the greyhound curled up under it. The sergeant was at first incredulous at Romilly's statement that she was the prisoner's wife. Father Mellowes had to corroborate her. He seemed to do so with a peculiar pleasure. Romilly had never before seen in him a hint of something so reminiscent of a worldly gloating at the sergeant's incomprehension and astonishment. The priest had the air of almost enjoying the awkwardness of this part of the interview.

"Had you then no suspicion of his guilt, Miss Mellowes—or Mrs. Kavanagh, I should say? Surely there——?"

"Let us not speak of guilt, sergeant," said Father Mellowes.

"But it is quite evident, Father. We have the proofs. And in any case surely his reputation was well known. Surely even you had heard of his association with Annie Lee, Father? Did she never tell you of it herself?"

"That is neither here nor there, now," said Father Mellowes. "She told me certain things—among others, that you yourself had made an appointment with her for the very night on which her body was found."

The sergeant began to say something and then stopped. His long face, with its long upper lip, shut down on itself in a blankness, wall-like. One long, tapering paw, looking feathery and boneless, stuck out from under the desk.

"The superintendent said I would be able to see my husband," Romilly said.

The sergeant called a guard and Romilly was brought to an office at the back of the building. She was left alone in a small room used for visitors while the guard went to the cell for Kavanagh. She had crossed an unknown frontier and was in a desolate land. She had left the flat with the dirty plates and cups that she had not yet washed up, piled in the little kitchen, she had left the sergeant's office with a fire burning in it, the dog lying under the desk and only a pane of glass between it and the evening street with its bicycles and carts, and stepped into a place from which the world was shut out. She had thought the room behind the shop had been the last and lowest corner of hopelessness, but there had been the gleam of the fish, of the mackerel in the boy's red hand, even the smell was a living smell, while here there was already the scent of stagnation, of the nothingness that the prison casts around it.

She had put down the bag she had brought on the floor beside her chair and now she felt that the few homely things in it could have hardly any use here; it was like bringing them to the grave.

Ah, what a long way she had come since last night, step by

step, following him down to this last, desolate room. The very wood of the table and chairs had to her a ghastly, bleached look as wood gets after years of exposure to the sun. But it was not the sun that had seeped into the furniture. It seemed to her to have gone dry and rotten with a death-rot, with the rot of being immersed in too much time and waiting.

When Kavanagh came in with the guard he saw her almost without seeing her. He had longed to see her so much that now she was there in front of him he could hardly see her, her face not at all; his eyes rested on her breast. He was so intensely aware of her that the impact blurred the vision of her. In a kind of blindness, he took her hand. He felt a pain in his chest. His eyes had gone into his breast like a pain, and the fire of his loins that had blazed as he had stood beside her in the passage this morning had gone into his breast.

She was speaking to him and the words were coming to him from the world and they were wounding him with the sweetness of the world. He was listening to them so intently, hanging on them, that to her he had an air of not seeming to listen at all, of being somewhere else, regarding, not her face, but her breast with an absent glare. She wanted to say something else, but she could only think of mentioning the things, the useless things that she had brought with her. They were still standing in the middle of the room, not yet having the presence of mind to sit down.

She was both relieved and disappointed that he did not kiss her, but took her hand. The guard sat down at the table and at length Romilly and Kavanagh sat on two chairs a little way apart in front of him.

"I brought your things," she went on, "and some cigarettes. What else is there you want? Would you like me to cook you your meals and have them brought in to you?"

They talked for a few minutes with a strained awkwardness. It was only at the end of the visit that she felt that he was glad that she had come. He was sitting on the upright chair with one of his hands on his stick and the other clenching the seat of the chair under his thigh. He said: "Were you waiting in there at the back of the shop this morning?"

"Yes."

"Eh, what a queer girl you are, Romilly," he said, calling her by her Christian name for the first time.

"I'll come to-morrow," she told him, getting up. "I'll come every day as long as you're here."

She held up her face to him. He still seemed hardly to see her, but then she felt his mouth on hers, burning on hers, and she tried not to stiffen against him. She was faint with disgust and love.

CHAPTER XVIII

THE
GOOD
BRUTE

■ ALL THE leaves had fallen from the crab-apple tree in the garden and the wet beds were full of yellowish, flowerless tufts, of long, wet stalks. The crab apples burned in the still, damp air, and over the garden there was a damp, smouldering light that rested on the long, broken stalks, on the yellowish globes of cabbages and the pale, top-heavy crowns of the seeding onions.

Margareta gyrated slowly beside Ezra down the gravel path along the hedge. He had brought her with him to show her the garden that he had spoken to her of in cellars and on hungry, comfortless evenings. She was looking everywhere, at the dim corners between the shrubs, at the strip of earth between the path and the hedge. Especially her eyes were drawn to those nooks and crannies where it seemed that all had been slumbering, black earth and roots and stalks, untouched through the years.

Aunt Nuala had been taking her afternoon rest when they arrived, her little maid, Jenny, had told Ezra.

"Better not wake her, Master Ezra," she had said, "or she'll come down in one of her contrary fits and then there's always the devil to pay."

So they had left Kavanagh's car in the lane outside and had gone to wait in the garden.

Ezra had not told Margareta much about Aunt Nuala, nor did he translate for her what Jenny had said. He did not want her to have any more scares or be subjected to any more bullying, and he was glad that she was sheltered from many things by her complete lack of English.

She was soon glad to go in and sit down in Aunt Nuala's small sitting-room that was so unlike the sitting-room above the fish-shop. From upstairs they heard Aunt Nuala's voice with its strangely deep, vibrant note to which Ezra always instinctly tried to be deaf. There was something so secretly angry and frustrated in it, with a potency of hidden anger greater than almost anyone else's, that he didn't want to hear it. Even when she was only calling down to Jenny to bring her something, there was sometimes this deep, musical, breaking note in her voice that could turn his blood cold. But Margareta heard it without emotion.

Without them having heard her descend the stairs, the old woman was standing in the doorway. She did not at first glance look old. Her stocky figure and full, brownish-yellow face radiated a bitter, smouldering warmth.

"Hello," she said. "It's you, is it? The long lost wanderer." He kissed her cheek as of old and felt the down on it with an uprushing of the past.

"And which of the young ladies is this?" the old woman asked. She was a downy, yellow wasp dying under a glass and ready to vent her venom on whatever could be stung.

She talked to Ezra with that vibrating undertone in her voice, and everything that she said seemed to mean something else. At the end of each few sentences there was the small, bitter barb, and he could feel it tearing out of her at him and at life.

"Upon my word, you took a long time about making up

236

your mind to come down and look us up. But I suppose you had other things to do. It must be pretty expensive living in a hotel, as I heard you were doing." Her mouth stretched into a derisive little smile between its yellow corners.

But much as money meant to her, he knew that it was not so much the cost that she grudged. The idea of living in a hotel without responsibilities and duties roused rage and fear in her—the ever-present fear that others might be enjoying life without paying the price while she was always paying the price and not enjoying it.

"I'm sharing a house with some other people," Ezra said. "I wanted Nancy to come there too, but it didn't appeal to her."

"Didn't appeal to her? By the hoaky, I don't suppose it did!"

She sat there in her mannish and worn clothes and her heavy boots and talked at him, and he felt the core of her grudge like a small, hard growth in her, somewhere in her bowels or her womb.

Much that she said was the truth. That was what made it so bitter. To have this little growth of truth and rightness in her was helping to kill her.

Ezra saw the spasm growing inside of her, her face turning dark, the wrinkled brows, under the wispy grey hair, dark and the mouth wet and yellow. Her voice was rising—rising to a strange, almost operatic pitch in which there was something incongruous and terrifying, coming out of the little, mannish old woman. The sudden, sensual ring of frustration and rage in the middle of a sentence filled the small, cosy room.

"You can dance for a bit, but the day comes when you've got to pay the piper," she said. "There's many a one that's thought he could live without giving a tinker's curse for anyone but himself, himself and their own desires. Such people allowed nothing to stand in their way. If they happened to be married and wanted another woman, then there was always a dozen good reasons for it. They knew how to abandon their nearest and dearest and still play the fine fellow, but for me they've never been anything more than damned little scuts who hadn't the spunk to face up to life like men.

"By the holy Paul, if I was a young woman, I'd sooner go and lie down in the straw with the pigs out in the yard than have one of them lay his hand on me!"

She glanced at Margareta with her mouth twisted into what might once have been a smile of contempt, but was now stiff with the inner poison, a grimace on her thin lips to whose corners drops of saliva were clinging.

"I've no doubt you'd laugh at me if I was to quote anything so old-fashioned as the Bible to you," she went on to Margareta, "so I won't say what was in my mind to say. But I'll tell you this, young lady, whatever else you may be: you're a fool into the bargain, a fool to come over here and put yourself at the mercy of his lordship here. Do you think he won't let you down as he let down all his other friends and boon companions, as he's let down everyone who ever raised a hand to help him, not counting the others? Do you think you're the first of his female friends that he's brought down here to visit me? He's brought others with fine names, introducing them to me with his charming, offhand airs as though there wasn't a breath of harm in it; to have seen him you'd have thought it was his sister he was presenting to me. Bringing them here on the way back from the races. Drinking round the country with his fine friends and the money pouring like water between his fingers. And then, when the notion took him, careering off to the Continent and for years letting none of us know whether he was alive or dead. But our lordship took too good care of his own skin; his wife needn't have worried about him. I often said to her: 'Mark my words, he'll turn up in his own good time with some foreign janey in tow.' And so he has."

She had to break off to wipe her mouth, from which the saliva had run down to her bristly chin. Ezra felt nausea at the scene. Her rage roused in him no counter-anger. He saw her face dark and livid and her small, thick body as though convulsed, and he was ashamed to look at her as if she had been naked. He could not look at her; he waited to let the spasm go over. Then he said: "There's no good talking to Margareta, because she doesn't understand a word you're saying."

The spasm had passed. Aunt Nuala went dry and brittle; she was now like a dry stalk that he could break between his finger and thumb.

Jenny brought in the tea-things, the lustre teapot and the cake-dish, and arranged these things that gleamed with a light that for Ezra was of another day. Aunt Nuala poured out the tea in a dry, brittle silence. After she had finished at the tea-table, she sat back in her chair, munching her bread and butter with a bitter, little, exhausted grinding of her strong jaws. The square face of the old woman was now greyish and under the eyes were leather-coloured stains.

After tea there seemed to Ezra nothing to do but to depart. He was still too shocked by the spasm that had passed through the small, dry body as though for a few minutes it had lain in the embrace of an invisible, venomous power. He could not say what he had come to say. He saw Aunt Nuala climbing up to her room with her heavy mannish tread, and heard Jenny whisper: "Don't mind her, Master Ezra. She takes these turns lately and there's no pleasing her. You don't know the time I have with her. If you and the young lady'll sit down again I'll make you a fresh cup of tea."

He did not want to stay, but the little maid persuaded him. She told him that the old woman would as likely as not later enquire for him, and then there would be the devil to pay if Jenny had let him go.

"It's her kidneys. The doctor says her kidneys are eaten away as if there was a vermin inside of her, gnawing at them.

239

I must go to her now and rub her with the liniment that he ordered, though I dread putting my hand on her, for it's never right, however softly I do it. You'd think her whole back was a raw wound to hear her, the poor creature."

But it was Margareta who went up to the old woman. She hobbled into the old-fashioned, low-ceilinged bedroom whose windows were open on to the autumn garden. She was aware of a scent as of newly-laundered chintz and pressed rose-leaves, an age-old and sweet scent that reminded her unexpectedly of her own childhood.

The old woman, whose name she did not even know, was sitting on the edge of the big mahogany bed with the buttons of her man's shirt undone and her scant grey hair down over her shoulders. The bottle of liniment was on the table by the bedside and she had just taken out the stopper.

When Margareta let herself down on to the bed beside her the look of derision and surprise passed from the old yellowish mouth. The slow and crippled movements of Margareta were a reassurance to Aunt Nuala. She had only seen the girl sitting and it was a shock and at the same time a singular kind of comfort to recognise in the contortions of the girl a kinship with herself.

Margareta took the bottle in her hand. She recognised by its smell what it was. But the old woman had a horror of exposing her body, and when Margareta tried to draw off her blouse she submitted only out of exhaustion and a hopeless resignation.

Her waxy torso was shrivelled and emaciated, and it had only been her broad shoulders and the loose cut of her blouse that preserved the air of stockiness that she had when dressed. The dry breasts hung like empty bags on the ribs. Margareta unbound the Thermogene wool from her lower back and began to gently massage the dry flesh.

The old woman submitted without protest. She felt the girl's hand had a quite different touch to the hard, rough hand of Jenny. But it was not only that Margareta's hand was larger and more fleshy; there was also in its touch a soothing gentleness that the other lacked.

Margareta rubbed in the liniment with a slow, circular motion. Dusk was falling into the garden outside the open windows and she saw the apple tree, the two cypresses and the other trees standing in the clear autumn evening with their steadfast stillness, stationed in stillness. Gradually the frown which had lain on her brow as she had entered the room dissolved. She had come up to the room with that impatience with which she carried through certain small tasks that she set herself. But now her brow cleared and her dark eyes took on a deeper, more brooding serenity than ever.

"Why must you carry on so?" she said to the old woman, speaking in her own language. *"Ei, ei.* Isn't it time we bowed to what death has to say, and not go on with our foolish mocking of him. . . ."

Aunt Nuala heard the soft, outlandish words and they were a relief from the bright words of Jenny, the bright, birdlike smile and the persistent avoidance of the horror. No one would ever come and meet her in the isolation of her dying. All avoided being with her in that inner, secret place of her death. They did all for her, but they left her alone in the place of her death. Only now had this stranger come and seemed to go straight down to that secret and not be afraid of sharing it. In the tone of her voice and the quality of her touch there was a knowledge that none of the others would dare to have.

Margareta held the bottle on her lap, between her thighs, warming it as she slowly massaged the old, crumbly flesh that began to glow faintly under the rhythmic motion of her hand. When one hand was weary she poured some of the liniment into the other and began afresh. Her eyes rested on the old woman's dressing table with its surface of some dark, highly polished wood on which were neatly laid out silver-backed brushes with short, yellow bristles worn down almost to the roots, some photographs in small silver frames, in one of which she thought she recognised Ezra as a child, small satin-padded boxes and other things too far dissolved into the dusk for her to make out.

Aunt Nuala would not remain in her room. She put on her blouse, brushed her hair and struggled into her boots again and clumped down the stairs and into the lamp-lit sitting-room. But when she appeared, Ezra saw that there was a change in her. It was more as he remembered when he had come off the train and he had been up to his room and come down again. There was a hint of the old homeliness that clung to Aunt Nuala and her house. She settled herself in her chair and reached for a paper spill with which to light her cigarette from the fire with the same careful deliberate gesture that he remembered. He got up and shut the shutters, leaving a small crack open as had always been done, and he knew that she was watching him out of the corner of her eye and was pleased at his remembering.

There was a little talk on and off, and then Ezra said: "I thought it might be a change for you if you'd come and stay with us for a week or two. There are rooms enough and the priest's sister is a good cook. And we could have some games of cards in the evenings." The old woman was fond of card-games, playing them with an intent and maddening slowness and deliberation.

But what would happen to her livestock if she was to go away for even a week, to her calves? The invitation came as a shock to her. It disturbed her. What was he offering her, now that it was too late? There was a half-ashamed longing in her to escape from all her cares and responsibilities and to go with Ezra and this foreign girl and abandon all that she was still struggling to cling to. She gave a sly glance at Margareta from under her thick eyebrows as she leant forward to poke the fire. It was almost as if she too had been let into the secret, as though she shared with Ezra the secret of the girl's attraction.

She began to refuse, to speak of the cattle, of Daisy who would not thrive if she did not bring her her morning and evening milk in the bottom of a bucket. The yard-boy had not a good hand with calves. But gradually her resistance crumbled. She was leaning back in her chair, the lamplight gilding the down on one cheek, her stubby hands playing with the black-tipped spill of paper, folding and unfolding it.

Margareta sat with her at the back of Kavanagh's car, which, with Romilly's permission, Ezra had taken. They drove back with her through the mild Irish autumn night to Altamont.

She was installed in Kavanagh's room, and there persisted the wordless understanding between her and Margareta. She went with Ezra or Margareta to the cinema, she played bridge or rummy with them in the evenings, and she enjoyed these things with a peculiar, intense pleasure. There were these last small pleasures and there was the sitting-room above the fish-shop where she sat by the fire reading or being read to by Ezra or writing letters in her small, energetic script. At times she was seized with the old spasms of rage and venom, the yellow corners of her mouth settling into the derisive smile. If Margareta happened to be about, she would put her big, gentle hands on the old woman's shoulders and look at her with a frown on her wide brows and speak to the other in her, Margareta's, own language: "For mercy's sake don't take on so. What is done is done, and what will come will come. *Ei, ei.* What is death going to take from you but a few calves and some trinkets? It will take what you don't need. And who can say what it may not give you? Let it come; say only like I said to that good brute, Bogusky: 'Be gentle.' Death too is a good brute if you don't resist him. 'What has an outlet must have an inlet,' as Bogusky said to me when he saw me hobbling back from the out-house. *Ei.* So it is. There is always the coming and going, the going out and the coming in, and no real end to it, if you ask me. There's the going out, there's darkness and rotting in the grave, but there's another side to it as there's another side to everything. The going-out side and the coming-in side. . . ."

The old woman would tremble with a sense of affront under the girl's hands and then gradually subside, and the derision and rage would pass from her old mouth. The corners would flicker with a smile of amusement that she would try to check, and she would end up by blurting out: "Upon my word, you're a caution! I don't know that I care for this mauling, but at least you've got a straightforward mug on you, though the devil knows what you mean by all that foreign palaver."

The old woman had never known such direct and simple contacts as here with the others. Death was not so terrible as it was when she was alone with it and with Jenny and her few other friends. Here it was not a spectre never to be mentioned, to be banished by a few bright words and false, bright smiles. She was conscious of its presence here, that those around her were not strangers to it.

She never read the papers, therefore the name "Mrs. Kavanagh" meant nothing to her, and she was not especially curious about Romilly's constant visits to Dublin to see her husband. She did not enquire what business her husband was engaged on, and when the others spoke of him she gathered that there was some sort of shadow hanging over him and Mrs. Kavanagh, but she never felt it necessary to get to the bottom of it.

She saw less of Romilly than the others because she was much away in Dublin during Kavanagh's trial. When it was over and Romilly came back, she was much of the time busy in the kitchen and with the house-work. She would only be allowed to see Kavanagh once more, on the eve of his execution. That last visit she longed for and dreaded, prayed for and prayed to be spared, at the same moment. She said to her brother: "How is it possible for men to invent situations that are beyond the mercy of God to invent? Because, left to God, the worst situations have a merciful dimness and uncertainty; the last hour is never put down in black and white; there is even often a loophole."

"Better fall into the hands of God than into the hands of men," said Father Mellowes. "Better the kidney disease of Ezra's Aunt Nuala than human justice."

"What shall I say to him, though?"

"You will find it in your heart what to say when the time comes," he told her.

At times she felt nothing, only apathy and inertia, and then she did not know how she was going to appear before him at the last. It was too much for her, she felt, too much for anyone to stand alone between another being and the grave; to have to stand, not even within hand's-reach, before him and be for him all, everything that he might have need of at that hour.

When it was too much for her, she turned from it and busied herself in the house, cooking and cleaning. At mealtimes or in the evenings, Aunt Nuala sometimes gave Romilly one of her sly appraisals out of the corner of her eye. In the moments when her old corrosive resentment gnawed at her she asked herself in what relation this Mrs. Kavanagh stood, or had stood, to Ezra. Because she could not altogether get it out of her head that she had somehow been tricked into coming here. Tricked into coming here and tricked now that she was here.

She thought she could never know what was really going on here. At these times she felt the old rage consuming her. She wanted to know; she had a right to know; and she could not get the truth from Margareta whom she trusted, because they could not exchange a single word.

So in the end, one evening when she was alone with him, she asked the priest. The very fact of the priest's presence reassured her, but when the old bitter rage began to ferment in her and Margareta was, as it sometimes happened, powerless to soothe her, she was not even sure that this was any guarantee.

"Does it never strike you, Father, that this is a rather queer sort of household? Are you never uneasy at what may be going on in it, I mean?" she said.

"What may be going on? Haven't you lived with us long enough by now to know what is going on? The tree is known by its fruits. And have you too not had the taste of the fruit of friendship?"

"Friendship is a much misused word, Father, especially in the case of men and women joined by no ties of blood."

"Don't you eat with us and sit with us and sleep with us under the same roof, day by day and night by night?" said Father Mellowes. "And can't you feel in your heart what shape the days and the nights have? Have they not the first groping shape of shelter and peace? Judge by what you see and hear and by the air you breathe and the bread you eat and not by the whispering voices. Ah, I too know the whispering voices, and sometimes they turn to howling voices. I know them. I hear them, louder and more insistent than you can ever hear them."

With these enigmatic words she had to be content. And, strangely enough, she was, apart from brief moments, content. She had no more desire to question or to be on the watch. In the early mornings when she opened her eyes on the darkness and listened and did not hear the small, early sounds that she waited for, and as all over again the awareness of where she was came over her, it began more and more to be a sense of homecoming. This was something that largely wore off during the day. During the day she was still a visitor, but in the dark early hours in which she always woke since her illness there was this knowledge that was both precious and of which at the same time she was ashamed. If Ezra had been there, if he had come in to her room at that hour she did not know what folly or sentiment she might not have been capable of. Yes, had he been beside her at that eerie hour of revelation in the dark before sunrise, before cock-crow, she might have had the courage or the stupidity to say to him words she had never spoken to anyone, except sometimes alone half in fun and half in pain to a pet dog or a favourite calf.

CHAPTER XIX

THE
SMILE

■   "I am poured out like wa-
ter, my heart is as wax. . . ." Father Mellowes read from the
same psalms for Kavanagh as he had after the funeral of Aunt
Nuala. He did not read: "Though I should go down into the
shadow of death, I shall fear no evil, because Thou, Lord, art
with me." Because there *was* fear—untold fear. And he would
not take any words that in the mouth of those who had died
would have been false. He abhorred the very breath of complacency. Romilly had come back to him, waiting outside the
prison, from her last visit to Kavanagh and he had seen on her
face the sign. He had seen the sign set on the face of the child,
of the small, vivid brown face of the little girl; the years in between dissolved at that moment and it was the child's face that
came out of the prison gate with that despair on it. It was the
child's mouth that opened under the shadow of the prison
wall and out of which came the sound of retching and then a
slimy, yellowish stream of vomit. He had taken a handkerchief and wiped the bitter taste from the child lips.

Nothing did he say or ask. Later she would speak, or perhaps she would not speak, but there was nothing that he
would say because any words would have a taint of complacency.

Let there be the dark, profound and untampered at. The dark must have its hour and there was no good trying to stem it when it came, with complacent words. It could not be held back as the sea could not be held back. It was like the sea, the cold unfathomable sea, balancing and counteracting the dry land and the teeming, human dry-land activity.

Father Mellowes knew the dark. He knew that man could not bear very much of it. When a little of it got into him the very heart dissolved like wax and the bones melted like water and the stomach and belly revolted. The first physical symptoms were often vomiting or diarrhœa, but these were accidents of the flesh.

The dark. Manifold were its shapes and tides, as he had known it.

Ezra was waiting. There was this question that he wanted to ask, and which he did not know how to ask. They were sitting at the table in the sitting-room and the priest's tattered missal lay on the table. He had not opened it. He had repeated the words by heart. He had not wanted to turn to a book and open it. That too would have been a subtle evasion and falsity at this moment.

"All the destructive pain," Ezra said, "what can come of it? All the pain that cannot be borne or submitted to. What condemned men go through and children and others. Can there be any point in it or isn't it the sign of chaos?"

Ezra and the two women waited for an answer. Even Margareta was waiting, knowing from the tone of Ezra's voice that he had asked a question. Ezra looked up. He saw Father Mellowes' smile, the smile that he would never get quite used to, resting on them, and he knew that that was the nearest to an answer that they would ever come.

AFTERWORD

Original poetry and fiction have their own histories, independent of their composers, though often influencing the course of their lives.

So it has been with me and the tale is a long one going back to 1942 when a German professor at Berlin University warned me that by spending the war there, and occasionally speaking on the radio, I was, as a writer in English, gravely damaging my future.

Looking back a long way, half a century, it is difficult to recall without distortion what was my instinctive response, instinctive because not being a very precise thinker, that is how my mind and system operates. Logically there could be no ambiguity, what the professor said was plain and simple sense. This sort of sense, known as "common", has never been abundant with me.

If I told the truth as I saw it in my work I would be denounced and ostracised by contemporary critics of English – and American – Literature.

Did I not take it seriously? Oh yes, that is not the reason for my ignoring it. As far as I can cross the threshold and enter the past, as I was at the time, I believe I told myself – a deep corner of my consciousness – something else: that there is a vacuum waiting to be filled by someone who sees it as his or her destiny. Or, put more pretentiously: history demands that certain events have a counterpart, something similar to the notion that the picture hanging on one side of the fireplace goes some way in determining what hangs on the other.

The Allied picture of what the Second World War was all about, and the manner in which their own side waged it, obtained – naturally – a wide consensus in English-speaking, and several other, countries. The picture on the other side of the fire completed a balance and gave the room the psychic lifestyle and feeling of those days, a harmony it would otherwise have lacked. That was my belief then and is so still, when I would have a perceptibly larger, if still small, percentage of agreement.

I saw myself as some kind of recorder, not a recording angel, far from it, but with some of the flair and inspiration of a prophet, as have all those – the Old Testament ones among them – who approach reality at a time of wish-legend.

When, having gone to Paris with a train-load of mostly French expatriates shortly after the end of the war to present myself (I had even an idea of playing the Prodigal Son) at the Irish Embassy and make a plea for help in getting my lover, Madeleine, whom I later married, out of war-ravaged Germany, I was unrealistic enough to entertain hopes of success. And this despite the fact that I had a wife Iseult, in Dublin and that furthermore her half-brother, Sean MacBride, was Minister of Foreign Affairs.

Oh, I committed folly on folly, of which, because I am not a fool, I was and am not proud. But of what I am modestly proud is what came out of it, the novel *Redemption* and which could have only emerged from these ridiculous miscalculations.

The narrator of the novel returns from Germany after the war to his native Ireland, an Ireland that has sat out the world conflict on bacon and tea – with the odd pint; and whom Ezra affects to despise and says so to his estranged wife, Nancy. He, as she and some others close to him realise, is the despicable one and the title of the book suggests that he is finally redeemed.

When Victor Gollancz published the novel in 1949 he splashed the words across the cover: *"Francis Stuart's Redemption"*. That is as may be, but this brief history of the novel, as it lived a life of its own, is an attempt to make sense out of what might seem a series of accidents and misconceptions. This I attempt of course primarily for my own sake, not for peace of mind which I have long relinquished hope of, but that by coming to terms with private and personal apparent chaos, I might accept and even welcome the harsh realities of life on this planet.

Francis Stuart,
Dublin,
July, 1994